D0113783

THE
CAPITALIST

Also by
PETER STEINER

The Resistance

The Terrorist

L'Assassin

Le Crime

THE CAPITALIST

PETER STEINER

THOMAS DUNNE BOOKS ✼ ST. MARTIN'S PRESS NEW YORK

THOMAS DUNNE BOOKS.
An imprint of St. Martin's Press.

THE CAPITALIST. Copyright © 2016 by Peter Steiner. All rights reserved. Printed in the United States of America. For information, address St. Martin's Press, 175 Fifth Avenue, New York, N.Y. 10010.

www.thomasdunnebooks.com
www.stmartins.com

The Library of Congress Cataloging-in-Publication Data is available upon request.

ISBN 978-1-250-06503-2 (hardcover)
ISBN 978-1-4668-7154-0 (e-book)

Our books may be purchased in bulk for promotional, educational, or business use. Please contact your local bookseller or the Macmillan Corporate and Premium Sales Department at 1-800-221-7945, extension 5442, or by e-mail at MacmillanSpecialMarkets@macmillan.com.

First Edition: February 2016

10 9 8 7 6 5 4 3 2 1

For Jane

History repeats itself: first as tragedy, second as farce.
—Karl Marx

THE
CAPITALIST

I

WHEN THE FIRE ALARM SOUNDED, Abinaash Chandha, a sixteen-year-old seamstress, jumped up from her Singer and ran toward the exit.

"Back to your station!" yelled her supervisor. "It is only a test of the alarm system."

"Everyone back to work!" yelled the other supervisors, waving their arms and blocking the aisles. "It is only a test! It is just like on Monday." It was true: There had been an alarm on Monday that had amounted to nothing.

Abinaash went back to the Singer while the alarm continued sounding. She finished hemming the silk pocket square with the embroidered "Pascal" logo in the corner and slid it to the finishes box. She earned ten rupees for every ten pocket squares she hemmed. The hems had to be sewed neat and straight with tiny stitches, which took time. She had been hemming squares for more than a year. On a good day she could earn two hundred rupees, over two US dollars, which meant she could send money home to her family. Abinaash finished another square before she smelled the smoke.

The Kavreen Style factory in Lahore, Pakistan, an immense six-story building next to the mosque a half block from the old Lahore

Canal, was on fire. Bolts of cloth stored next to the generator had smoldered for a while before bursting into flames. The factory walls were brick, but the stairs and floors were wood and were littered with fabric scraps that ignited with explosive fury.

The supervisors had disappeared. Abinaash ran with the others to the stairs, but the stairwell was filled with billowing black smoke. You could see flames below and hear the screams of the workers on those floors. Pandemonium broke out on the sixth floor. Women and men screamed and wailed and ran about, first in one direction then the other. One old woman—her name was Safia Atwal—sat at her Singer with her eyes closed, her lips moving, her hands folded on her lap, and her body rocking gently back and forth.

Smoke was seeping up between the floorboards. All the windows were covered with iron bars. Abinaash ran to the farthest window where a young woman and a man squatted on the sill kicking furiously at the bars. A wailing siren came closer and then stopped below. The woman and man continued kicking. When the woman fell back exhausted, Abinaash took her place kicking at the bars. The bars did not move, but the two kept kicking.

Down below, the firemen dropped the ends of their hoses into the canal and turned on their pumps. Great gouts of brown water surged through the hoses and struck the fire with a hissing noise. More fire trucks arrived and soon there were hoses crisscrossing everywhere. The firemen aimed the nozzles into the flames. But the building was an inferno that no water could quench.

The firemen could not go into the building. They could not even get near enough to place a ladder against it. And even if they had been able to, their longest ladder would have reached only the third floor. They could only point the hoses and gaze into the fire with shiny, sooty, despairing faces. Many hundreds of people, mostly women, had come out of the building. They stood behind the firemen, staring into the roaring inferno or looking away toward some imaginary place where this could not happen. No one came out after that.

On the sixth floor the bars on the window, which opened onto a side alley, suddenly came loose and crashed to the ground twenty meters below. The young man screamed at the crowd on the road until someone noticed and began yelling and pointing in his direction. The first person to jump was gravely injured, and people rushed in and carried her off. Abinaash and the young man tried to hold others back while people below piled up debris under the window—old furniture, palm fronds, mattresses, upholstered chairs, blankets, anything they could find that might break their fall. Some women had tried to make a rope from sheets of uncut silk pocket squares, but when they hung it from the window, it went down only eight meters. The heat was terrible. It made it hard to breathe.

People pushed past Abinaash and jumped, sometimes two at a time, landing in the tangle of those who had jumped before them. Abinaash looked around. The sixth floor, mostly empty now, was burning. Through the thick smoke she could see all the sewing stations in flames, like so many pyres, along with the carts that had been used to carry away the finished work. Safia Atwal, the old woman, was still sitting by her Singer. She was on fire and still rocking back and forth, back and forth. Abinaash slid down the silk rope as far as she could and then, after a moment's hesitation, let go.

II

THE COUTURIER PASCAL, with offices in Paris and New York and showrooms in Paris, New York, London, Berlin, and Hong Kong, learned of the Kavreen Style factory fire when *The New York Times* called. "I'm working on a feature about the safety conditions in the factories of your South Asian suppliers," said the reporter.

"Well, I can assure you," said Serge Palmer, Pascal's vice president in charge of public relations, "that we regularly inspect the facilities of all our suppliers to make certain they adhere to the highest safety standards."

"Did you inspect the Kavreen Style factory? If so, you must know that it was a fire trap. The alarms were faulty, there were bars on all the windows, there were no emergency exits, no fire extinguishers, and there was highly flammable litter everywhere."

"Why are you asking about Kavreen?" said Serge.

"It burned to the ground in June," said the reporter. "Two hundred and seventy-four people died, and many hundreds were injured."

"Two hundred and seventy-four?" said Serge. "My God. That's horrible," he said, and he meant it. "But Kavreen is not one of our suppliers. We used them once, but after an inspection of their factory, we stopped using them. We haven't used them for two years."

"And yet," said the reporter, "their logbooks show orders from Pascal, which were being fulfilled the week of the fire, which was just a few weeks ago."

"That isn't possible."

"It is not only possible, Mr. Palmer, it's true. Pascal has a new line of neckties and pocket squares, among other things, called '*Insouciante*,' that came out this summer—a striped field with an embroidered logo—that was manufactured by Kavreen. I can show you the logbooks, the order numbers, the shipping bills."

There was silence at the other end of the line. Finally Serge said, "I'm certain your information is incorrect," although he had a sinking feeling that it wasn't as he hung up the phone.

The *Insouciante* line, which included ties, scarves, skirts, shirts, blouses, bags, pocket squares, and other items, all with narrow charcoal and dove-gray stripes capped with the embroidered silver *P*, was enormously successful. The products were prominently displayed in exclusive shop windows. The pocket squares sold for two hundred and sixty dollars, the neckties for three-fifty, the scarves for nine-fifty. They couldn't keep them in stock.

Pascal *had* sent someone to inspect their Asian factories two years earlier. They had then left it to their overseas agents to find new suppliers to replace those factories found wanting, either for quality or safety reasons. The agents mostly waited until the inspector—a junior executive—left the country, never to return. "And make certain that those items are taken care of," said the junior executive one last time as he was being driven to the airport. He shook his finger to show that he was serious.

"Yes, sir," said one agent. "You will certainly see that has been done when you are next here. It will all be taken care of, sir." Once the junior executive was gone, the agent renegotiated the company's arrangements with the factories, including a small consideration for himself to ensure that the factory would remain in the supply chain into the foreseeable future.

"Yes," Abdur Pandit admitted, "of course ours is an old building." He was the owner and founder of Kavreen Style. He had built the business from nothing, sewing on an ancient Singer he had bought while still a boy. The machine had been old and in serious need of repair and had cost him almost nothing. Abdur had taken it apart and replaced all the worn gears and frayed wires. He had collected cotton remnants and sewed aprons day and night, which he then sold to the local Mutual Department Store. Before very long he was able to hire others—first only those with their own machines—to do the sewing while he searched for new outlets. Through an agent he had finally gotten a contract for Russian aprons and housedresses.

Abdur expanded his operation, moving from one cramped space to another, until the abandoned colonial hospital became available. He bought the building and had been making improvements ever since, adding a freight elevator to move supplies to the six floors and then to remove the bundles of finished products to the first floor, where they were inspected and packed for shipment. He reinforced the sagging floors, rebuilt the stairs, and installed dozens of sewing stations on each floor. He installed a generator to deal with the incessant power outages. "It is an old building, but it is perfectly safe, with exits on each floor that lead into wide stairwells. Not like our competitors, with their narrow, steep, unlit stairwells and cramped and dangerous work spaces. It was once a hospital, after all." He was sweating. He mopped his brow.

"It might be a jail the way it is now," said Vikram Rob, the agent. "There are bars on the windows." He studied the checklist of violations his junior executive had left behind. "There are no toilets."

"Without the bars, people steal my cloth by the yard. By the bolt, I should say. They throw them out the windows to their confederates below. Without the bars, I am out of business. What am I to do?"

"And what are people to do if there is a fire?" The discussion had spiraled around in that manner with promises that toilets would be installed, that a fire escape ladder would soon be installed, until the revelation came that the junior executive had instructed Vikram Rob to find a more compliant supplier. "I am very sorry. It is out of my hands. If it were up to me . . ." Finally a figure had been named and Vikram Rob signed the new contract.

III

THE NEW YORK INVESTMENT BANKER, St. John Larrimer—he pronounced his name *SIN-jun* in the English manner—always wore a pocket square. The *Insouciante* by Pascal was his favorite. It added the perfect note of luxury and discernment, peeking from the chest pocket of a Savile Row suit.

St. John had been born into modest circumstances, and yet, despite all odds and by dint of sheer hard work and struggle, had managed to build a thriving and successful enterprise. Of course luck had played a role. Things had gone his way often enough. But he had had his share of setbacks at well. Essentially he was the author of his own success. He thought of himself as a self-made man. He had built his career carefully, thoughtfully, conscientiously, paying attention to every detail. It was his conviction that if you studied your chosen field of enterprise thoroughly, left nothing to chance, worked harder than everyone else, you would succeed.

St. John knew what was important, what made a difference between an ordinary investment banking operation and a superior one. He understood that his clients were the lifeblood of his enterprise, the means and reason for his success. So Miss Maypoll, the statuesque receptionist seated at the broad desk in the glass front office, greeted clients with a smile and by name the moment they stepped off the elevator, as though she had been waiting for them, and only them, to appear. Then Lorraine Usher, St. John's longtime assistant, came out of her office and walked them down the thickly carpeted hall.

St. John slipped into his jacket, stood before the mirror and adjusted his tie, and raked his fingers through his hair before he came out to greet them. He took their hands in both of his and led them into his capacious office. "Please," said St. John, gesturing toward the chairs and sofa, "make yourselves comfortable."

His office, even more beautifully appointed than the anterooms through which the visitors had just passed, spoke to the caution and care he took with the assets he managed. There were fine antique Persian carpets on the floor and a leather and velvet sofa by the window. Several Barcelona chairs faced one another around a glass coffee table. There were fresh flowers in a Qing dynasty celadon vase in the center of the table.

St. John's desk and its chair, art nouveau pieces of beautifully worked oak and mahogany, had once belonged to Andrew Carnegie. The shell blue walls of the office were hung with prints by Dürer, Holbein, and Goya. A Rembrandt etching of Jesus driving the money changers from the temple hung on the wall behind his desk. The Rembrandt was a small irony St. John allowed himself, the money changers having been the investment bankers of their day.

He and the clients sat making small talk until Miss Usher brought refreshments on a handsome silver tray: assorted cookies from Petrossian artfully arranged on a gold-rimmed Limoges plate and tea or coffee in matching cups. St. John treated each client as though they were his only client and nothing could be more important to him than their happiness and well-being. He never smoked in their presence, though he allowed them to smoke if they were so inclined. He lit their cigarettes with a Waterford crystal lighter carved in the shape of a swan.

St. John was fond of reminding his clients how seriously he took their trust. "Your trust," he said, leaning forward a bit, his voice dropping half an octave, "is your most precious asset. It is worth more than your money." He paused a moment while this admonition sank in. "Guard your trust carefully. And don't give it to anyone—*anyone*—who hasn't earned it."

The minimum initial investment at Larrimer, Ltd. was two hundred thousand dollars, which guaranteed that every client, while not necessarily rich, had at least accumulated significant wealth. For some, it was their life savings; for others, it was less important money. But in every case, it was an amount that assured St. John that they had given the prospect of investing in Larrimer, Ltd. due consideration before committing to it.

St. John insisted that every prospective client read through the firm's prospectuses and disclaimers, including the audited financial statements and all the fine print. If possible he spoke with each of them in person, warning about the fluctuations that always occur in financial markets. "If you are extremely averse to risk," he said, "then perhaps you should rather invest in bonds or treasury bills. Of course there is risk in every investment, including bonds and T-bills—the risk that inflation will consume your earnings and eat into your principal, for example. But there are levels and varieties of risk, and you should carefully consider which are appropriate for you.

"In order to make use of the entire spectrum of financial instruments"—this was a phrase his clients loved; *financial instruments* implied something beyond crass money, something elegant, something surgical, or musical—"and in order to continue to provide the high levels of return to which our clients are accustomed, some risk is necessary, even desirable. However, this level of risk may make you uncomfortable. In that case our investment strategy may not be for you." He warned them again and again against placing their money with him whenever they revealed even the slightest hesitation. But the more St. John sought to discourage prospective clients, the more they wanted him to manage their money.

If a client asked to see Larrimer's trading room, as some occasionally did, St. John escorted them upstairs, where Jeremy Gutentag, his chief trader, oversaw a roomful of men and women sitting in front of multiple computer screens with graphs and pie charts and numbers crawling across them. Jeremy walked smartly among the traders, gesturing left and right. He was slim and elegantly dressed. He had straight black hair and coffee-colored skin, a shy smile and large intelligent eyes that swam earnestly behind shell-rimmed eyeglasses. He explained in a whisper what the clients were seeing.

The trading room was void of all decoration. There was no noise—no ringing phones, no shouting as one found in other trading rooms. It felt like a library. "Actually, it's more of a scientific laboratory," Jeremy explained in his plummy Oxford accent. He had gotten a first in economics and management at Oxford and then a master's degree from the London School of Economics. He spoke with the kind of refinement guaranteed to make wealthy Americans swoon. "What goes on here is financial science. The invisible hand of the market at work on your behalf." He nodded deferentially toward the clients. "No magic here; just a great deal of meticulous research and hard work." The thick gray carpet, the sleek black and silver furnishings, the traders at their stations, and Jeremy Gutentag overseeing the entire operation gave the impression of a smooth and efficient enterprise.

At the end of each month, every client received a statement printed on heavy, cream-colored stock with three holes punched along the edge. Each statement reminded them of the total amount they had invested, as well as its percentage of growth over various periods—months, quarters, years—and its actual growth in dollars over the time it had been invested with Larrimer, Ltd. The total value of their holdings was in bold type at the bottom of the statement just above the amount they had invested. The total value figure climbed steadily and never failed to impress. In each month's statement, there were also charts with reassuring upward curves so that each client could see how well he was doing compared with the stock market, which was also rising but not at such a rapid rate.

Then in the fall of 2008, the stock market's various indices, suddenly, without much warning and in unison, stopped rising and turned downward. Banks began to founder, one after the other, first Bear Stearns then Lehman Brothers. Venerable, well-established institutions everyone had assumed would always be part of the banking landscape vanished into the cataclysm, leaving chaos and debt and broken dreams behind. The entire world economy threatened to collapse.

Despite the cataclysm, Larrimer's value had more or less held its own, showing only modest losses, and then, after a brief interlude of modest correction, inching upward again. The avoidance of a collapse in value in Larrimer shares was, as the most recent statement explained, thanks to Larrimer, Ltd.'s early reading of the overheated real estate and financial markets and its timely investment in various leveraged instruments and hedges against just this eventuality. "The indications as early as last spring were that we were overdue for a severe correction, and I am happy to say Larrimer, Ltd. was able to take appropriate defensive positions without putting your assets at increased risk. Your assets are as safe as they ever were. We are in for a bit of a rough ride. But I am confident we will all come out the other side in excellent shape."

The defensive positions St. John described in this, his newest and, as it turned out, final monthly statement were not precisely as he described them. In fact, as his clients were soon to discover, there were no defensive positions or hedges or leveraged instruments in place. And not only that: The charts showing Larrimer's continued growth against various stock market indices were nothing more than elegant fabrications. Dreams and confabulations. As astonishing as it might seem, every one of Larrimer, Ltd.'s investments and trades and audited statements and gains, not just now, but going back over the previous twenty-five years, was an invention of St. John Larrimer's mind. The general stock market indices were the only true thing in Larrimer's monthly statements. There were no astute readings of market trends; there were no cunning investments. In fact, there were no investments at all. They did not exist. They never had.

IV

THE TRADERS IN THE LARRIMER trading room were buying and selling shares and financial instruments, or at least they thought they were. They were executing sell and buy orders, puts and calls, and other financial maneuvers as they were instructed. But their orders went nowhere. They disappeared into the vast and ephemeral cyberworld. In fact, except as a name embossed on stationery and painted in gold leaf on the door of a suite of fancy midtown offices, Larrimer, Ltd. did not exist.

The most recent modest profits Larrimer had posted were merely St. John's means to gain a bit of time, to prolong his clients' trust for the few days he required to remove the last of their money to various safe and secret offshore accounts and to then remove himself to a location beyond the reach of his clients and, more important, beyond the reach of the New York attorney general, the United States attorney general, and all the other law enforcement officials who would soon be eager to interview him.

St. John used the Waterford lighter to fire up one of the Havana cigars he favored when he was alone. He held the lighter in his rock-steady hand and puffed and puffed until he was enveloped by a cloud of fragrant smoke. Call him a thief, if you must. But what he was doing was what the financial system was ultimately designed to do—to take other people's money. He leaned back in Andrew Carnegie's chair and blew smoke at the ceiling.

St. John was not stupid or venal; he was a realist. He did not wish investors ill, even the most ill informed. He was driven by his belief in the marketplace in its purest form. He was not one of those ordinary investment bankers who actually used their clients' money to buy equities and then sweated bullets waiting to see what went up and what went down. He believed the financial and stock markets had moved beyond that outmoded model of decades earlier and had arrived at a pure, clear, unadulterated system of capitalism: an economic system characterized by private or corporate ownership of capital goods; by investments to be determined by private decision; and by prices, production, and the distribution of goods determined mainly by competition in a free market. Period.

The market was now as it should be: a zero-sum predatory system of success based on advantage-seeking, whether the advantage be a millisecond's head start because your computers were closer to Wall Street, or advance knowledge of an earnings report. Insider trading was an outmoded concept. They were *all* insiders now. Or they were dead. It was an economic system, not a moral or a political one. And to function successfully, it needed to be free of moral and political constraints.

While the moral and political world had imposed interfering rules and laws on them, every banker and trader worth his salt was finding ways around those laws. To those who balked at the notion of a predatory economic system, St. John would have suggested they just look around. The natural world was in essence an economic system, and what in the natural world was *not* predatory? By taking down the zebra, the lion kept the zebra population in check and kept nature in balance. It was not pretty, but it was the way of the world.

Madoff had been reckless and had therefore been taken down by the marketplace, not by morality or politics. The marketplace was the ultimate regulator: cold, indifferent, relentless. St. John had kept his ambition in check and made certain that his fictitious earnings reports, while usually, but not always, superior to those of the market, had remained within the margins of credibility.

Thanks to his caution and good sense, over the twenty-five years of Larrimer, Ltd.'s existence he had stolen an amount just shy of three billion dollars. Real money certainly, BIG money even, especially for an operation such as his. But still small potatoes compared to Madoff. And compared to some other Wall Street thieves he knew about too.

Unlike Madoff, St. John had injected dips and setbacks in his reported returns, losses any fund would necessarily have experienced. He had also kept his annual returns sufficiently within reason to avoid alerting the SEC. And even when the SEC *had* come calling in the person of half a dozen lawyers, alerted by someone or other with an ax to grind—a jealous competitor or a nosy accountant—they had, after as thorough an examination as their limited means allowed them, given Larrimer, Ltd. a clean bill of health, which he of course cited in his next newsletter as though it were an endorsement. "Here is what the SEC recently wrote—after a thoroughgoing audit of our investment strategy: 'Larrimer, Ltd. has used careful market analysis and prudent strategic investment to earn substantial returns on investment without exceeding any SEC guidelines or violating any laws or regulations.'"

Bernard Madoff had just been too damn greedy. He had never reported a down year. How ridiculous was that? St. John had been tempted more than once to blow the whistle on Madoff, for his stupidity if for no other reason. Except that doing so might have called attention to himself.

There were plenty like St. John in the money business. Many specialized in devising new market derivatives and other arcane and ultimately bogus strategies. The main purpose of these strategies was of course to earn unreasonable amounts of money, but a secondary purpose was to allow these financiers to avoid thinking of themselves as thieves while they were stealing. St. John knew plenty of them personally. He even used their services when he needed corroboration for the worthiness of some particularly arcane investment strategy.

And they used him when they needed similar bona fides. "Do you know St. John Larrimer of Larrimer, Ltd.?" they would ask their clients. "Take it from me: Larrimer wouldn't be buying these bundled mortgages if they were not an extremely reliable investment vehicle."

That was not to say St. John's clients (or his fellow thieves' clients) were idiots. A fancy rug or an expensive print on the wall was not sufficient to persuade them of anything. And they regarded Larrimer's brochures and financial statements with healthy skepticism. At least at first they did. Once they saw the returns, all skepticism vanished.

Larrimer's returns had an almost erotic power, a gorgeous and ultimately fatal allure that could not be resisted: a 2 percent loss in a year when the Dow was down 14 percent, then a 4 percent gain in a flat year, then 13 percent up, then 21 percent, then 8 percent, beating the market by just a few percentage points. Of course, with returns like that, few clients withdrew their money. They understood the magic of compounding; they left their money to grow with Larrimer, Ltd. and added more when they could. When someone did withdraw money, there was always sufficient new money coming in to pay them off, including even their fabulous gains.

Bernie Madoff was a fool. Had he really thought the market would continue to climb and, by its continued climb, cover his scheme forever? What was the point of the entire exercise if you were going to be called to account, to have all your gains stripped away and end up spending the rest of your days in a nylon jumpsuit, living—if you could call it that—in a steel and concrete cell surrounded by convicts and guards and razor wire? In St. John's eyes, Madoff was the biggest sucker of all, because he had had the most to lose.

St. John had seen to his interests, which was what you were supposed to do in the capitalist system. He had given enormous donations to museums and dance companies and charitable causes. But he had also donated substantially to the election campaigns of New York senators and state and national representatives. The mayor was his friend, as were a number of New York City assemblymen and a great many policymakers in prominent positions. These precautions made it certain that he could speak to pretty much anyone he wanted, when he wanted, about matters that affected his business.

"C'mon, Tim. You were in the business. You know there's already an unreasonable amount of reporting accompanying each trade. Much of it is redundant."

The treasury secretary chuckled. "I *was* in the business, St. John, but I'm not anymore." St. John paused long enough to make the secretary uncomfortable. "All right, St. John, I'll see what I can do."

"Just lean on the SEC."

"I'll see what I can do."

"It will be good for all investors, Tim. And for your people. Who could be against eliminating unnecessary paperwork?"

"I'll see what I can do."

It was a conversation Abdur Pandit of Kavreen Style would have recognized and keenly appreciated. "Yes, yes!" he might have said, brimming with admiration and envy. "Oh, yes. You Americans are the masters of business, no doubt. It is how I would like to speak to Mr. Vikram Rob, the independent agent who keeps throwing up barriers in front of me. It is how things are done in the capitalist world. It is how business is done. The world is like a sewing machine. It must be kept in good repair; it must be cleaned and oiled, so that it can continue to sew. It doesn't mean terrible things won't happen, which are no fault of our own. Catastrophes even, yes. But these have nothing to do with the system. They come like a meteor, from outer space. The fire that happened, I could not have foreseen or prevented it. Oh, it was a terrible thing. I weep for those people who died. But it does not change anything. We know how the world works, do we not? And we do what needs to be done, even when it is difficult. Isn't that so? And by the way, Mr. St. John Larrimer, forgive me if I appear forward and immodest, but I must tell you: It was I who manufactured that lovely pocket square peeking from your suit pocket. It pleases me enormously to see you wearing it so handsomely."

V

St. John knew there was no way he could expect to stay in the United States in the immediate aftermath of absconding with three billion dollars, and he had planned accordingly. After thoroughly researching the extradition and penalty questions, he had settled on France as a place where he would be able to live safely once the bottom fell out. France's politicians were as corruptible as their American counterparts, and its extradition laws and treaties sufficiently malleable to provide him a reasonable expectation of security and protection. He had acquired a French passport and set about arranging things with the responsible French authorities years ahead of time, spreading enough money around to see that he would be properly insulated against unwanted assaults from law enforcement entities, French, American, or otherwise.

St. John owned a penthouse apartment looking over the bay at Cap d'Antibes and had a large yacht moored nearby, its staterooms made up, its crew at the ready. He entertained the French president and his beautiful wife, as well as the leaders of the opposition parties and anyone else who might eventually be of use to him. The French president was intoxicated by wealth. He counted St. John among his close friends. They sailed out on cruises together.

The president and his wife sported gold Rolex watches, gifts from

St. John. They took ski vacations and luxurious African safaris. Besides New York and Cap d'Antibes, St. John had homes in Saint Moritz, Mexico City, Paris, and Hong Kong. But his preferred residence was his beach complex not far from the large stone outcropping called Pain de Sucre on Terre-de-Haut, one of the islands in the Caribbean Sea, a part of the French department of Guadeloupe and therefore under French jurisdiction.

The stock market had been overheated for months. It was just as St. John had written in his last report. Signs of strain were showing. Questionable investments were being called in; many legitimate assets were overvalued. The big investment banks were enormously overextended, having borrowed a hundred dollars for every dollar they invested. And in the frenzy to make money, they had constructed fantastical derivatives with no intrinsic value, and then sold them to unsuspecting clients—individual and institutional, clients whom the traders and executives derided. "They're Muppets," wrote a Goldman Sachs vice president in an e-mail he would later come to regret, by which he meant they were gullible fools.

On that Monday afternoon when the market took its most precipitous slide to date, and coincidentally just after St. John had gotten a warning call from one of his contacts inside the SEC, he called Nigel on Terre-de-Haut. "The moment has arrived, Nigel. Things are about to unravel. I'm on my way."

"*Oui, Monsieur St. John. Bien. Tout est prêt.* Everything is ready."

St. John had over a thousand clients, and he understood percentages. He knew there had to be dangerous criminals among these clients, people who would be disposed to use force to try to get back what he had stolen from them. That was why he had Nigel. Nigel was efficient and fastidious, and he also had a lethal side. In an earlier life he had been a French Foreign Legionnaire, then he had been a mercenary in the Congo. After that he had spent a few years overseeing operations for Blackwater in Somalia and Iraq. Once he was in St. John's employ, however, Nigel was satisfied that he had found the perfect position for his particular set of skills. He hired six other strong-arm specialists—former colleagues from the Legion and Blackwater—whose job it became to ensure that St. John could continue to live in unmolested and tranquil splendor.

St. John's car drove right onto the tarmac at JFK and parked by the small silver jet, as was St. John's privilege. He took a hundred-dollar bill from his chest pocket and pressed it into the driver's hand. He boarded the waiting jet, which immediately taxied to the runway and took off.

St. John watched as the shore fell away behind them. He pushed aside a vague sense of regret. Seeing his sons would be more difficult now, although he had rarely seen them even when there had been no impediments to doing so. He had ensured that they were well provided for. Now they had their own lives apart from his. He lit a cigar and watched the clouds passing, watched the ocean beneath them turn from gray to azure blue. He had known all along this day would come. That was as it should be. Every ending was a new beginning.

After three hours, the two small islands of Les Saintes appeared on the horizon ahead. The plane banked, then dropped over the hills and onto the runway that ended at the water's edge. St. John came down the stairs and got into the waiting car. Nigel signaled the French customs official—whose meager government wage St. John subsidized—and the customs man waved them on their way.

Five minutes later the electronic gate in the mighty wall around St. John's estate slid open. "It's good to be home, Nigel. Everything all right?"

"Yes, sir," said Nigel.

Coconut palms lined the curving pink-gravel drive like two rows of soldiers. The car sped past the guard barracks. After another minute the plantation house came into view, a great sprawling structure made of stone and weathered wood, completely surrounded by a deep veranda. Clusters of upholstered wicker furniture sat here and there around the veranda. Ceiling fans turned in an uncoordinated and lazy rhythm. Breezes ruffled the curtains in the open French doors.

Servants moved about silently, making sure everything was perfect for the master's arrival.

Since buying the property from a Pakistani computer mogul, St. John had enlarged and upgraded the house. He had built extensive garages, along with guard, servant, and guest quarters. He had made the pool into a lagoon with caves and small hidden bays. He had added tennis courts and a voluptuous tropical garden that fell away to the sea. St. John had spent part of every winter here, running his financial empire and preparing for the day—*this* day—when the stock market would finally collapse under its own weight.

The collapse had not been his doing. But as it had come about, the financial swamp would now drain, and the bottom-feeders—at least those who had not made provision—would be exposed, trapped in the shallow pools that remained, swimming in ever smaller circles, gasping for air until they succumbed.

VI

AFTER THE WAR, Jack Larrimer, St. John's father, brought Millicent, his English bride, home to Milwaukee. Jack found work as an accountant in the city's tax department while Millicent saw to the children, Margaret and Audrey, and six years after Audrey, St. John. They named him St. John because it sounded noble and grand. His name represented their hopes and aspirations for their only son. It also told of the pain of Millicent's exile and her yearning for England.

St. John was short and chubby and had a funny name, and was relentlessly teased by his schoolmates. He arrived at school at the last possible moment and fled as soon as the final bell rang. When he found himself at an elite college preparatory high school, he felt his fortunes change. There were plenty of smart, rich kids who wanted nothing to do with him. But his intelligence was appreciated by other students and by the teachers. He was bright and capable and won a scholarship to Yale.

Once there, he cast around for a major course of study. But while everything was initially enticing, it was eventually repulsive, or at least boring. One afternoon in the Yale Museum, St. John saw a small exhibition of religious statuary by the medieval German sculptor Tilman Riemenschneider. Each of Riemenschneider's sublime wooden figures radiated such unshakable conviction and solidity that

St. John decided then and there that he would study art history. Adrift on a great sea of uncertainty, it was conviction he sought, the answers to questions, the fulfillment of his longings, belief that was beyond belief.

Of course art history offered more questions than answers. There was no certainty to be found there. He tried history, then sociology, then philosophy, all with the same disappointing result. He finally settled on religion because time was running out and he had to settle on something in order to graduate. He wrote his senior thesis on "Tilman Riemenschneider's Faith: The Banishment of Doubt Through Artistic Expression."

St. John was intent on going on to study at the Union Theological Seminary, where he was sure certainty must reside. But an economic history course in his final semester—a required course he had been avoiding—changed his mind yet again. Six weeks after graduation, he found himself in New York, working at Goldman Sachs and drawing what was, for someone just out of college, an enormous salary. His task for the first year at Goldman was to learn the American financial system inside out, to which he devoted himself with the same zeal and intelligence he had directed toward the works of Riemenschneider. And it was here, in the world of money, that he finally found what seemed like certainty to him: a system of thought governed by a set of indisputable truths. Of course the only indisputable truth was the money. Lots of it. But it was there for the taking.

After that first year, St. John was given several accounts to manage, and he did so with efficiency and ruthlessness. The ruthlessness was a new quality in his personality, but he adapted to it instantly, since it accorded entirely with his sense of how capitalism worked and how finance must be done. There must be no sympathy, no forgiveness, in short no human qualities beyond cold, hard logic.

St. John understood that the capitalist system was a system in name only. What he failed to understand—then, but also later—was that the capitalist system is so enormous and multifaceted that even an intelligence as encompassing and nimble as his own could not begin to apprehend its complexity. It is like the Milky Way, whose name is a completely inadequate designation for an immensity of stars and asteroids and black holes and various matter from the gargantuan to the subatomic that are themselves mostly unnamed and yet all together enormous enough that they could, and someday will, consume our entire solar system in an instant, an instant in which everyone, the billionaire St. John Larrimer, the teenage Abinaash Chandha, and everyone in between—all of us—will be instantaneously united in fire and nothingness.

St. John did not know or care about the fire that had decimated the Kavreen Style company or the old lady who had burned to death rocking in her chair in front of her sewing machine or the many others who had been injured or perished. And without knowing or caring about the fire, how could he, or anyone, claim to understand markets, economics, and capitalism, since humanity and the things St. John sought to banish from the system—sympathy, forgiveness, but also greed and venality—lay at its heart?

The old lady—Safia Atwal was her name—rocking in flames and chanting something, at least Abinaash thought she had been chanting—could be said to have been situated in the instant of her death, as closely as anyone was, to the epicenter of the capitalist system. The necessity of that old woman's labor—to her, to her family, to Kavreen Style, and on up the economic ladder to Pascal couturier and beyond to the moguls and predators, along with the horror of her exploitation and final hour—made her a sort of fulcrum on which the entire system was balanced. There are, of course, other possible fulcrums; one could posit *infinite* fulcrums throughout the system and infinite ladders leading from them up through poverty, through comfort, through prosperity, wealth, and beyond. And, oh, if only the fire brigades who showed up at the Kavreen fire had had such ladders!

Abinaash Chandha did not perish in the fire. Once she had lowered herself to the bottom of the rope made of *Insouciente* pocket squares,

she was still nearly twelve meters above the alley below. She hesitated only a moment before she let go. She woke up two days later
with her body swimming in pain. She cried out. She opened her eyes
to see a woman peering down at her. The woman held her hand and
called out to someone who was out of Abinaash's view. "She's awake."

The other person came into view. "This will stop your pain." And
whatever they did stopped the pain. When Abinaash awoke again,
she recognized that she was in a bed. Dust mites danced in pale light
slanting across the room from a high window. The pain was duller
than it had been and somewhat removed from her so that she felt it
as though it belonged to someone else. There was a bag of pale fluid
hanging from a pole above her that fed through a plastic tube into her
arm. She tried to turn her head, but couldn't. A different woman
came into view. "You're in hospital. Do you know what happened?"

Abinaash lowered her eyes to indicate she did.

"You've got a broken back and two broken legs and some cuts and
bruises."

"What else?" said Abinaash. The strength of her own voice surprised her.

The woman smiled. "We think that's the worst of it, but time will
tell. You are in extreme traction because of the breaks. That is why
you cannot move."

"What will happen to me?"

"Your wounds will heal. Your back and left leg should heal with
time on their own. You will have surgery on your right leg, which
has multiple fractures."

"I don't have money for surgery."

"You will have the surgery; do not worry about the money." The
woman, a doctor, took Abinaash's hand and gently squeezed it.
Abinaash let out a little cry.

The hospital notified Abinaash's family where she was. Her
younger brother and her mother came from the village and stayed
by her side. They were allowed to sleep on mats on the floor beside
Abinaash's bed. Her mother fed her broth and lentils and rice. She

caressed Abinaash's hair and wept to see her eldest child in such a state. She told her stories of the village. "Mrs. Niim has run away from her husband again. He is mostly too sick to get out of bed. But sometimes he can, and then he beats her. 'I have had enough of his abuse,' she told me. 'I take care of him, I feed and wash him, and what does he do? He beats me. I have had enough.' She has gone to her sister as she always does." She paused. "You will come home with us when you are well enough. You can work with us in your father's field."

"And what will one more of us working there accomplish?" said Abinaash. It was a discussion they had had before.

"Your sisters want you home. Your brother wants you home."

"I do," said her brother. "I want you home."

"It makes no sense, Mamaji. We need the money I earn here."

"Your life is not worth money, Abinaash."

"There is fire in the village too, Mamaji. I could burn up there."

"And what will you do when you are out of hospital?"

"I will find work. It won't be hard. I am an excellent seamstress. My skills are in great demand."

"And if you do not find work here?"

"I will find work. Don't cry, Mamaji."

VII

IN SEPARATING THE GULLIBLE from their money, St. John believed that he played a crucial role in the capitalist system, performing a kind of radical surgery on the failing economy. It had long been understood—since Adam Smith and even before—that the economy was a self-correcting mechanism. By exploiting weaknesses within the system, St. John helped it excise these weaknesses and make the necessary corrections, just as one might have a tumor excised from one's body so the body can rehabilitate itself and grow stronger.

To his everlasting dismay, St. John was only rarely able to expound on this philosophy these days. Of course many of the powers that be thought exactly as he did. He had met them—senators, presidents even, judges, business leaders, and entrepreneurs who confessed to worshiping at the altar of the Marketplace. Of course they would never have admitted to sharing a predatory worldview. That would have meant admitting, albeit tacitly, what was true: that they were the lords of the universe and thieves, and that the great masses of everyone else were there for their convenient exploitation. Therefore they spoke in an opaque code: "Business drives the world economy. That is why the world needs new markets," said the French president, shooting his cuffs and flashing his Rolex.

"Of course," said St. John, "we need to encourage the creation of

new markets, but"—he raised a forefinger in a cautionary gesture—
"while protecting the least of those among us." He did not know who
the *least among us* might be, but he felt a kind of warm sympathy for
them, like what he felt for his sons. He could never have imagined
Abinaash or the world she lived in, given the world *he* lived in. St.
John and the French president stood on the deck of the *Enterprize,*
St. John's yacht, watching the crew going about their tasks. St. John
gestured out across the open water, as though there might be yet
undiscovered lands beyond the horizon, where people were just waiting to be swept into the world of capital and markets.

"Yes, the unfortunate," said the president. He looked wistful,
since he thought of himself as unfortunate, at least compared to the
American billionaire.

"By the same token," said St. John, "the unfortunate must not be
allowed to drag the economy down. Those unwilling to pull their
weight, well, we can't encourage sloth and dependency, can we?
Forty-seven percent of the people of the world"—he may have made
up the number, which caused him to repeat it for emphasis—"forty-
seven percent, nearly half, expect their government to provide them
with health care, clothing, food, you name it. . . ."

Only when St. John was in the company of Richard J. Smythe
could he speak freely. He was fond of the argument in its unvarnished
form. And though Richard knew it by heart, St. John became animated each time he brought it up. "We—you and I—are the purest
of capitalists." In St. John's mind purity was the necessary condition
that excused many things.

Richard had been two years ahead of St. John at Yale, so the two
had not known each other there. Richard was on the crew team and
in the secret society Skull and Bones. And while St. John still had
lofty aspirations, Richard was already discovering his own criminality. Richard eventually became a lawyer and then went on to found
a small and very profitable bank whose main business was laundering money.

Richard and St. John first met at Goldman Sachs, where Richard had come to propose a joint enterprise between his young bank and Goldman. The two men discovered their Yale connection. They also discovered a shared a fascination with medieval art. Their friendship did not blossom right away. It was only after St. John had left Goldman and had founded Larrimer, Ltd., after his study of capitalism and finance had led him finally to embrace untrammeled capitalism—for its philosophical purity, of course, but also for its promise of extreme wealth—that their purposes intersected and their friendship was sealed. St. John remained, in part at least, a true believer, while Richard's motives were less complicated. He just wanted other people's money.

Their shared passion for medieval art became, as their wealth multiplied, a passion for collecting rare and expensive things, *priceless* things if possible. Their passion was for the value rather than the thing itself. And their passion was competitive. They would meet at one or the other of their various residences to show off the latest acquisition. Richard had only recently acquired a Gutenberg Bible. He donned white cotton gloves and slowly turned the heavy vellum pages—they made a deeply satisfying rustling sound—while St. John watched.

St. John in turn had a new Picasso, *his* new Picasso, a musketeer, painted very late in the artist's life. "It's one of his last paintings and one of the best in the series. I got it for six million. It's worth twenty at least." As enthusiastic as each man was about collecting, both were more or less indifferent to the beauty of the things they collected. All that mattered was to own something of great value.

Neither man knew many particulars about the other's business. Each would have considered it imprudent and unwise to ask the other how he came by his wealth. They had known each other long enough that they could guess the rough outlines of the other's dealings, but for the sake of plausible deniability, they preferred not to speak of it. They were content to revel in their mutual success and to celebrate capitalism and its triumphs.

They celebrated in tufted leather chairs beside the great fireplace at the Yale Club, or on the deck of Richard's yacht in Bali, or St. John's at Cap d'Antibes, or on the grand marble terrace on Biscayne Island watching the black water spill over the edge of Richard's enormous pool with Miami spread out before them.

St. John turned to Richard with a smile. "We agree then," he said as though the premises had all been stated, as indeed they had many times before, "that capitalism is the biggest con game of all." Both men barked with laughter. They sought to outdo each other in the cynicism department. Each found the other's audacity bracing and reassuring. Cynicism protected them from the anguish of the hoi polloi.

"I mean, seriously, it depends on more and more people buying more and more things they don't need, doesn't it? Produced by ever-growing industries that by all rights shouldn't exist.

"Everyone dreams of being as rich as we are. That's the necessary part of it, isn't it? Whether they're hawking Vitapunch or Mercedes-Benzes or shares. What's the difference? What's the difference between laissez-faire capitalism and a pyramid game? Nothing, really; there's no difference. Each depends on more and more consumers in pursuit of more and more stuff."

"No difference," Richard chimed in, affirming his friend's assessment of things. He studied his whiskey glass. He shook it lightly so the ice cubes clicked against the crystal. "It might be different if there were infinite, ever-expanding markets," he added, as though it were an afterthought. "But there can't be, can there? The world is finite, isn't it? The population is finite. Those down at the bottom end up holding the bag."

"As they should," said St. John. He could not imagine those down at the bottom.

Neither could Richard. "Indeed. As they should."

"Well," said St. John as though he had just thought of something. "Maybe there's one small difference." Richard turned toward him expectantly. "Well, the pyramid game is invisible, isn't it? While the capitalist game is entirely visible, right there for everyone to see."

"If only they would look," said Richard.

"But, wonder of wonders, nobody ever does. Or if they do, they don't see. They just believe."

"Well," said Richard, "believing is faith, and faith is the end of thinking, the end of seeing—"

"And the beginning of confidence." St. John raised his glass in Richard's direction. "To confidence," he said.

Richard returned the salute. "To confidence!" Their conversations always ended with this toast to confidence in its myriad of meanings.

VIII

AMONG THOSE WHO HAD RECEIVED Larrimer, Ltd.'s last statement there were some whose suspicions had finally been aroused beyond soothing. They realized Larrimer could not possibly have anticipated the extent of the devastation, nor could he have hedged his investments sufficiently to avoid massive losses. Bear Stearns was gone; Lehman Brothers was going. Larrimer's good returns were simply not possible.

On Monday morning when Lorraine Usher came into the Larrimer, Ltd. offices—she was always the first to arrive—the phone was ringing. Without taking off her coat or laying her purse aside, she answered the phone.

"Put Larrimer on the phone."

"He's not in yet, Mr. Ballard. I'll have him call you as soon as he arrives." Winston Ballard, a retired tire manufacturing executive, had several millions invested with Larrimer, Ltd.

"When will that be?"

"Any minute, Mr. Ballard. He's usually here by now. I expect him any minute."

Ballard snorted. "You're covering for the son of a bitch while he makes off with our money."

"I assure you, Mr. Ballard—"

But he had already hung up.

After the third or fourth such call, Lorraine called St. John's cell phone. She got a busy signal. She tried his home number. It was busy as well. Every number she had for him was busy. She tried Jeremy Gutentag and got no answer. She went up to the trading room, where everything seemed normal, except for the absence of Jeremy. No one knew where Mr. Larrimer or Mr. Gutentag was.

She went back downstairs and into St. John's office to see whether she might find some indication where he might be—an airline itinerary or a calendar entry she had missed, something like that—but she found nothing. When she turned to leave, Lorraine saw that the little Rembrandt was gone. Jesus and the money changers. The other prints remained, but the Rembrandt was missing from its spot on the wall. Her hand flew to her mouth. She knew in that moment that St. John was not coming back and that he had taken the money with him. "He's gone," she whispered.

Lorraine went back to her desk and sat down. She thought of all the people who had their money with Larrimer. She stared straight ahead; her vision grew cloudy as her eyes filled with tears. Lorraine Usher felt sorry for herself of course—she had all her savings with Larrimer. But she also felt sorry for all the others who had invested their money with Larrimer and lost it. And then her sympathy went pinwheeling outward. She thought of the millions, even billions, suffering fates far worse than hers.

The phone would stop for a moment and then immediately start again. She came to imagine it was the suffering of the world calling. She could not bring herself to answer.

Lorraine had worked for Larrimer, Ltd. for most of its twenty-five years. She had saved assiduously over the years until she had $150,000. As a favor to her, Larrimer had waived the investment limit so she could invest in his fund. Some favor. Now she knew why. The file drawers behind her were full of the names of clients. There were associations and charitable institutions among them. But mainly it was individuals who had invested with Larrimer, just as she had.

"You had better go home, Francine."

Francine Maypoll looked at Lorraine uncomprehendingly. "What? Why?"

"I think Mr. Larrimer is gone. I think he stole all the money. He's gone."

"Gone?"

"Gone."

"How do you know?"

"I just know."

Once Miss Maypoll was gone, Lorraine went back to her office and sat at her desk. She turned in her chair and looked at the file drawers. She got a yellow pad from the supply closet, opened the top drawer, and pulled out a handful of files. She began making notes.

At the end of the day, she put the thick folder of pages she had filled into her purse. She got up from her desk, put on her coat, and left the office, carefully locking the door behind her. She had briefly considered taking something of value as compensation for all she had lost, one of the remaining prints perhaps. She decided against it. She was not a thief.

IX

Quite a few of Larrimer's investors—some of the endowment and fund managers in particular—while not exactly thieves themselves, could be said to have behaved in a thievish way. In fact by their behavior, they confirmed one element of St. John's philosophy: that in order to function as it was designed, capitalism needed its constituent population to generally harbor and exercise larcenous inclinations. Capital could not grow if people did not want to get their hands on other people's money.

Even lending money for interest was, ipso facto, a larcenous enterprise. Laws and regulations had been put in place to keep banks and other lenders from charging more than was seemly. But what was seemly, and who decided what was seemly? Anyway, even with strict laws in place, banks found ways through and around the laws, thanks to teams of skilled money managers and lawyers, who behaved, in fact, not unlike Vikram Rob and Abdur Pandit and agents and factory owners and bankers and lawyers across the suffering world. They managed to charge preposterous interest rates on consumer debt and make it seem a benevolent and virtuous act.

"We can help you manage debt," they said.

"We are helping society to grow and prosper," they said.

"We are working for you," they said.

"We have your interests at heart," they said.

"We are building a more prosperous world, the world of tomorrow," they said.

"Why rob a bank when you can found one?" A character in one of Bertolt Brecht's plays had said something like that, and most bankers would secretly have agreed.

The small EisenerBank in Zurich, Switzerland, while not exactly founded by thieves, had been founded with them in mind. It lent money, to be sure, and actually at reasonable rates of interest. But its main profits came—as did Richard Smythe's—from laundering money. The EisenerBank found lucrative investments for its clients and collected a percentage of each investment's worth. The difference from Richard Smythe's enterprise was that the EisenerBank was prevented by Swiss law from asking where the clients' money came from, although there could be very little doubt that they knew.

Seeking the best returns for the bank's customers, Lorelei Steinhauer, the president of the EisenerBank, had invested a substantial amount of the bank's holdings with Larrimer, Ltd. When it became clear that St. John had absconded with the money, Lorelei went into hiding. After all, some of her clients were mobsters—Saudi, Indian, and above all Russian—to whom she had promised that their money would grow.

Then there was the Greenwich Fund, a mutual fund founded and directed by Summersby van den Heuvel. After an initially promising flurry of subscriptions, the fund's client roster began to shrink as it became clear that Greenwich's portfolio was doing poorly even in an easy bull market. Van den Heuvel had no experience managing money. But he was from a wealthy Greenwich family and had been able to raise considerable amounts of money from family and friends and neighbors.

In fairness to Summers, as he was called, he was slightly less lazy than the fund's other directors. He at least wanted to improve earnings, and not only in order to improve his and his fellow directors' 3 percent management fee. He was concerned for the people who had invested their money with him, since they included his mother, his sister, and any number of cousins and uncles. How would it look if their holdings diminished while in his care?

Summers had looked around and found Larrimer, Ltd. and its amazing returns. He invited St. John Larrimer to lunch at the Millennium Club in the City. The deal was arranged before the second cocktail. Greenwich would pay Larrimer a 1 percent management fee, and Larrimer would take over the investment of the entire forty million dollars still left under Greenwich's management.

The change in Greenwich's fortunes was immediate. Within weeks the fund rose to the top 10 percent of the value-investing sector of funds. *Forbes* magazine did a feature article on the turnaround at Greenwich. Financial advisers and investing newsletters started recommending Greenwich, and new money came cascading in. A charity devoted to impoverished Holocaust survivors invested its entire endowment with Greenwich.

Even allowing for the 1 percent that Greenwich paid Larrimer, Summers's and the other Greenwich directors' fees increased exponentially. Before long Greenwich had eighty million dollars under management. The number had risen to almost a hundred and twenty million when the dam broke and St. John went missing.

X

THE FRENCH VILLAGE Saint-Léon-sur-Dême sits surrounded by small farms in the narrow Dême River Valley. Saint-Léon was called Dombona in Roman times, but was later renamed to honor Saint Leonardo di Carronna, martyred during the second crusade while plundering a mosque in what we today call Jordan. He had ridden his horse up the steps and into the mosque and was stuffing silver chalices into his saddlebags when a Saracen warrior beheaded him from behind. Leonardo was elevated to sainthood in 1180 by Pope Alexander III.

That irony about the town's namesake suited Louis Morgon. He had come to believe that most saints were anything but and that virtue was ephemeral at best. Louis was a retired state department and then CIA official who had made Saint-Léon his home for the past forty years. His relatively brief US government career was far behind him now.

That career was, in a life with plenty to regret, the thing he regretted most. It had torn him from his family, which was bad enough. But it had also led to the death of several people, and though they were by no means innocents, their deaths still troubled him. He had come to believe that intrigue of the kind he had engaged in had caused and continued to cause a great deal of the world's misery and suffering.

Louis still had nightmares that made him cry out in his sleep. When she was there with him, Pauline would hold him until he woke up.

"Louis, Louis. It's all right. I'm here."

"Where?"

"Here. It's all right."

"I fell down on my face." He wiped his hand across his lips. "My mouth was full of sand."

"I know."

"I could feel it in my own mouth. It was me."

"It wasn't you. You're all right."

It was early morning. The first gray light was showing through the window. He looked around. The familiar sight of the barn and the poplars silhouetted against the dawn was reassuring. He lay in Pauline's arms. When she awoke again, the sun was high in the sky and she heard Louis rattling around down in the kitchen.

They ate breakfast on the terrace. They wore their jackets with collars up and wrapped their hands tightly around the steaming coffee bowls. The croissants didn't need butter, but they slathered butter on them anyway, and blackberry jam, which Isabelle Renard had made.

"What time is your train?" said Louis.

"One-thirty," said Pauline.

"From Saint Pierre or Vendôme?"

"Saint Pierre. I have patients coming first thing tomorrow. Listen, there's a Max Beckmann show at the Pompidou. Why don't you come with me?"

"I can't. But do we have time for a walk before the train?"

They drove the old Peugeot to Rochecorbon, which was almost to Saint Pierre. They walked east along the left bank of the Loire and then up into the vineyards above Vouvray. The sky went from

brilliant blue to gray and back again. At its brightest and bluest,
it suddenly started to rain. They looked up; there wasn't a cloud in
sight.

"Are you worried about money?" Pauline asked; she didn't know
why.

"Only a little," said Louis. He lived from his modest savings.

"It's getting worse," said Pauline. The bank collapse and market
crash had hit with full force in the United States. And the housing
market was falling off at an alarming rate.

"It will come here too," said Louis.

"I know. But your money's there. Some of it's with Jean-Baptiste."

"Only a little," said Louis. "Anyway, so is yours."

"Not all of it," she said.

"It should be safe," he said. "Well, relatively."

"Show your paintings, why don't you?" she said. "You might sell
some."

"What does Jean-Baptiste say?"

"About your paintings?"

He laughed. "About our money."

Later that same day, when Pauline opened the door to her apartment and saw the light on the answering machine blinking, she knew
somehow that something bad had happened. The message was from
Thierry, her middle brother. His voice sounded strangled. Jean-
Baptiste, the money manager, their youngest brother, had killed
himself. He had cut his wrists in his New York office.

"He bled to death," said Thierry.

"Oh, God," said Pauline. She pressed the phone to her heart and
wept.

Jean-Baptiste was thirty-eight. He had managed a small portfolio for family and friends. He had lost much of the money, including
all of Thierry's and some of Pauline's.

Louis had lost two thousand dollars that he had only recently
placed with Jean-Baptiste, mostly because he loved Pauline and she
loved Jean-Baptiste. Pauline had not lost a great deal of money either.

But she had lost a brother. "He was just a boy," she said. "I'm going to New York," Pauline said. "To bring him back."

"Shall I go with you?" said Louis.

"No," said Pauline.

She and Thierry flew to New York together. They did not speak much during the flight. Sometimes they held hands.

"What is the purpose of your visit?" said the customs officer at Kennedy Airport. When Pauline hesitated, the officer looked up.

"Business," she said finally.

He stamped her passport. "Welcome to the United States," he said.

XI

PAULINE AND THIERRY TOOK A taxi into Manhattan.

A young man from the French Embassy helped them collect Jean-Baptiste's body for shipment back to France.

Jean-Baptiste's secretary, Diane, had found the body. She helped Thierry get permission from the police to take personal items from the office. She went along to the building, but would not go up. "I'll be here in the coffee shop," she said. A policeman escorted Thierry into the office. They ducked under the yellow tape across the doorway. POLICE LINE—DO NOT CROSS.

The carpet by the desk was stained with Jean-Baptiste's blood. Thierry collected a few personal items: photos of their dead parents; of Thierry and Jean-Baptiste on a sailing vacation, arms around each other; Jean-Baptiste with Thierry's children; Jean-Baptiste with Pauline.

"May I look in the files?"

"No," said the policeman.

Thierry shrugged. He put the pictures in a cardboard box and left.

A different policeman went with Thierry and Pauline into Jean-Baptiste's apartment in Brooklyn. It was a small one-bedroom. You could tell that Jean-Baptiste didn't spend much time here. Yet you could also feel that it was Jean-Baptiste's.

"I know his clothes," said Pauline. "His shoes. His umbrella." There was nothing remarkable about any of it, and yet he was everywhere. His books, his computer, his letters. His scribbled notes. "All of it." She paused. Louis waited silently with the phone to his ear.

"I'm in the Park East Hotel looking out at Central Park," she said. "Do you remember the view?"

"I do," he said. "Two years ago. It seems like a lifetime."

"Have you heard of St. John Larrimer?" She pronounced it *Saint John*.

"Who?"

"St. John Larrimer."

"No," said Louis. "Who's that?"

Jean-Baptiste had studied economics at the Sorbonne, then gone to work for BNP, a French bank, in their international investments department. He worked hard and was soon promoted to a position where he was managing a small portfolio. He invested astutely and got good returns.

"You should be in business for yourself," said Thierry.

"Who on earth is going to give me money to manage?" said Jean-Baptiste.

"I will."

When Jean-Baptiste started his own business, Thierry turned some of his investments over to him and was soon glad he had. His returns increased, and more important, Jean-Baptiste flourished. He seemed to have found what he was meant to do. Pauline gave Jean-Baptiste some of her savings as well, and so did other relatives and friends.

Jean-Baptiste was grateful to everyone for their trust in his abilities. He decided that he really ought to be at the center of the financial world if he was going to find the best returns, and, with the encouragement of his clients, who were his family and friends, he moved to New York. He made new contacts and discovered new opportunities.

He had not been there very long when he learned of St. John Larrimer's extraordinary earnings record. Some of Larrimer's methods were proprietary, but from what Jean-Baptiste could see, the exceptional earnings seemed real. When he happened to meet the man himself at a party the following week, it seemed like destiny. St. John exuded confidence. He lamented the disappearance of honor and integrity from the business of money management and investing. "When I began, over twenty years ago, your word was your bond. Those days are gone. Bernard Madoff ruined that for everyone."

"Yes, but he must have begun with the best of intentions," said Jean-Baptiste. "Don't you think?"

St. John thought for a long moment before replying. "I don't think so," he said. "No. I find it inconceivable that he did. No, no. It's just impossible. A human being doesn't undergo that sort of transformation without having harbored evil and malevolent intentions from the beginning."

"But his family would have known, wouldn't they? His wife, his sons?"

St. John gave Jean-Baptiste another long look. "You just can't know what's in a man's heart." St. John invited Jean-Baptiste to visit his offices and see his trading room. He introduced him to Jeremy Gutentag, who gave him a tour of the premises. St. John gave Jean-Baptiste his prospectus and the last several issues of his monthly report. Jean-Baptiste studied Larrimer's publications. He read articles in *Fortune, The Wall Street Journal, Mutual Fund,* and *Fund Market Trader,* and everything else he could find on the subject of Larrimer, Ltd. Everyone, even the SEC, gave Larrimer a high rating.

Jean-Baptiste understood money and investing, but he was an innocent when it came to people. The fact that Larrimer spoke French and held dual American-French citizenship seemed significant to him. The proprietary nature of Larrimer's trading strategy also aroused his admiration rather than his suspicion. The problem was Jean-Baptiste knew nothing of greed or malevolence. He was in some ways, as Pauline had said, just a boy.

To his way of thinking, earning money by investing in shares and bonds and commodity futures and currency and every other financial entity was only possible if every transaction was based on mutual trust. He trusted those in the business to be honest; he had no choice but to trust them. After all, the financial entities they traded in—including currency itself—were all abstract constructions. They had value only because they were exchanged, and that value was determined by implicit agreement. Which meant trust. Without trust, there could be no honest value, and every exchange became predatory and false. Without honesty and mutual trust, the financial system was nothing more than a shell game.

After carefully weighing the risks and benefits, Jean-Baptiste decided to put a large portion of the money he was managing into what he perceived to be the superior system. Being a cautious investor, he kept some money in US treasury bills and bonds, municipal bonds, money market funds, and other guaranteed investments. But his job was to increase the savings of his family and friends to the best of his ability, and if Larrimer, Ltd. offered a better and more dependable means of doing so, then he really had to take advantage of it.

Jean-Baptiste learned of Larrimer's criminality from the newspaper. When he could not reach Larrimer, Ltd. by telephone, he went around to their offices. He found the door locked and sealed with yellow police tape, the same tape that now sealed Jean-Baptiste's office and Brooklyn apartment. He called the Securities and Exchange Commission offices where, after a very long wait, he was connected to an official who confirmed for him that St. John Larrimer did appear to have absconded with the entire sum under his management.

"And who are you, sir?"

"Jean-Baptiste Vasiltschenko." Jean-Baptiste told the official who he was and that he had invested more than half of the money under his management in Larrimer, Ltd., including his own money and that of several dozen clients.

"What is the name of your organization again? And the address and phone number?" Jean-Baptiste gave the official his name and address, which the man wrote down.

"And what has been your connection to St. John Larrimer?"

"My connection? I have no connection to him. I invested with him. My clients' money."

"Where are you from, sir?"

"I am from France."

"And your clients?"

"Are all from France."

"I suppose, sir, you know what a feeder fund is?" The official did not wait for an answer. "Larrimer, Ltd. was supplied by a number of feeder funds, funds that were set up to look like separate investment entities, but were designed specifically to supply Larrimer, Ltd. with cash. This is an illegal activity in the United States and in France as well."

Jean-Baptiste did not reply.

"Well," said the man, finally, "we will need the names of your clients and the amounts of money each has invested and lost. And we will want to examine your books. Our agents will ascertain whether, and to what extent, you might be complicit in this affair. I would urge you, sir, not to leave the country and to cooperate with our investigators. I would also suggest that you retain legal counsel."

Jean-Baptiste held the phone to his ear long after the man had hung up. He saw in his mind's eye his brother, his sister, his cousins, and friends who had each and every one trusted him with their savings.

Jean-Baptiste swiveled his chair around and looked out the window. New York, which only a short time earlier had seemed welcoming—the embodiment of opportunity—now looked hostile and forbidding. In his mind Jean-Baptiste heard a great steel door slamming shut. The towers across Fifth Avenue seemed to lean toward him, their windows a thousand accusing eyes. A siren passed on the street below, as they often did in New York. Then it stopped. It sounded to Jean-Baptiste as if they were coming for him.

Jean-Baptiste turned back around to his desk. As the blank windows watched, he composed a letter to his clients, begging their forgiveness.

> *My dear ones—*
> *You have entrusted your hard-earned money to my safekeeping, and I have betrayed your trust. You are the very dearest people in the world to me. You do not deserve this. I cannot go on living, knowing the harm I have done. I hope you will someday forgive me for the misery I have caused.*
> *With love forever,*
> *Jean-Baptiste*

XII

On a breezy Saturday in October, Jean-Baptiste was buried next to his parents in the Père Lachaise cemetery in Paris. His family and friends, many of whom had been his clients, were there.

"Poor Jean-Baptiste. Why did he have to do it?" said Anwar, Pauline's former husband.

"He probably blamed himself," said Louis.

"That's what we do, isn't it?" said Anwar. "The only ones who *don't* blame themselves are the ones who should."

Louis looked at Anwar. Anwar smiled. "Not you, Louis." He took Louis's arm and drew him close. "I'm talking about the Larrimers, the Madoffs, the thugs, the brutes, the sociopaths. They all sleep like babies."

At the wake at the Bistrot des Platanes, Louis stood alone, looking into a glass of red wine. Marianne—Anwar and Pauline's daughter—walked up and kissed him.

"Marianne." He kissed her in return and held her head against his shoulder.

"Poor Jean-Baptiste," she said.

"Yes. It's awful," said Louis.

They stood together and watched the others for a while.

"Did you have money with Jean-Baptiste?" Marianne said.

"A little," he said. "Did you?"

She smiled. "I'm a schoolteacher, Louis."

"Yes. Of course," said Louis.

"Tell me, Louis, what do you think about this Larrimer guy?"

"I don't think anything," said Louis. "Why?"

"I don't know, I just wondered," said Marianne. "It's awful that there are people like that."

"Yes."

"They've kind of been your specialty, haven't they, Louis?"

"My specialty?"

"Scoundrels, I mean?"

"I guess so. In the past. Not anymore."

"Why not?" she said. "Why not anymore?"

Louis didn't answer for a while. "I don't know," he said finally.

Marianne tried another tack. "He's French, you know."

"Who?"

"Larrimer. St. John Larrimer." She emphasized the *Saint*. "*Saint* John."

"He's French?"

"Well, he's got a French passport."

"How do you know?"

"It was in the papers. Did you know he stole three billion dollars? No Bernard Madoff, but still . . . I wonder what makes somebody do such a thing."

Louis studied Marianne's face. She pretended not to notice.

"Nothing will happen to him, will it?" she said. "He probably stashed the money in Swiss banks."

"Probably," said Louis.

"You know he has an apartment in Cap d'Antibes," said Marianne.

"No. I didn't know."

"And an apartment in Paris, and who knows where else, probably all bought with stolen money. He'll get away with it, won't he?"

"Will he?" said Louis.

"I think he will, don't you?"

"Not necessarily. Interpol is pretty good."

"They're pretty good?"

"They're *very* good," said Louis. "They're very good."

XIII

ON THE INTERNET, Louis found an endless string of articles and news reports describing the magnitude of Larrimer's crimes. There were lists of Larrimer's victims and how much each had lost. There were indictments of his moral turpitude and conspiratorial speculations about who his accomplices might have been, including everyone from the American president to the Chinese, even al Qaeda.

There were reports from happier times too: society page accounts of St. John's 1988 marriage at the Plaza Hotel to Carolyne Bushwick of the New Haven Bushwicks. St. John's notable charitable involvements were also documented. He was on the boards of the Museum of Modern Art and the Metropolitan Opera, and had at one time been a Yale trustee. He had made large donations to Republican and Democratic candidates alike. There were pictures of St. John and Carolyne at glamorous events. And there were articles documenting their contentious and very public divorce in 2000. Carolyne had lived in Greenwich, Connecticut, with their two teenage sons until they went off to college. Louis looked back at the list of Larrimer's victims and found Carolyne's name among them.

Pauline saw a file folder labeled LARRIMER lying beside Louis's computer.

"I'm just curious," said Louis.

"Just curious? You're never just curious."

"It's an interesting case," he said.

"It's not a case."

"No, it's not. You're right. But it interests me. That's all. I just won-der, will they find him? Will he go to jail? Will justice be served?"

"Please don't, Louis," she said.

"Don't what?"

"Because," she said, dropping the folder with a thud for emphasis, "it's not your business. You don't need to do this. It really isn't your business."

"No. It's not my business." He paused. "But then, whose business is it?"

Pauline heard one of Louis's provocative disputations about to begin. "I don't know," she said, trying to cut him short. "Just not yours."

Louis smiled. He kissed her sweetly. "You're right. It's not my business." Then: "I'm a changed man."

She gave him a look.

They went to the kitchen. Louis cut two large wedges of tarte tatin, slid them onto plates, and set them on the table while Pauline brewed tea. The smell of apples filled the room. They ate the tarte and sipped tea. "Besides," he said, as though there had been no interrup-tion, "it's not about justice. I shouldn't use the word. It's something else, something . . . more difficult." He waited for a response, but got none. "Don't you think?" he said finally.

"It's your argument," she said. "You tell me."

He set the teacup on its saucer. He said that what he was think-ing of was as bad as it was good. If there had been a map plotting out human motives, Louis would have located what he had in mind where justice and revenge intersect. Louis was speaking about Larrimer, but he knew all too well from his own experience pre-cisely where justice and revenge came together. It was an intersec-tion that was heavily traveled and dangerous.

Forty years earlier, in the back alleys of Cairo, Louis, then in his early thirties, had met secretly with a smuggler and arms dealer he knew only as Ali. Ali was an odious human being, a bully and a sadist, proud of who he was. He was known to have committed more than a few brutal crimes just for the pleasure of doing so. Though his work was often dangerous, Louis rarely carried a weapon. But he did whenever he met with Ali.

Ali was worth meeting because, among other questionable enterprises, he procured young women for various people, including an Egyptian general and a fundamentalist mullah, both of whom were enemies of Egypt's president, Anwar Sadat. Ali claimed to have information about a plot against Sadat and was now offering it for sale to the Americans. It was Louis's job to assess the value of the information and pay Ali what it was worth.

Louis quickly decided the information was worthless. It was more in the nature of rumor, and there were few specifics, no names of anyone involved, no dates or places. He kept his hand on his gun as he told Ali there would be no payment. Ali knew Louis had a thick envelope of bills inside his jacket. He also knew that Louis had a gun. Louis watched as Ali weighed the two factors one against the other.

Ali walked away muttering. It was the last time Louis saw him. A week later his bloated body was fished from the Nile. There were multiple knife wounds in his back and about his neck. It was the mullah who had had him killed. But the father of a teenage girl Ali had raped and then passed on to the mullah was arrested for the crime, tried, and imprisoned.

"Well," said the station chief, "Ali was a bastard. He needed killing. Sometimes you don't get to do justice. It just gets done for you."

"And what about the wrong guy going to jail? Is that justice?"

The chief shrugged. "No. That's just tough shit."

Louis had stopped believing in justice. Justice? Whose justice? Such concepts—justice, virtue, good, evil—sought to project a false sense of clarity onto the world. Louis *did* still care, however, about what he called "the balance of things." He cared that a kind of equilibrium be maintained. He called this "happiness," by which he did not mean anything more than a reasonable calm. "It seems like the best we can hope for. Somehow, though, even this seems like a utopian dream. Notions like good and evil always get in the way.

"Much of humankind pretends to be happy so they don't have to face the fact that they're not. *Justice will prevail*, they think, because they can't stand to acknowledge the injustice in their own lives—*our* lives, I should say, and which we in turn inflict on others.

"Think of the wars waged back and forth, think of Israel and the Palestinians, think of Shiite and Sunni, think of Hindu and Muslim, think of the people in prison around the world because of false evidence, faulty testimony, misapplication of the law—" Louis stopped speaking abruptly and sipped his tea. "I'm sorry."

Pauline smiled a not particularly happy smile.

From then on, Louis kept a tight rein on his interest in sorting out St. John Larrimer. He continued to read news reports about Larrimer's crimes and followed the speculation in the press about his whereabouts, about whether and how and which authorities might actually get involved. But he let the file he had assembled sit by the computer, unopened. Pauline was right. There was nothing he could or should do.

Louis painted the shutters. He planted a new hedge of *charme* on the downhill side of the garden to protect it from the north wind. He planted rosebushes along the drive. He tended the beans and lettuce and the last tomatoes. It had been hot and dry, so he had to water the garden daily. The beans had mostly been eaten by rabbits, but the tomatoes had been especially good this year. Gardening seemed a much better pastime than St. John Larrimer. Until Jennifer called.

XIV

THANKS IN LARGE PART TO Louis, neither of his children had had a particularly easy life. He had allowed his career to keep him away from home for long periods when they were young. And even when he was home, he spent long days at the office. He blamed the demands of the work, but eventually he came to realize and admit that he was uncomfortable at home. He felt ill suited for family life. The best that could be said for his fathering was that he had, by his long absences, prepared his children for the day when he left for good.

To his credit, he worked later to reconnect with them. For years they would not answer his letters or take his phone calls. They were stubborn and wounded and would not relent. After all, they were his children, and he was nothing if not stubborn and relentless. And so the more they resisted his efforts, the more resolute he became. He wrote long letters about his life and sent little gifts that went unacknowledged. He knew of course that the past was past. But he was determined to make up as best he could for his absence from their earlier lives by being a presence in their lives from now on. And eventually they let him. First Michael, the younger of the two, and then Jennifer.

Louis thought that Jennifer had suffered particularly from his absence. If he had been there more, she might not have dropped out of college, married early, and then quickly divorced, or so he told himself. (His theoretical debates with himself about justice were of little use when it came to measuring his own culpability.) Jennifer might have gone off the rails—it had almost happened—but instead, after her divorce she had gone back to college and studied nursing. Louis was back in touch with her. He paid for her school. Then, to his delight, she started and ran—more or less single-handedly—the Arlington Nursing Clinic, a storefront walk-in medical center on Arlington Boulevard that served the indigent and poor of Arlington, Virginia. She found quarters, persuaded foundations and hospitals to underwrite the clinic, and got doctors and nurses to volunteer their time. The day the clinic opened, there was a line of people down the block. Jennifer's tenacity filled Louis with admiration. He sent money for the clinic when he could. And eventually he and Jennifer became friends.

"Have you heard of someone called St. John Larrimer?" she asked.

"I know who he is," said Louis. "I know what he's done."

"The clinic, Dad." Louis heard her voice crack.

"What about it?"

"It closed."

"It closed?" he said stupidly. He did not want to hear what was coming. "Why?"

"Larrimer, Dad. I don't know. It's these *fucking* times!"

"Tell me, Jennifer."

One of the mainstays of support for Jennifer's clinic had been Fred Cohen, a Virginia real estate developer. He owned the storefront that housed the Arlington Nursing Clinic, and he had allowed Jennifer to rent the space at a greatly reduced rate. He also donated funds for medical supplies. His contributions had amounted to a significant part of her budget.

But he had invested nearly all his money with Larrimer, and now he was ruined. Jennifer had tried to make up the budget losses though her hospital contacts, but she had been unable to find anyone who could take up the slack. And worst of all, because Fred Cohen couldn't make his mortgage payments, the building that housed the clinic was in foreclosure.

"We have two weeks to get out."

XV

LOUIS SAT ALONE at a table on the terrace in front of the Hôtel de
France and waited. He wore a wool jacket and a scarf around his neck.
His hands were wrapped around a coffee cup. His white hair flut-
tered in the breeze. Christoph came out to see whether he wanted
anything more.

"No, Christoph. Thank you. I'm fine."

Christoph inclined his head in the direction of the police station
across the square to indicate that Renard had just come out.

Louis acknowledged Christoph's gesture, but did not look.

Renard saw Louis and smiled to himself. Louis sat like that sometimes, alone on the hotel terrace, a coffee cup in front of him, when
he wanted something from the policeman. He could have come to
the office or called, but usually he preferred to sit until Renard came
over. Louis fiddled with the coffee cup or looked at the rose climbing the hotel wall beside him. Renard wondered whether this odd
behavior might be a holdover from his CIA days.

Louis had helped Renard with some of his cases, despite the fact
that Louis held many of the laws and regulations Renard had sworn
to uphold in low regard. Renard admitted—although not to his superiors, *never* to his superiors—that a partnership between a servant of

the law, such as he was, and a man like Louis could be and in fact *had* been fruitful.

Louis had been on the wrong side of the law often enough. And each time, the wrong side had somehow ended up being the right side in terms of justice or morality. One read about such moments in novels. But it had been edifying to Renard to encounter such a situation face-to-face. Thanks to Louis, Renard had been instrumental in solving some cases involving assassination and kidnapping and international terrorism, big cases where great men were culpable and small-time villains turned out to be innocent of wrongdoing.

Thanks to Louis's history and to his unconventional, not to say unlawful, intervention in these cases, their successful resolution never made the papers or even the official police reports. It was as if they had never happened. But in every case, justice—which Louis did not believe in, but Renard did—was served.

"Hello, Louis," said Renard. He was unaccountably happy to see Louis, even though he knew he was about to be distracted from his official duties. "I've only got a few minutes."

Louis smiled and stood, and the two men embraced, as they always did these days. Renard sat down. Christoph brought him coffee.

"Do you know who Bernard Madoff is?" said Louis.

Renard laughed. "Who doesn't?" he said.

"What about St. John Larrimer?"

"Larrimer? No. Who's that?"

"Another Madoff on a slightly smaller scale. You should swear out a warrant for his arrest."

Renard laughed again. "Last night I arrested Guy Labillout. He broke into a house in Villedieu and stole a computer and some money—"

"So why haven't you sworn out a warrant?" said Louis, ignoring Renard's implication. It's just a matter of filling out a form, getting a judge to—"

"You know why," said Renard, looking at his watch.

"Humor me," said Louis.

"Okay. Because his crimes, whatever they are, did not occur within my jurisdiction."

"But they *did*. Larrimer stole money from *me*."

Renard hesitated only a moment. "I'm guessing the money wasn't stolen here."

"And if the guy you arrested . . ."

"Guy Labillout."

"If Guy Labillout had stolen money elsewhere?"

"Don't treat me like a fool, Louis." Renard was getting impatient. "I can only arrest him if he's here, or if the crime was committed here, or if there is an outstanding warrant. If Madoff or . . . or . . ."

"Larrimer."

"If Larrimer were here, then perhaps I could arrest him."

"So, if I got him here?" Louis smiled.

"To Saint-Léon?" Renard studied his face to see whether he was serious. You could never tell. "If he were here, and I had an outstanding warrant . . ." Renard hated discussions like this, although they served as a useful warning that Louis might be up to something. "Why are you interested in Madoff and Larrimer?"

"I already told you. The question is why aren't *you* interested?"

"It isn't my job. That's why they have the SEC in the United States, Interpol, the OLAF—the Office Européen de Lutte Antifraude— here, and other enforcement entities."

"And you think they will—"

"Listen, Louis. I don't have any way of knowing *what* they'll do. But they got Madoff, didn't they?"

"He turned himself in."

"The main thing is he's in jail. My guess is they're after this Larrimer, if he's defrauded people and stolen their money. There are lots of guys like that, unfortunately. Some French fund manager killed himself in New York. They're probably after him. . . ."

Louis reached across the table and touched Renard's hand to stop him from going further. "Jean, that was Pauline's brother Jean-Baptiste."

"Oh, no. Really? Jesus. I'm sorry."

"You met Jean-Baptiste. Remember?"

"Yes, I remember now."

"Pauline is heartbroken."

"But they say he's being investigated by the SEC. *And* the FBI."

"And they'll probably find wrongdoing," said Louis. "Even where there's been none."

"How do you know?"

"Because that's what they do. They're under pressure from the politicians and the press. Remember: They missed Madoff and Larrimer before it was too late. They have to find somebody to blame. To protect their budgets, to keep their jobs. Who better to blame than somebody who's dead?"

Renard wished he could say "you're wrong."

Louis told Renard about Jennifer's clinic. Men like Larrimer and Madoff played with people's lives as though there were no consequences. "They're sociopaths. They live by taking advantage of the tenderness and decency of others. They see their advantage as the highest good."

"If *I* had said that, you would say I was oversimplifying," said Renard. He sipped his coffee and peered over the rim of the cup, waiting for the reaction.

"Yes," said Louis. "You're right. But you would never have said that." Renard waited. "You," said Louis finally, "*you* live in the world, and I live outside it. Your work requires your belief in the prevailing truths. My work—"

"Painting?"

"Okay, not my work, but my . . . inclination means that I test truths, assault power—"

"That's a little grandiose, isn't it? Louis Morgon, the avenging angel?"

"Yes. You're right too."

"Too?"

"Pauline said the same thing. It *is* grandiose. Forgive me."

The two men sat in silence. They turned their gaze from each other to across the square and into the fields above town. Two tractors crossed back and forth, tilling the ground. The wind kicked up eddies of dust behind them. The farmers—Bernard and Patrick Godin—would be back the next day to plant wheat. In a few days thin green lines would show in the gray soil. The wheat would grow until the cold put a stop to it. In the spring it would grow again, would ripen into a gorgeous golden mass. Then it would fall under the thrasher. The plows would come and turn everything under, and the whole cycle would begin again.

"So," said Renard, almost afraid to ask. "Tell me what you're thinking."

"I'm thinking many things at the same time. Confused. I'm confused."

"Do you really think there's anything you can do?" It seemed a ridiculous question on the face of it. What could any one person do?

"No. Yes. Something. Maybe. I don't know." Renard could see that Louis was groping, trying to find a place to put the lever of Archimedes in order to move the world. Louis was over seventy, and yet he was still at war, with the world and with himself. He wanted to interfere, to at least throw handfuls of sand in the works so that malfeasance ground to a halt. Renard admired and loved Louis's passion and anger. At the same time he feared where they might take him. Louis's curiosity had turned to a desire that Larrimer pay dearly for his greed, for his arrogance and insolence, for his contempt for others, for everything he and his kind had caused to go wrong.

Of course many other people wanted the same thing with the same intense passion. But it would never have occurred to most of them that they could do anything to bring that about. To Louis's way of thinking, the massive apparatus of government and order and the economy, the apparatus of the world, was an indifferent monster, a leviathan inching along on its bed of slime, devouring the many and cherishing the few, not out of any feeling for or against them, but because the many were available and the few took massive advantage of the world's dark realities. One such reality was that the many were available for devouring. Another was that wealth and power protected the culpable.

In some important ways, Louis was like St. John Larrimer, thinking he could turn the prevailing truths to his advantage. "So," said Louis, "what if one—"

"One?" said Renard.

"All right: I. What if I seek out the gaps, the penetrable moments in Larrimer's defenses, his self-deceptions and pretensions? That could work, couldn't it? Then the lavish protection I'm sure he's built around himself might suddenly become vulnerable. I might be able to get at him." Renard was looking at him in disbelief.

Where Louis seemed to see only disorder and chaos, Renard saw order, and when order had been disrupted, he struggled to restore it. That must have been what Louis meant when he said Renard lived in the world while he, Louis, lived outside it. Renard's objective was necessarily more modest. That was where arresting Guy Labillout came in, arresting him, bringing him to trial, seeing that he was punished.

But Louis refused to be distracted or intimidated by the size and scope of Larrimer's infraction, or by what he called "niceties" like jurisdiction or legality. Renard picked up his coffee cup and put it to his lips even though it was empty. He smiled across the table at Louis as though he were not a madman. "And how," he said finally, "do you propose to go after Larrimer? What does that even *mean*?"

"I haven't the faintest idea," said Louis. "Even if I could track him down, then what? After all, how do you translate an insane idea into a plan of action?" And that might have been the end of it, if the answer to Louis's hypothetical question had not come from a most unlikely source.

XVI

St. John Larrimer was a man divided. Richard Smythe, his only true confidant, had seen St. John's dark side, his venality and cold-heartedness and quintessential ruthlessness. He knew St. John as avaricious and aggressive and a surreptitious but vicious bully. St. John would do anything necessary to have his way. Being of a similarly larcenous, albeit more congenial, disposition, Richard did not mind St. John's dark qualities. In fact, he found them amusing. And St. John kept this side of himself carefully hidden from everyone else.

On the other hand, Lorraine Usher, his longtime and faithful assistant, knew St. John's other side, his quotidian ways, his efficiencies and inefficiencies, his good and bad moods, his kindnesses and his unkindnesses inside out. She knew from the moment he arrived in the morning what his frame of mind would be, what business he might want to conduct and what he would want to leave for another day.

"Lorrraine, bring me the . . ." and she would be there with the required file or report before he could complete the sentence.

She knew exactly when to interrupt a meeting. She was able to make hotel or restaurant reservations without instruction beyond "Lorraine, I'm going to Paris on the twenty-sixth." She arranged for his pilot to have the jet ready, for a Rolls with his favorite driver to be waiting to transport him to Le Bristol, and for the Cuban cigars and single malt scotch whiskey that accompanied him everywhere to be in his suite when he arrived. His favorite valet was on call. So was François, the barber, if he was needed, and it was Lorraine who decided if he was needed. She knew nothing of his prostitutes; that was up to the valet.

Lorraine knew that when St. John tugged at his ear, he was about to make a phone call, as though he were preparing that organ to hear nuances it might not otherwise notice. She knew that he liked his steak buttered, that he did not like vegetables, except potatoes, or fruit, except mangoes. He always kept a hundred-dollar bill folded in his silk pocket square, just in case.

She knew his personal history as well. When his sons were little, he had sat by their beds and read to them. He had read *A Tale of Two Cities* when they were still far too small to appreciate it, followed by something by Edith Wharton and then Henry James. It didn't matter that they were too young. He read it all in a lively and vivacious way, even doing all the dialogue in different voices. The boys would drift off to sleep but, when he tried to tiptoe from the room, they would call him back to read some more. When his sons were older and St. John was no longer interested in them, he gave them money instead of attention.

Throughout the years of her employment with St. John, Lorraine became essentially invisible to him. He would sing in a high, off-key tenor when he thought he could not be heard, and she knew he was happy. Of course she did not know that his happiness derived from the latest larceny or a particularly artful and satisfying piece of vengeance.

St. John liked certain cigars for certain occasions. Lorraine thought she could have written his biography with only the butts and ashes he left in the ashtray as her source material. She knew he drank black coffee. Except when he decided he preferred a cup of tea. Before he could ask, Lorraine appeared with the small Limoges teapot. St. John always laughed, discomfited and delighted at the same time. "You read my mind!" he said.

To her great regret, she had not read his mind on the larger questions. However, on making the bitter and belated discovery that St. John was a crook, Lorraine decided she would learn everything she could about his criminal enterprise and how he had done it. After all, it was right there, in those drawers behind where she had sat all those years. And it had been put there—itemized, notated, organized, and alphabetized—by her. She had overseen the files without knowing that they represented the record of a vast criminal enterprise. Every day she had taken files out, updated and inserted documents, stored them away, month after month, year after year.

So, on that morning of her rude awakening, after swiveling around in her chair and after staring through tears at the bank of steel filing cabinets, she had stood up and pulled open the first drawer. "Aaron, Frank; Aaron, Philippa and Marcus; Abaddo, Martha and Joseph; the Abbaccus Foundation . . ." Lorraine realized she was reciting the names without reading them. And not only that, she was seeing the faces and hearing the voices that went with the names. She had over the years, without ever intending to, learned Larrimer's entire client list—now victim list—by heart. She knew their investing history, when they had first come to Larrimer, on whose recommendation, how much they had deposited, whether or not they had made withdrawals. She knew whether they took tea or coffee, how they dressed, their manners and ways, and what St. John thought of them.

Lorraine had information in her head that any prosecutor would find indispensable if and when St. John was arrested and the case came to court. It was her civic duty, she believed, to make useful sense of what she knew. As the telephone continued ringing that first morning and then afternoon, Lorraine went through file drawers, seeking particular files, which she now saw revealed irregularities— things St. John had brushed aside when she had tried to point them out, but that now would certainly be of interest to the law. At the end of that long, bitter day, Lorraine stuffed the sheaf of notes she had made into her briefcase and went home to her small house in Queens.

When she returned the next morning to continue her research, the door had been padlocked, sealed, and covered with police tape. She could not enter, but it did not really matter. She had already collected information on over a hundred files that represented a thorough record of St. John Larrimer's irregular transactions.

Lorraine returned home and studied what she had. She then wrote letters to some of the most grievously afflicted of Larrimer's victims. She explained who she was and expressed her sympathy for their loss. She explained that she was collecting evidence against St. John Larrimer to present to the SEC. If they knew anything about Larrimer's crimes that they thought might be helpful in his prosecution, she asked them to please send such information to her at the above address or to the SEC. She spent the better part of two days typing and sending the letters. Then she wrote to the SEC telling them who she was and that she was ready and willing to testify against St. John Larrimer.

Two days after she sent the letters, five agents with pistols on their hips and wearing blue jackets with FBI in huge yellow letters on the back presented themselves at her front door. One held a search warrant in front of Lorraine's face while the others brushed past and fanned out through the rooms of the house. They took her notes, her computer, and various other papers they thought might be relevant.

"Why are you taking my things?" she said.

The agent in charge gave her a long look. "We're conducting a criminal investigation, Miss Usher. That should be obvious. These things are evidence."

"How—?"

"If you read the search warrant, you'll see that it allows us to collect evidence."

"But it's not—"

"May I offer a friendly suggestion, Miss Usher? You should consult with your attorney before saying anything more."

Lorraine Usher was a small, pear-shaped woman. She wore plain glasses and had her thin gray hair pulled back in a no-nonsense ponytail and held in place with a rubber band. There was nothing remotely intimidating about her. And yet when she stuck her chin out and stepped toward the agent in charge, he paused.

"What is your name, sir?" she said.

"I am Agent Salvator Morconi," he said and produced his badge. "And—"

"Agent Morconi, I recently contacted the SEC about what I have learned about St. John Larrimer's theft of his client's money. My own money is among the millions he stole. I worked for the man for more than twenty-five years. I have collected evidence against him and am prepared to assist in his prosecution."

Morconi's hesitation was only temporary. He was going to the Fordham University Law School at night and had already learned, and come to relish using, the vocabulary and syntax of official moral indignation. "First of all, Miss Usher, it is our place and not yours to investigate crimes. As you can see, we are in the process of doing so. If you hinder us in our work, you might be arrested and charged with obstruction of justice. A serious crime has been committed. Now, you will certainly be interviewed about your part in this matter, and you may be asked to give testimony at the appropriate time."

Morconi paused for effect. He turned away as though to oversee the ongoing operation. Then he turned back. "For now, Miss Usher, I suggest you retain a good criminal attorney. To my eyes, at least, it seems highly unlikely that Larrimer could have done everything he did without your knowing and possibly abetting his crimes. Take it from me, lady: get yourself a good lawyer."

XVII

Once Lorraine was alone, the seriousness of her situation began to dawn on her. She had managed to discern a great deal of St. John's treachery from a quick overview of some of the office files. So one could reasonably wonder why she hadn't been able to see these things earlier if she could see them so readily now. And what about those letters to St. John's clients and to the SEC? Wasn't that an elaborate ruse to mislead investigators and to feign innocence?

"But I lost my entire savings," she heard herself saying in her imaginary courtroom testimony. "I'm a victim as much as anyone."

Her imaginary attorney rolled his eyes; the imaginary prosecutor thundered. "So you would have us believe, Ms. Usher. But where, Ms. Usher, are the millions you have hidden away, the millions you were paid for filing false reports with the SEC and the IRS and for helping Mr. Larrimer steal nearly three billion, THREE BILLION dollars?"

Her imaginary attorney was on his feet. "I withdraw the question," said the prosecutor quickly. But the damage had been done.

Lorraine Usher would have given anything to stop all those letters from going to all those clients. But some had already been received

and opened and read. Those to more distant addresses were still ar-
riving or would arrive soon. Pauline's letter arrived six weeks after it
had been mailed. It was addressed to Jean-Baptiste and had been sent
to him while he was still alive but had arrived after he was dead. The
envelope had been addressed by hand, and so the police assumed it
was a personal letter and forwarded it to Pauline, who was listed in
their records as Jean-Baptiste's next of kin.

"What kind of letter is it?" said Louis, trying not to appear too
interested.

"It's a peculiar letter," she said. She read it to him.

"May I see it?" He read through the letter. "Do you know anything else about this person?" he asked.

"Nothing," said Pauline. "It's strange, isn't it?"

"A little."

Louis looked up Lorraine Usher and found her listed among
Larrimer's victims.

"Why would she write such a letter?" said Pauline.

"I don't know," said Louis.

"Maybe she was an accomplice and she's trying to cover her
tracks."

"Maybe," said Louis. "She seems like an obvious suspect. But she
seems a little *too* obvious to me." He thought for a moment. "According to reports, she lost one hundred fifty thousand dollars. But the
minimum you needed to invest with Larrimer was two hundred
thousand. So he made an exception for her. Which he probably
wouldn't have done if she were an accomplice. You see? It makes her
name stand out. Maybe she's angry and desperate, and now she's in
trouble. Writing this letter was a big mistake."

"Why?"

"Well, *you* thought she might be an accomplice."

"That's just me," said Pauline.

"No. It's a reasonable conclusion. I'd bet that's how the SEC will
see it. And others too." Louis didn't elaborate on who the others

might be. "They'll think, she worked in his office for who knows how long. She must have known something."

"Unless?"

"Well, unless she didn't. Smart people can see wrongdoing and not recognize it. If they're not criminals, they're not looking for criminal behavior. She trusted this guy, maybe even admired him. He probably paid her a nice salary, bought her flowers on Secretary's Day, gave her a Christmas bonus. He made an exception so she could invest in his business, which she must have seen as a favor.

"She sat in this guy's front office every day. She took his phone calls, made his appointments, met his clients, typed up his correspondence, his reports. Whether she knew what he was up to or not is almost irrelevant. She knew the circumstances of his life. She knew him."

"Do you think I should write her back?"

He paused and thought. "No," he said finally.

"Why not?"

"Well, you know I'm going to visit Jennifer and Michael in Washington."

"Yes. . . ."

"I think maybe I'll stop in and see Lorraine Usher on the way."

XVIII

Louis did not elaborate on who else besides the SEC might think that Lorraine had been St. John's accomplice. He didn't want to alarm Pauline, but he was certain that among the many innocent people who had had their money stolen, there were a good many villains as well. Louis had noticed on the Web site, for instance, that the EisenerBank had lost all its money to Larrimer, and since the bank was in Zurich, it seemed likely that many of Eisener's clients had a serious interest in hiding their money, and an equally serious interest in getting it back when it went missing. They were probably not engaged in the sort of business that allowed them to write off their losses.

Lorraine Usher's doorbell rang at eight-thirty one Sunday morning. She looked through the curtain and saw a man, sixty-five or seventy maybe, not tall but trim, with unruly white hair drifting above his head. He stood with his back to her, looking out at the street. When he turned to face the door, it was as though his blue eyes locked on hers, even though there was no way that he could see her watching from behind the curtain. She let him knock again before she opened the door.

"Yes?" she said. She left the storm door latched. And her right hand rested on the baseball bat she always kept leaning against the wall just out of sight.

"I'm Louis Morgon," said the man, "and I've come to speak to Lorraine Usher."

"What's it about?" she said, not admitting that she was Lorraine Usher.

"I got one of the letters Miss Usher wrote about Larrimer, that is, my friend Pauline Vasiltschenko did. It was sent to her brother, Jean-Baptiste Vasiltschenko, who—"

Lorraine opened the door. "Oh, God," she said. "That poor man. Please come in, Mr. Morgon. Please." She held the door and Louis stepped inside. "I'm so sorry about his death. I met him once— Mr. Vasiltschenko. He seemed like a lovely person."

"Yes," said Louis. "He was."

"Did his sister lose her money?"

"Some," said Louis.

"Is she all right?"

"She misses her brother."

"How awful." Lorraine wiped tears from her cheeks. "Did you lose money?" she asked with trepidation in her voice.

"An insignificant amount," said Louis.

"Insignificant?" said Lorraine.

"A small amount. I don't care about the money."

"No?"

"But I do care about Larrimer and his criminal behavior. What he did to people, to Jean-Baptiste and Pauline Vasiltschenko. Did you lose money, Miss Usher?"

She paused a moment. "I must tell you, Mr. Morgon, my attorney has instructed me to direct anyone who contacts me to the SEC. I have no intention of interfering with the SEC's investigation, and to the extent that I have done so, I am sorry. I regret having sent those letters; it was a mistake to do so."

"I agree with your attorney. I think it was a mistake to send those letters. To be honest, I'm not at all interested in the SEC's investigation. I don't think it will amount to much of anything. They will be looking for scapegoats. And you, I imagine, will be high on their list of candidates."

Lorraine stiffened. She was about to ask Louis to leave when a large orange cat emerged from behind the living room couch and planted himself between them. The cat, Arthur, stared at Louis with his glittering green eyes as though taking his measure. Louis watched for a moment, then stooped and patted his own leg. Arthur walked over and rubbed against him.

"Well," said Lorraine, as if Arthur had changed her mind for her. She sat back down. "What is it you wish to speak to me about?" She gestured toward the couch. Louis sat down, and Arthur jumped up beside him and stepped onto his lap.

"I am not with any agency—official or otherwise," Louis said. "I am here completely on my own initiative. Half-cocked initiative, my friends would say. *Have* said," he corrected himself and smiled. "But I've been thinking how nice it would be to find St. John Larrimer and turn him over to the law. I don't intend to exact any sort of revenge. I only want to—how should I say this?—'guide' him into the hands of the law and then to . . . compel the law to deal with him."

Lorraine looked at Louis with astonishment. "*Guide* him?"

Louis stroked Arthur; Arthur closed his eyes and purred.

"You intend to do this by yourself?"

"I can't possibly do it by myself."

"No, I wouldn't think so."

"And I have to confess, I have no idea how it might be done."

"I see," said Lorraine, not seeing at all.

"That's one reason I've come to see you," said Louis.

Lorraine's eyes grew wide. Louis expected her to bring up her lawyer again. Backing away from the affair entirely was the most prudent course of action and what anyone—lawyer or friend—would have advised her to do. What she said, though, was "would you like some coffee or tea?"

"A cup of tea would be very nice," said Louis.

Lorraine went to the kitchen and returned a few minutes later with a pot of tea and some scones and jam on a tray. She had used the time to think over what Louis had said so far. "How do you mean to find Mr. Larrimer?" she said as she poured the tea.

"Well, as I said, I don't know yet," said Louis, "although I suspect finding him will be easier than getting close to him. Or his loot."

"And why are you doing this?"

"Well, I don't think the SEC will—"

"No, no," she said. "No. You already said that. Why are *you* thinking of doing it? Why you."

"The answer is long and complicated and probably boring," said Louis.

"Then what's the short answer?"

Louis gave her a sharp look. "Pursuing crooks is sort of a hobby of mine," he said. He wanted to put a stop to her questions.

Lorraine did not look away as he expected she would. She met his eyes and held them. Lorraine Usher had just been betrayed by St. John Larrimer, to whom she had devoted the better part of her professional life. She was alone and without employment prospects or any other prospects she could think of. She was in trouble with the FBI and the SEC, to a sufficient extent that she had had to ask her brother-in-law, Bruno, a tax analyst and attorney in the New York City housing authority, to act as her lawyer until she could get out of this mess.

"As it happens, I'm looking for a hobby," she said.

"I beg your pardon?" said Louis.

"I'm . . . looking . . . for . . . a . . . hobby." She spoke the words as though she were speaking to a foreigner. She did not smile.

XIX

Lorraine told Louis everything she knew about Larrimer, Ltd.'s operations. That the FBI had taken her notes seemed to make little difference; most of the crucial information was in her head. She told him about Jeremy Gutentag, who had run the trading room and who seemed to have vanished from the face of the earth.

"Did he, this Gutentag, know what Larrimer was up to?"

"I don't see how he could not have known. He oversaw all the trading."

"That doesn't necessarily mean anything. But what can you tell me about him?"

"He grew up in England, but he looked to be Indian or something. A nice-looking boy. Very polite and very well-spoken. Smart. But he kept to himself. He came from London. He was thirty years old. He went to Oxford University and the London School of Economics. This was his first job."

"How long had he been working for Larrimer?"

"Six years."

"Was he well paid?"

"He was very well paid."

"But his name is not on the list. He didn't invest with Larrimer?"

"No," said Lorraine. She frowned as though realizing the implication for the first time.

"Where did he live?"

"His address was the Carlton Plaza Hotel."

"For six years?"

"I always wondered about that. I asked him more than once whether he didn't want to get an apartment. 'No,' he said. 'There's no need.' He seemed to me to be someone whose life was mainly lived somewhere else."

"Somewhere else?"

"Well, he didn't seem to have much of a life in New York. He was either at the office or at the Carlton Plaza."

"Do you think that somewhere else may have been London?" said Louis.

Lorraine guessed it was, but she didn't know. "He was from London, but I don't think he had any family left. I don't think he went there in the six years he was here. Even though he had been here for six years, it was always like he had just arrived. And like he was just about to leave. But I don't know for where.

"Maybe living in a hotel just suited him. I once had to pick up some papers there. He was surprised when I showed up at his door. He had me wait in the hall while he got the papers. 'The next time, Miss Usher, call first and I'll meet you in the lobby,' he said. He was polite, but firm about that."

Lorraine told Louis what she knew about the rest of the trading room staff, but that wasn't much. They were mostly young business school graduates. They had mostly kept to themselves. And now they had all retained lawyers and gone into deep seclusion.

She was still able to recite most of the client list from Aaron to Zylinski. Louis stopped her when she mentioned names he knew from reading the accounts—individuals or corporate names. He was particularly interested in banks and other financial institutions. Of course in most cases she did not remember many specifics. But some accounts revealed peculiarities about Larrimer's transactions, and she offered those peculiarities to Louis to the best of her recollection.

She knew now that there was evidence in the files of accounting inconsistencies including the backdating of trades. Larrimer was not actually buying or selling securities, so by dating his buys and sales to his advantage, he "documented" his exceptional returns. His trades had been verified as legitimate by his accountants, Robert Feather and Sons in Greenwich, Connecticut. Larrimer had explained away the backdating to Lorraine as a result of his having neglected to enter the purchase or sale when it was actually completed. Lorraine had had no reason to doubt any of it, until now. She gave Louis the accountant's contact information.

She also gave him Larrimer's social security number, credit card account numbers, and whatever she knew about the banks through which Larrimer had conducted his business transactions. "I suppose Mr. Larrimer will have moved the money somewhere else."

"He will," said Louis. "Even the offshore banks will have changed. But the old banks and especially those he owes money—mortgages, loans—could be useful. You never know."

Lorraine also had the addresses of St. John's various properties around the world. She had a good idea, she thought, which one he would probably prefer as a hideout. "Les Saintes . . . Terre-de-Haut," she said.

"Where is that?"

"Guadeloupe," she said. "He loves it there."

St. John's whereabouts did not seem to concern Louis. "Not yet," he explained. "Eventually. But not yet."

"But won't he get away if you don't get him soon?"

"It's unlikely," said Louis. "He's lived grandly for a long time, hasn't he? That's not an easy habit to break. Plus he's got no experience at hiding. Anyway, we're not going to 'get' him. Someone else will have to do that."

Lorraine was a fount of information. Louis had already filled one yellow pad with notes and was starting on the second. He could decide later what was of value and what wasn't. It was possible that she was deliberately misleading him, that she was still on Larrimer's payroll, still running interference for him, but Louis doubted it.

"Tell me about Larrimer himself," he said.

"What about him?"

"His life—friends, family, whatever comes to mind."

"Well, he never talked with me about his personal life or included me in it. I met his children a few times and only saw his wife a couple of times. In all the years I worked for him, he never invited me for lunch or for anything else. Never. He said, when he hired me, and then more than once after that, that it was better that we keep our relationship strictly business. Now I see why. Still, there was stuff you couldn't help knowing. He was not punctual; he was unpredictable and undependable. He wasn't always where he said he'd be."

His wife, Carolyne, had apparently had a similar experience. After they had been married a few years, she discovered St. John had been having an affair with a wealthy client in Los Angeles. Carolyne had thought he was on a business trip when, she learned by accident, thanks to an errant phone call, that he had in fact been holed up in the client's Beverly Hills mansion. After that St. John moved to the Park Avenue apartment. Seven-forty Park Avenue, where all the big shots live. Carolyne took the two boys and moved to Greenwich. St. John paid her a huge settlement along with alimony and child support.

"Was the divorce nasty?" Louis said.

"It wasn't. She said what she wanted, and he paid."

Carolyne bought a real estate business. As far as Lorraine knew, St. John and Carolyne had little to do with each other after the divorce.

"Maybe," said Louis.

"But he stole her money."

"Yes, maybe. But he also gave her plenty. You never know," said Louis. "It might be useful to both of them to have her on that list of victims. And what about the lover? Is she on the list?"

"I never heard her name, but I think she must be. There were a few clients from Beverly Hills. One of them, Mona Liebling, may be the lover."

Louis studied Lorraine's face. "I have to ask you an indelicate question. I hope you will forgive me. Were you in love with St. John Larrimer?"

She did not hesitate. "At one time I think I was. When I first started working for him, the business was exciting and there was something exciting about the travel and meetings, the fancy office suite. But then I realized one day, it wasn't romantic at all, and he seemed small and boring."

"Small?"

"In spirit," she said. "He did not seem to care about others. Except for his boys. He loved those two boys, at least when they were little. But everyone else . . . ? I don't think he loved anyone. He drank a lot. He didn't have much of an imagination."

"Forgive me," said Louis. "I had to ask."

"I know."

St. John Larrimer had led the life of a typical businessman: long hours, dull meetings with clients, boring tasks, late restaurant dinners. It was true he was stealing. But in a way, organizing a theft of such complexity and magnitude was even more time-consuming than the actual investing work would have been. Nearly everything St. John did had to be falsified on paper, which meant being meticulous and fastidious in a way that ran counter to his nature. And as the deceptions multiplied and deepened and became intertwined, it took more and more effort and concentration to keep it all sorted out. In his own way, St. John was a hard worker. He had spent long hours in the dreary office of Robert Feather and Sons (there were no sons; there was only Robert) going over accounts, tax returns, SEC filings, in essence getting and keeping his story straight.

Except for the apartment on Park Avenue and the villa on Terre-de-Haut, he rarely visited any of his properties. In fact, he had acquired most of them as places to put money. Real estate was safer than banks; St. John knew from experience just how easy it was to bilk banks.

Nothing Lorraine had said about Larrimer had surprised Louis until the moment she mentioned the prints that hung in St. John's office. "He took one of them with him when he left," she said. "It was an etching, I think. By Rembrandt." Louis's eyebrows jumped up into the middle of his forehead.

"Really?" said Louis. "Do you remember what it was?"

"It was Jesus and the money changers."

"Was it an original?"

"Oh, yes. He collected them."

"Really? Do you remember what else he had?"

Lorraine did not remember. "They were always changing," she said. "Except for the one by Rembrandt. That was his favorite. But he was always buying new ones. Paintings too. He got catalogs from all the auction houses, and he bought stuff all the time."

"How much stuff?"

"He told me once he owned more than two hundred prints and paintings. He was on the board at the Metropolitan Museum, you know. He said they were going to have a show of his collection."

"Really. And where did he keep his collection?"

"Some of it went to his apartment, but I don't know where he kept the rest of it. Probably his houses. I don't think anybody knows where they all are, except Mr. Larrimer."

"Does he have favorite artists?"

"I don't know who they all were," said Lorraine. "I don't know much about art. Picasso maybe."

"He bought Picasso?"

"Oh, yes. Quite a few. And some other French painters. Famous ones. One starts with *R*, I think. Rard or Rond."

"Renoir?"

"No, not him. Rar? Something with *R*? Or . . . Is this important?"

"Bonnard?"

"That's it. He painted his wife washing herself?"

"Yes. Who else did he like?"

"Matisse. Mondrian, I think." Lorraine could not remember most of the names.

Finally she recounted how, over the past several weeks, she had gotten letters from several dozen clients in response to her letter. At least she supposed they were in response to her letter, but she couldn't be sure. She had turned the unopened letters over to Bruno to forward to the SEC. And some people had actually showed up at her door.

"How many people?" said Louis.

"You're the fourth."

"And who were they?"

"I don't know. I didn't ask. I sent them away."

"Like you sent me away?" said Louis.

"If they had met Arthur, it might have turned out different. But no, I sent them away without opening the door." Lorraine and Louis had by now spent several hours together. The teapot was cold. Arthur had gotten bored and had left.

Louis leafed through his notes one last time. "Jeremy Gutentag." He paused. "You said you thought he was Indian?"

"I think so. From London, though."

"Do you know anything about his life there?" said Louis.

Lorraine thought for a moment. "No. Not much."

"Anything? His family, his friends, his studies?"

"Well, he was a very accomplished student. He was proud of that. He said his parents were both dead. His father had had a shop of some kind."

"Did he speak with an accent?"

"Oh, he spoke beautifully. Like an educated Englishman. Which he was."

"But no Indian accent?"

"Not that I could tell. But I'm not that good on accents."

"Do you remember anything else?"

"No. Jeremy didn't say much about his life."

"Did his name strike you as odd? Gutentag? It's a German name."

"It did, actually. I mean, he was dark skinned, and I found it odd that he had a name like that."

"His father could have been white," said Louis.

"I don't think so," said Lorraine. "He said once it had been hard for his parents, being Indians in London."

"Did he say Indians? Did he say where his parents were from?"

"I don't remember. I just remember him saying they were immigrants from . . . I don't think he said where."

"Not India?"

"I don't think so. I don't remember."

"Not Pakistan or Bangladesh or Sri Lanka?"

"I just don't remember. I'm sorry."

"I think that's enough for now," said Louis, closing the notebook. "You have been extremely helpful. I can't thank you enough." He gave Lorraine his number in Saint-Léon in case she thought of anything else.

XX

Jeremy Gutentag was on the run. Not so much from the law as from his own guilty conscience, chased by his own recently reawakened sense of right and wrong. His guilt rushed after him like a pack of baying hounds. The magnitude of his crime cast a dark shadow over him. He could think of only one place where he would be safe.

He had been plucked from obscurity by the great St. John Larrimer and given a seat at Larrimer's trading desk. After a brief apprenticeship there, he was put in charge of the other traders. Larrimer had seen something in the young economist. Jeremy had thought it must be his academic achievement and his native intelligence. While still at Oxford, he had published articles in several important journals. He had references from leading economists who described Jeremy as someone for whom success was "an inevitability."

For St. John, Jeremy's smooth charm, tony accent, and most particularly the falsified bits of his history—not surprisingly St. John had an eye for such things—added up to a man primed for larceny. "Tell me about yourself," St. John had said. It was their first meeting. Jeremy sat across the table from St. John. Lorraine had just brought them coffee and sweets.

Jeremy was supremely confident, as though he were in his natural domain. He sat comfortably, his fingers interlocked on his lap, one slender pinstriped leg draped across the other. His dark eyes met St. John's. "Well, Mr. Larrimer, you know from my résumé about my academic and professional history. . . ."

"What else should I know?" said St. John.

"You must know that I'm very eager to be part of an enterprise such as yours," said Jeremy. "I confess, Goldman has offered me a terrific deal, but, frankly, being part of a large, conventional establishment doesn't interest me."

"Conventional. Goldman Sachs is conventional?"

"I think it is. And large. One could say too large to succeed in the sense that I think an investment bank can succeed. And in the way that they do investment banking, yes, I think they *are* conventional. And woefully predictable, once you have their business model pegged."

"And do you? Have their business model pegged?"

"Yes, I do."

"I see." St. John liked this boy. "And tell me about the rest of your life, who you are."

Jeremy shifted in his seat. He recited his biography: born in London of hardworking Indian immigrant shopkeepers, work after school in the family shop, then Oxford on a Kings' Scholarship, then the London School of Economics. Parents deceased. "I think that's about it," he said.

St. John seemed satisfied. He offered Jeremy a job. Over the next several months, he allowed Jeremy small glimpses of the questionable corners of his operation. Nothing that could incriminate him, but details that a like-minded financier might recognize as not entirely aboveboard. St. John did so with complete confidence. He knew his man, better than Jeremy knew himself.

"But how could you be sure that I wouldn't go to the SEC?" Jeremy asked one day. St. John had recently upped the ante and revealed an unmistakably illegal bit of business.

"Well, by then you were already involved, so you couldn't, could you?"

"But earlier, when I first arrived, before I . . . knew much?"

"Well, you always knew something was up, didn't you?" said St. John.

"I suspected. But—"

"Well, in the same way, I knew *you* from the start," said St. John, tasting the Burgundy he had ordered, a 1986 Andrées. He rolled it around on his tongue, then nodded his approval to the sommelier. They were at Per Se, celebrating Jeremy's ascension to head of the trading room.

"Knew what?" said Jeremy.

"I knew how much you valued the game."

"The game," said Jeremy. The word made him uneasy. He was unaccustomed to both his newfound authority and the fact that it was part of a criminal enterprise. Like St. John, Jeremy had long ago concluded that the economic system was something to be dominated and manipulated by those with the means to do so. It was a neutral, amoral system, like the weather or geology, except that it was rigged and could be manipulated. Anyone with the means to do so, should do so. This imperative was part of human existence. But how had St. John known?

"I just knew," said St. John, holding his wineglass high and waiting for Jeremy to raise his.

XXI

JEREMY HAD BEEN WATCHING the tickers, so he knew, almost before St. John did, that things were coming apart—bank shares were plummeting while the Fed was making alarming noises. Without so much as packing a bag, Jeremy took a taxi to JFK and left for London. He stayed in London only long enough to conduct some business, which consisted mainly of removing his savings to a secure location. Then he bought a suitcase, some clothes, and a first-class plane ticket for Lahore, Pakistan.

Jeremy presented his passport and his ticket at the gate. The other passengers had already boarded the plane. The gate attendant produced a boarding pass and then fed Jeremy's passport through the scanner. "Welcome, Mr. Kapoor," she said. "Have a pleasant flight." As Jeremy went down the gangway, they closed the gate behind him.

Jeremy had been born and had grown up in Lahore as Charanjeet Kapoor, the privileged only child of Mohan and Golapi Kapoor. Mohan was the founder and owner of several businesses, among them the Fine Fabric Works, manufacturers of fine cloths of cotton, linen, and rayon, including what was widely considered to be the world's very best muslin.

Mohan and Golapi were generous and unstinting in their love for their son. They wanted more for their Charanjeet than even they could provide. They understood from the start that his future lay in the larger world, and that one sure path to that larger world led through the British public schools—which is how Charanjeet found himself at Trinity, a boarding school in the Gloucestershire village of Tronklin-on-Wye. After graduating from Trinity with high honors, it was on to Exeter College at Oxford University. Mohan and Golapi happily paid the fees, which were considerable, as long as Charanjeet did the work, which was also considerable.

Taking the name Jeremy Gutentag—he liked the ring of it—had been Charanjeet's idea. At first Mohan and Golapi had found the idea shocking and distasteful, but they soon saw the wisdom behind it. Charanjeet did not tell them about his invented biography with the deceased shopkeeper parents. That would have hurt them too much. Through the years, Charanjeet wrote long, newsy letters home, always signing "With love, Jeremy." Sometimes he telephoned. "Hello, Mummy, it's Jeremy."

This was his first trip home in ten years. He had left home a boy, but he emerged now from the crowded international arrivals terminal a handsome and accomplished young man. Mohan and Golapi laughed with delight when they saw him, for he was proof incarnate of the success of their collective project. Their driver took Jeremy's attaché and rushed off to retrieve his suitcase. Jeremy's announcement that he was returning home had been sudden and unexpected, but what did that matter? Mohan and Golapi were thrilled to have him there.

"How long can you stay, Jeremy?" said Golapi, caressing his cheek.

"Mummy, I am Charanjeet again," he said, and kissed his delighted mother's forehead. "I have left Jeremy in New York, and so must you."

XXII

CAROLYNE BUSHWICK'S REALTY OFFICE WAS in a strip mall a short walk from the Bridgeport train station. Louis had decided to use a false name with Larrimer's ex. "Hello, Ms. Bushwick, I'm Louis Coburn. I'm sorry to be late."

"It doesn't matter," she said. "I've got plenty to keep me busy. Please." She gestured for him to sit down. She saw that he was looking at the sign over her desk. "The company came with the David Reis name—I bought it from Janet after David died. It seemed prudent to keep the name. It's a familiar one in these parts."

"Of course. I understand," said Louis. "I suppose it helps avoid unwanted attention."

"Attention?"

"The Larrimer connection."

"I see." Her face had gone cold. "You said on the phone that you are interested in a second home."

"Yes, that's right."

She leafed through a folder. "I only have a few listings right now that meet your criteria. They're all in Greenwich."

"Really? I'm surprised. I mean, the market hasn't been that—"

"We deal exclusively in upper-bracket properties; they are mostly immune to the downturn." She passed a folder across the desk. "Here are four properties that might interest you."

Louis leafed through the listings. "May I have copies of these?" Carolyne got up and went into the next room. The office where Louis sat seemed entirely impersonal. A cheap desk, two chairs, a filing cabinet. There were no pictures—of her sons, for instance, no computer, no calendar, no personal diary anywhere. He could hear her fiddling with the copy machine. She didn't know how to use it.

"Can I help?" he said and got up and walked toward the copy room. As he passed the desk, he took a quick look in the top drawer. It was empty. The filing cabinet drawers had no labels. He knocked lightly on the side, and you could hear it was empty too.

"I've got it," she said, and the machine started whirring.

"They're lovely properties," he said, stopping in the doorway. "They seem priced for a better market than we're having."

She turned and smiled at him. "I'm sure the prices have some flexibility built in."

"I would hope so," said Louis.

"Shall we go look?" Carolyne drove Louis down to Greenwich, where they looked at the four houses. "Cavernous" was how Louis later described them to Renard.

"They're all four marvelous," said Louis. "I'll have to give them all serious thought."

They drove back to Bridgeport. "We have relationships with several banks, Mr. Coburn. We can help you get financing on good terms. It's added value that we provide."

"Forgive me, Ms. Bushwick, but you keep referring to 'we.' Are there other partners in the David Reis Realty, or are you in business for yourself?"

Carolyne gave Louis a long look. "Why do you want to know, Mr. Coburn?"

"Well, I just like to know exactly who I'm dealing with, that's all."

"You're dealing with me, Mr. Coburn."

"So that means you are in business for yourself?"

"Mr. Coburn. I thought you said you were interested in buying a home. If that's so, then let's stick to business."

A few minutes later Louis watched from the coffee shop across the street as Carolyne came out of the office, got in her car, and drove away.

"You buying a house?" said the young woman making his coffee.

"Maybe," said Louis.

"From her?"

"Maybe."

"In Bridgeport?"

"Greenwich. Why?"

"Well, you're the first customer I ever saw come out of there. I don't think they move a lot of houses."

"You see everyone that comes and goes?"

She made a sweeping gesture. "We're not real busy."

"You think it's a front or something?"

The young woman shrugged.

The real estate sales and tax records at the town hall confirmed what the coffee maker had surmised. David Reis Realty had not sold a single house in the entire time that Carolyne Bushwick had been its proprietor.

XXIII

LORRAINE HAD HAD FOUR UNIDENTIFIED visitors, and Dimitri Adropov had been the very first. Dimitri was a major customer of the EisenerBank, having only recently entrusted that institution with many millions of Swiss francs, which they had then turned over to St. John Larrimer. Dimitri was one reason Lorelei Steinhauer was in hiding. In fact he could easily have tracked her down and taken his revenge. And Dimitri had to admit, killing her had been a momentary temptation. It was what his colleagues on the board at Gazneft, the huge Russian oil conglomerate, all wanted. "But," Dimitri asked them one by one, "how does that get our money back?" He went around the big steel and glass table asking each of them. "You want your fucking money, don't you?"

Even in a fancy suit with a smooth shave and a two-hundred-dollar haircut, Dimitri looked like a killer. His shoulders were wide, and he was tall. He all but filled Lorraine's front doorway. His narrow eyes were arranged in a permanent squint. When he smiled, the temperature seemed to drop twenty degrees. Lorraine half expected a little forked tongue to come flicking through the space between his front teeth. She had kept her right hand on the baseball bat, but a lot of good that would have done. It turned out, though, that Dimitri liked cats, so who knows what Arthur might have decided if Dimitri had made it inside.

"My attorney has instructed me to direct everyone to the SEC," said Lorraine.

"I understand," said Dimitri with a smile. He turned and left. All he had really wanted for now was to know where she was. When the time was right, he would find out from her where Larrimer was. Then he would extract the money from Larrimer—including interest and expenses. He would probably kill Larrimer and his accomplices. Usually Dimitri left that sort of thing to his underlings, but when it came to situations like this—in a foreign country with vast sums of money at stake, Dimitri preferred to do the job himself. He didn't know whether this Usher woman was an accomplice. But she was a witness, so either way she had to go.

From that day on, Dimitri Adropov or an associate sat in his car and kept watch on Lorraine Usher's house. Dimitri saw Louis arrive, and he watched him leave some hours later. This man was old. But in Dimitri's business (not the oil part of his business) he had learned to judge men, and there was something about this man he did not like.

As Louis got out of the cab in front of his hotel, the sun came out from behind the clouds. A passing shower had swept the air clean. The light was golden and clear, and the air, despite the humidity, was cool and invigorating. Such light and air were like a magnet for Louis, drawing him outside to walk, no matter what else he had to do.

Walking was not just a passion for Louis. It was part of who he was, a central aspect of his disposition, a quality of his being. He walked the way most people breathed. He walked to put things in perspective, to figure out what needed to be done, but also, as he saw it, to stay alive. He had walked the length and breadth of France. One of the things he loved best about that country was that it had given him walking.

Louis had long made it a habit to wear only good walking shoes, no matter what the venue. He had two pairs of such shoes—the broken-in pair he was wearing now and the newer pair he was breaking in back home, lug-soled leather lace-ups that came to his ankles. Without even thinking about it, Louis set out up Fifth Avenue, went a block east, and continued up Madison. He moved at a brisk pace. He liked seeing the shops. They were, to his mind, part of an exotic landscape.

Just above Ninetieth Street, he turned west and headed into the park. He followed the meandering paths where they led. He stopped at the reservoir and leaned on the fence, looking west to the apartment buildings on the other side. They were perfectly reflected in the mirror surface of the reservoir. A pair of mallards skidded onto the water, and the reflection broke into pieces.

Louis turned and continued in a southerly direction. Once he left the reservoir, the paths meandered west then east then west again. He came upon a quartet of musicians playing. A saxophone case lay open in front of them. He dropped some money into the case and sat down on a bench to listen. It was an unseasonably warm day. He took off his jacket and rolled up his shirtsleeves. There was a thin film of perspiration on his arms.

Louis did not usually pause like this when he walked. The rhythm of the walking, the steady pounding of his feet, the swinging of his arms were part of what he loved. But when he was being followed—as he was fairly certain was the case now—an instinct from his earlier life broke into his consciousness like a discordant note and turned it in a more vigilant direction. His attentiveness shifted from the park and pathways to the configuration of people around him.

The large, well-dressed man following him seemed not to care whether Louis noticed him or not, which made Louis careful not to give any indication that he had. Toward the south end of the park, Louis turned back toward Fifth and then went north until he came to the spot where he had gotten out of the cab.

He went into the office tower beside his hotel. The lobby ran perpendicular to the street for fifteen meters, then made a ninety-degree left turn to the concierge's desk. Louis rounded the corner and approached the concierge's desk, then turned abruptly, as though he had changed his mind. He walked back toward the blind corner, which he and Dimitri Adropov—the other man—reached at exactly the same moment. They collided, and Louis staggered backward and fell. Dimitri instinctively reached out to catch Louis by the arm, as Louis hit the floor.

"Sorry, very sorry," said Dimitri. And he *looked* sorry. The concierge rushed from behind his desk, and together he and Dimitri helped Louis to his feet. Louis wobbled a bit and leaned on Dimitri while the concierge brought a chair from behind his desk. Dimitri lowered Louis gently onto the chair. "You are all right?" he asked. He wanted to get away as quickly as he could, but to be too hasty might seem suspicious. Thankfully, Louis came to his rescue.

"Go on," said Louis with a wave of his hand. "I'll be fine. I'll just sit here another minute. I came in the wrong door. I thought this was the Park East Hotel."

"The Park East is next door," said the concierge.

"Should I go with you?" said Dimitri.

"No, really, I'm fine," said Louis. He stood up, steadier this time. He brushed off his clothes a bit. "Seriously, you go on. I'll be fine. It was my fault; I'm sorry." He offered Dimitri his hand.

"All right then," said Dimitri. "I go now." He shook hands with Louis, thanked him, thanked the concierge, and left.

Louis waited a moment, and when by his calculation Dimitri had left the building, ran to the revolving door, much to the concierge's astonishment. Louis watched as Dimitri hurried to a black Chevrolet Suburban and sped off.

From his room Louis called Lorraine's number, but there was no answer. He called Renard at home. "Do you know what time it is?" said the policeman.

"Midnight. You weren't sleeping."

"That's not the point."

"What *is* the point?"

Renard gave up. "Okay. What do you want?"

"I've learned some interesting things about Larrimer. I'll tell you all about him when I get home."

"I can't wait."

"But here's something more important. I was followed by a Russian, a mobster, I think."

"You think?"

"He was carrying a large pistol."

"How do you know that?"

"We bumped into each other. Do you think you could find out who he is?"

"What's his name?"

"I have no idea."

"So, how am I supposed to—"

"We had our picture taken. Arm in arm: the security camera at the concierge desk, 1012 Fifth Avenue. Today's date, about five-fifteen."

"What is it?" said Isabelle after Renard hung up the phone. She was smiling. She knew it would be a good story.

XXIV

Louis dialed the CIA switchboard in Langley, Virginia. He gave his name and said that he wanted to speak to Peter Sanchez. No one else. Peter Sanchez. He was put on hold. He had helped Peter out of a bad spot a couple of years earlier and, as uncomfortable as it was for Peter to admit it, he owed Louis his career. He would not be pleased to hear from Louis, but he could not afford to ignore his call. The next voice Louis heard said, "This is the duty officer, Mr. Morgon. Please give me your contact information."

Louis was fairly certain Renard would never get anywhere near that security film. But he was also certain he would try, driven by the need to watch over Louis, and probably also out of curiosity. Louis also knew that once Peter Sanchez knew that Renard had tried, then Peter would have to go after it himself, if for no other reason than to find out what Louis was up to.

Louis did not know who the Russian was or why he was following him. But he thought that it must be connected to the Larrimer case (in his mind it was now the Larrimer case), and he could only have found Louis by way of Lorraine Usher. Louis tried her number again, and this time she answered. She recognized Dimitri as soon as Louis began describing him. "He was here. He didn't give his name, so I don't know whether he's on the list of people that lost money or not."

"Do you remember anything about his visit?"

"I remember it very well. I referred him to the SEC, and he went away."

"He didn't insist or protest or ask any questions?"

"No. I was surprised that he didn't. But he left quickly, got in his car and drove away."

"His car?"

"A big black car. I didn't get the license number. I wasn't thinking that way then."

"New York, HBN-646?"

"Maybe. I don't know."

"If things get . . . tricky, do you have somewhere you can go, someone you can stay with?"

"Tricky?"

"Dangerous. My guess is this guy wants to find Larrimer pretty badly, and if he doesn't by other means, he will probably come back to see you. And he might not leave as easily this time. So is there somewhere you can go?"

"Not really, no."

"What about your brother-in-law, Bruno?"

"Renee—my sister—and their kid are both allergic to cats, so what do I do about Arthur? Do you think this really could get dangerous?"

"It could."

"Should I have a gun?"

"Have you ever used a gun?"

"No."

"I don't think that would be a good idea, Lorraine. But I may have a place you could go; I'll see what I can set up. Listen, Lorraine, one last thing before we hang up. Where did Larrimer buy his paintings and prints?"

"He bought at all the auction houses—Christie's, Sotheby's, sometimes smaller places."

"He had accounts with them?"

"Yes. They'd all send stuff over for him to look at. If he didn't like it after a few days, they'd take it back."

"And what about private dealers? Did he buy from any galleries or private dealers?"

Lorraine thought for a minute. "Sometimes. There was one guy. He called the office occasionally. Mr. Jones. No first name, just Mr. Jones."

The next morning after breakfast, Louis walked over to Sotheby's. At the entrance he was asked to sign a visitors' registry. He wrote "Mr. Jones." He took the escalators up to the fifth floor, where the pieces were being assembled for the upcoming auction. He found a wall of works by Picasso—three etchings, a lithograph, a painting. It was not long before a staff member, an identity card around her neck, was by his side. She was young and pretty and tall.

"It's a wonderful late work, don't you think?" she said, brushing her hair back with one hand. She stood admiring the painting before turning her head and smiling at Louis.

"Yes, it certainly is." Louis gestured vaguely with his hand toward the canvas. "This passage here . . ."

"Yes," she said. "The brushwork, the mix of colors. We can see the master in full and total control of his medium. He has reached the summit of the art universe and is now free to paint as he wants."

"Yes," said Louis. He leaned in to look at the ticket. "Nine million minimum," he said.

"Please let me know if I can be of any help," said the young woman. She turned to walk away.

"Actually," said Louis, "I have a client who may be interested in this painting. He can't be at the auction; he will want to bid by phone."

She was by his side again; her smile had returned. "Of course, sir. That can easily be arranged."

"He's bought from you before."

"His name?" She tapped her tablet and prepared to search for the client's name and account information.

"That's the thing," said Louis. "He'll want to bid anonymously."

"That can be arranged as well."

"In the past he's bought under his own name. It would be well known to you. The thing is he wants to remain anonymous to Sotheby's as well. Not only for his protection, but for Sotheby's."

"I think," said the young woman, "you should probably speak with our accounts manager." Louis gave the Picasso painting one last look and followed the young woman across the exhibition space to a heavy door. She poked at the small keypad and the door lock clicked. Louis followed her inside and down a short hall. She knocked on an unmarked office door and they went in. The accounts manager rose to greet them. He wore stylish eyeglasses with thick black frames, a black suit, a gray tie, and a plaid pocket square. The young woman began, "Mr. . . ."

"Jones," said Louis.

"Mr. Jones would like to make arrangements for an anonymous bidder for the November auction."

"I see," said the accounts manager. He gestured toward a chair and waited until Louis was seated before he sat down. The young woman left the office. "Now, Mr. Jones, please tell me what I can do for you."

Louis explained that he had been engaged as a consultant for a certain collector—a major client of Sotheby's and a frequent bidder at auction, particularly for works by Picasso, Matisse, and Bonnard. "He had in fact been expecting to have his print collection exhibited at the Met, that is until . . ." The accounts manager smiled and raised his hand to indicate that he already knew whom Louis was talking about.

"We understand . . . the situation," the accounts manager said, knitting his manicured fingers together. "We are of course aware of matters. I am delighted to learn that he wants to continue building his already formidable collection. In fact, I had thought of your client in connection with *The Lovers*, the Picasso you were looking at just now, but despaired that he would be in no position to acquire it. As you must know, it has been in a private collection for the last fifty years. It hasn't been seen since then. Of course Sotheby's must remain very discreet in this matter. Still, *The Lovers* would make a wonderful addition to his collection. A cornerstone work, really."

The accounts manager paused to tap on his computer keyboard. "Will he be bidding, or will someone be bidding on his behalf?"

"I feel certain he will want to bid himself."

"We will need his newest information in order to proceed. Including banks for payment purposes, that sort of thing." The accounts manager touched the keyboard, and the printer behind him began humming. "Of course we will need to verify everything once we receive the completed forms." He slid the papers across the desk to Louis.

"If he manages to acquire *The Lovers*," said Louis, "there is also the matter of delivery. As you can imagine his American assets have been—"

The accounts manager raised his hands again. "We will leave those matters to you. I'm sure the highest discretion is in everyone's interest—yours, your client's, and ours. When the time comes, we will direct you to insurance underwriters and shipping companies we work with on a regular basis, who are known for their reliability. And their discretion. It is all really quite manageable, Mr. Jones. I assure you."

"Thank you for your help." Louis stood up, the two men shook hands, and Louis left the office. On his way out he found the young woman and asked to take some digital photos of the Picasso. He took five or six while she watched. He thanked her and left the building.

Christie's did not have any Picassos consigned for their next auction. There was an excellent Georges Braque, which the young assistant thought might interest Mr. Jones's client. Louis met with the Christie's accounts manager, and the same scenario repeated itself until the accounts manager looked at Larrimer's account information.

"Ah," he said, "here you are. Hamilton Jones. I see you've been

Mr. Larrimer's agent for some years now, Hamilton. And you also represent . . . well, you already know who you represent, don't you?" He gave a great bellowing laugh Louis guessed was meant to draw attention away from his small stature.

"I think so," said Louis, laughing and leaning forward. "Let me see. Do you have everybody?"

The Christie's manager turned the screen around, and Louis was offered a look not only at Hamilton Jones's clients but at his complete contact information. Louis studied the screen.

"That's almost everyone; just one missing," he said. "Good show!" The manager's face fell. "Oh, dear."

"No, no, don't worry. He's new. You couldn't have known. He's an American collector living in France since the seventies. I found him quite by accident only recently. He has an extraordinary collection of paintings—Matisse, Picasso, Derain, Bonnard. All bought from private dealers, never at auction. He'd be interested in your Braque, except, like I said, he never buys at auction. I've tried to convince him to, but he won't budge. Once in a while he sells something."

Louis suddenly stopped himself. "Oh, my. I'm afraid I've already said too much. Of course I can't give you his name. He would never forgive me."

XXV

LOUIS CALLED LORRAINE USHER. "Was Larrimer's art buyer named Hamilton Jones?"

Lorraine thought for a moment. "That name sounds familiar. Maybe it was."

"Do you remember whether there was a Hamilton Jones listed among Larrimer's clients?"

Louis could hear Lorraine reciting the *J*'s to herself. "No," she said. "No Hamilton Jones."

Louis called the number he had gotten from the Christie's computer.

"This is Hamilton Jones." The voice was nasal and resonant and had the suggestion of an aristocratic English accent.

"Mr. Jones, this is Louis Morgon calling. I'm going to be liquidating my painting collection and I need some professional help in that regard. I understand you are in that business."

"Louis . . . ?"

"Morgon, Louis Morgon. *M-o-r-g-o-n.*"

"How did you hear about me, Mr. Morgon?"

"I would rather not say. Let's just say I heard good things."

"And you have a collection of paintings you want to sell? Tell me a bit about your collection."

"Well, I have several first-rate Picassos, some Cézannes, some Matisses."

Hamilton Jones was silent for a long time. "I fancy myself a Cézanne expert, Mr. Morgon. I know where most of his paintings are."

"Well, I don't suppose you know where they all are, then. But you are in the business of advising collectors on sales, aren't you?

"Yes, I am in that business."

"I know it's very short notice, but I'm only here in New York briefly. I'm flying home to France tomorrow, and I wonder whether you might have time to see me today."

Hamilton Jones paused again. Finally he said, "I'm sorry, Mr. Morgon, but I have some pressing business I have to attend to."

"Well, why don't you let me buy you dinner this evening, Mr. Jones? I can tell you about my collection and what I would like to accomplish. I think you'll find it worth your while. You pick the place."

Louis arrived at Le Vigneron a few minutes before eight. It took a few seconds for his eyes to adjust to the dimly lit room. Most of the tables were occupied by men in suits and women in dresses. Louis was wearing what he usually wore—rumpled slacks, an open shirt, and battered walking shoes. It was on the shoes that the headwaiter's eyes came to rest, as though he had just seen a cockroach scuttling across the floor.

"Monsieur?" he said. He fussed with the seating ledger in front of him so as not to have to meet Louis's eyes.

"Mr. Hamilton Jones's table," said Louis.

The headwaiter searched the reservations, hoping Jones's name was not among them. But it was. "This way, sir." Seating Louis immediately was better than having him hanging around the front of the restaurant.

The table was in a corner and apart from the other tables. Louis was handed an enormous menu covered in red leatherette with a thin golden rope around it and a tassel that promptly found its way into his water glass. He squeezed the water from the tassel while the head-waiter looked on in horror.

"An aperitif, monsieur?"

"I'll wait for Mr. Jones."

Louis was studying the wine list when Jones arrived. "They have a very nice Burgundy," Jones said, "at a not too outrageous price."

The Burgundy was sixty dollars. "I like the Chinon—the Médard. Does that suit you?"

"It's your nickel," said Jones. "Hamilton Jones," he said, and stuck out his hand.

Louis took it. "Louis Morgon. Thank you for coming. What do you recommend for dinner?"

"They do everything pretty well, but I'm told the calves' liver is very good, if you like that sort of thing. I prefer the filet mignon. The chef is Cuban, but he understands rare when you say rare. And they have an excellent crème caramel, so save room for that." Hamilton Jones was in his fifties. He had dark hair, a handsome square jaw, and a gap between his front teeth. He wore round glasses that he kept putting off and on, letting them dangle from a cord around his neck. He wore a blue blazer and a striped tie. A pocket square spilled from his jacket pocket.

The waiter came and Louis ordered the liver, medium rare. Hamilton Jones ordered the filet mignon, rare. The Chinon came. They raised their glasses and drank. "It's good," said Jones.

"I live near Chinon," said Louis.

"With your collection."

"With my collection. My rather large and excellent collection, if I say so."

"Tell me how it is excellent," said Jones.

"Well, as I said, I have some first-rate Matisse paintings, some Picassos, Cézanne, also Derain, Bonnard, Renoir, a Mondrian, Ensor, others. And some prints and drawings by most of them."

"Louis Morgon. And why haven't I heard of you?"

"Because I keep my collection to myself. I acquired it from private parties, many of whom had the paintings from the artists themselves. I bought a couple of Picassos out of his studio. I never lent paintings; I never bought at auction. I just collect and enjoy them myself. Or rather *collected*, past tense. I've finished collecting. Now I want to get rid of it."

"And why is that?"

"Because I'm finished with it. I'm alone now. Collecting belonged to a part of my life that's over."

"I see." Hamilton Jones sipped his wine and regarded Louis over the rim of the glass.

"I want to sell most of them, and I don't want to do anything foolish. I need the help of a professional."

"I would think so. Well." Hamilton Jones set down his glass. "Here's how I work. I have a rather extensive list of collectors who are looking for various works by various artists. I match buyers and sellers. It sounds simple, but it isn't. When I find a buyer for something you want to get rid of or a seller for something someone else is looking for, I take a commission of five percent from the buyer and five percent from the seller once the deal has been completed. For works that go for over a million, the fee slides downward to a minimum of three percent. You'll find that others have different fee arrangements than I do. But I've found it makes sense to structure things so that they suit me, and this arrangement suits me. And it seems to suit my clients."

"I presume," said Louis, "you will want proof of provenance, that sort of thing, before you take on a work to sell."

"Of course a clean provenance adds value to the work."

"And yet," said Louis, "even the greatest collections have their share of forgeries, stolen and plundered art, don't they?"

"Do they?" said Jones.

"Look at the Met," said Louis. "If you eliminated all the art of questionable provenance, you'd have a mostly empty building, wouldn't you?"

Jones smiled. "A clean and complete provenance is a wonderful thing, as I was saying. A desirable thing. But, alas, as you point out, it can also be a . . . difficult thing. We in the business always have to accommodate ourselves to the realities of the world."

"The realities of the world."

"Let's say no more about it for the moment," said Jones. "I'm sure every piece in your collection is of impeccable provenance. All in good time." He took off his glasses and let them dangle from their string. At that moment their food arrived.

Back in his hotel room, the telephone was blinking. There was a message from Peter Sanchez with a number to call. Louis dialed the number.

"Hello, Louis." Peter tried to sound casual and relaxed, but there was apprehension in his voice. "I was . . . surprised to get your message after so much time. What brings you to the US?"

"Hello, Peter. Do you know who St. John Larrimer is?"

"Larrimer, Ltd."

"That's him," said Louis.

"Did you lose money to him?" Louis thought he heard a hint of delight in Peter's voice.

"I did lose a little, as a matter of fact," said Louis.

"I heard that claims are being taken at the SEC."

"Are they?"

Peter remained silent for a moment. "So, you're not—"

"I'm not expecting much good to come from the SEC, are you? I'm doing some investigating on my own."

This time Peter's silence lasted longer. "Investigating," Peter said finally. "Aha. And what is it you want from me?"

"Actually, I've got something *for* you. I visited Larrimer's secretary the other day, and she'd had a visit from a Russian mobster—"

"You know he's a mobster?"

"I'm guessing. She had a visit and then the same guy turned up following me around Manhattan. I thought you'd be interested."

"Who is he?"

"That's what I'm hoping you'll give me in exchange for this information. You can find him on the security camera at 1012 Fifth Avenue, five-fifteen yesterday. That's November fifteenth, 2008."

"I know what day yesterday was."

"I find that very reassuring," said Louis.

XXVI

THE RAIN RATTLED on the roof. Rain on slate was the sweetest sound Louis knew; he was happy to be home. Pauline had come down from Paris. She had slept late. Louis carried breakfast to the bedroom. Soft-boiled eggs, croissants, grapefruit juice for him, orange juice for her.

"Breakfast in bed?" she said.

"I'm glad to be home." He eased himself into the chair by the bed.

Pauline studied him for a moment. "This Jones person you talked about."

"Yes?"

"What's he like?" Pauline dipped a point of her croissant into the egg yolk.

"I don't know," said Louis. "He could be difficult; he could be useful."

"Then you have a plan."

"Not exactly," said Louis.

"But the beginnings of one?"

"Not even."

"Then why did you go to New York? Why the visit to Larrimer's secretary and the art auctions and Hamilton Jones? Have I left anyone out?"

"No. That's everyone." Louis had not told her about the Russian. Peter Sanchez had called the night before: "Dimitri Arkady Adropov. He's from Chelyabinsk. It's just east of the Urals, an industrial town, a city actually, just north of Kazakhstan on the border between Europe and Asia, known mostly for its nuclear arms factories." Peter was happy to know something Louis didn't. "Adropov is a businessman—oil, gas, and arms manufacturing. But he's also a thug. He's been charged in the US with racketeering, bank fraud, and murder. There was a 2001 arrest that ended in a mistrial. He left the US, showed up again five weeks ago, left again this morning."

"This morning?"

"You must have scared him."

Louis allowed him his little joke. "Will you tell me if he shows up again?"

"*You* tell *me*," Peter had said.

"Well," Louis said to Pauline, "I went to New York because I need to assemble a cast of characters."

"You talk as though you're writing a play, not pursuing a criminal."

"In a way I'm doing the same thing a playwright does. I'm assembling a cast of characters, an Othello and a Iago, and hoping— depending on it, in fact—that they'll collide and get things going, whatever that turns out to be, hoping something leads to St. John Larrimer and his money."

"Are you the Iago or the Othello character?" Pauline said.

"I'm the Shakespeare character . . . I know, I know." He raised his hands before she could say anything. Of course he was being presumptuous. More than presumptuous. Not too long ago, he would have taken no note of it, or found the idea amusing. But lately there was a discordant note sounding in his head, a faint but distinct alarm warning, not of mortal danger, but of *moral* danger, hubris and arrogance.

Pauline had finished her egg. She was grateful that he had let her sleep and then made breakfast. Nonetheless she cast a skeptical look in his direction. Louis lifted himself from the chair with some difficulty—it was old (and so was he) and had collapsed in on itself so that the seat sagged only a few inches over the floor. He stepped to the window and looked out. The rain was coming down harder. The bare linden branches nodded and shuddered under the barrage. The last petals of the roses fell off.

"Hamilton Jones," said Louis. "I don't think Hamilton Jones is his real name, by the way. I think he invented it to lend himself credibility with art collectors and museum and auction directors, to facilitate his movement in that pretentious world. And I'm pretty sure his English accent is phony too. But he certainly seems knowledgeable about art and the art world, particularly its deceptions and illusions. He all but confessed to me that he would be willing to move art that is not what it seems to be. Meaning stolen or forged art. Forgery means nothing, he said. What matters, he said, is not whether it's a forgery or not, but whether it's a good painting. In fact he said that making a good painting in someone else's style is a sign of a certain kind of mastery."

"You liked hearing that, didn't you? I'm guessing you agree," said Pauline.

Louis laughed. "Maybe. He mentioned a Vermeer in the Frick. I went and looked at it, and I think he's right that it's not a Vermeer. In fact, it doesn't even look like a Vermeer—the color is wrong, the brushwork too. But it's an interesting and lively painting and so probably deserves to hang where it can be seen, in this case, in the Frick."

"You like him. Jones."

"I rather agree with his thinking. And, yes, I like him."

"You're about to forge some paintings, aren't you?"

"I've always thought Picasso was overrated, especially his late stuff. That nine-million-dollar painting in Sotheby's was done by rote. There's energy but no passion. At least that's my reading of it. Anyway, what better way to learn whether I'm right or not than to try to make a late Picasso? It would be an interesting exercise." Louis gave Pauline a smile that was meant to be reassuring.

"An exercise that is against the law," said Pauline.

"*Making* one isn't against the law; passing it off as Picasso's—*that* would be against the law."

"I received a box of Jean-Baptiste's personal papers while you were gone. I knew it was coming, but still it was a bit of a shock."

"I can imagine."

"Letters, notes, that sort of thing. Seeing his handwriting is eerie now that he isn't here. It's like he's still . . . somewhere, or part of him is, like he's still writing things. The papers had all been gone through of course."

"Yes."

"I don't know what to do with them. Maybe just destroy them."

"Are there any business papers? Correspondence, that sort of thing?"

"No. I'm sure that stuff remained behind as evidence. Except for this." She handed Louis a slip of paper.

"A wire transfer."

"That's Jean-Baptiste's Paris bank wiring money to Larrimer, Ltd. It was stuck to another envelope. It must have been sent by accident."

Louis studied the piece of paper. "PariBanque. That's my bank."

"Is it useful to you?"

"I don't know. It might be. It's got account numbers—Jean-Baptiste's and Larrimer's. Larrimer's will be closed out. But what would happen, I wonder, if I tried to wire money—say a hundred euros—to the Larrimer account number?"

"Why would you do that?" said Pauline.

"Well, they'd either return it to me as undeliverable or . . ."

"Or they'd forward it. Wouldn't they have to forward it if they could? You're trying to make the bank into your accomplice, aren't you?"

The next afternoon Louis sat in the small PariBanque office in Saint-Léon across the desk from Didier Lespagnole, the branch manager, and raised the same question he had raised with Pauline. What happens if you send money to an account that has been closed?

"Have you done that?" Didier asked. The banking system was

an orderly one, and even the suggestion of a small and innocent malfunction was disquieting to Didier. He pursed his lips, sat up straighter, and fixed Louis with a glare.

"It's a theoretical question for now," said Louis.

"Ah. Theoretical," said Didier and relaxed, as though that changed everything. "Well," he said. He opened the center desk drawer and withdrew a wire transfer slip. He held it facing Louis with one hand, and pointed with the other. "This is like the slip you would receive if you did such a thing. This number"—he pointed—"would be your transaction number, which includes your account number as well as the number of the bank where the transaction originated— these first four numbers here. This number is the routing number, which shows the steps of your transaction. And this space"—he pointed to the other end of the slip—"would contain the receiving bank's number, again the first four numbers, and the recipient's account number or, more likely, a reference number."

"Ah, a reference number. And what happens if the receiving account has been closed?"

"During the first sixty days after an account has been closed, money is automatically wired forward. Unless some irregularity such as a bank closing or criminal activity is involved, in which case the account is frozen and no transactions can be completed."

"Do you know who St. John Larrimer is?"

"Please, Monsieur Morgon. I'm a banker. Of course I know who he is."

"What would happen if I were to wire money to an old account of his?"

"Why on earth would you do such a thing?"

"Theoretically," said Louis.

"Ah. Well. I think you could expect to hear from the authorities."

"The authorities?"

"The American SEC, Interpol. You would be inviting trouble."

"And would I get a slip indicating where the money had gone?"

Didier gave him a long look. "You would. Theoretically."

XXVII

From the JFK Aeroflot first-class lounge, Dimitri Adropov contacted an FBI man he knew. They had a business arrangement. Dimitri gave up occasional gangsters in exchange for tips and information.

"Your Louis Morgon is connected to the CIA," said the FBI man.

"CIA? I thought there was something about him. How he is connected?"

"I don't know exactly; the record is unavailable."

"Unavailable?"

"Sealed. The record is sealed. But he's still on their roster. And here's something interesting: He's got an FBI file too."

"Stop with mystery. Why he has file?" Dimitri's Russian accent tended to get stronger when he was excited.

"When he was with the CIA, he got in trouble somehow. And later he was linked with a terrorist plot."

"This guy is terrorist?"

"There was a connection, but I don't know what the connection was. It looks like he was charged with something serious and then the charges were dropped."

"He is still in CIA?"

"Maybe. I can't tell."

"What he is doing for them, you think?"

"My best guess would be he'd be looking into money laundering, bank fraud."

"But EisenerBank is Switzerland, not fucking America."

"Maybe he's looking for the Larrimer money. In any case, he probably knows about you."

"But have you seen him? He is fucking old man!"

"Maybe so. But if I were you, I'd be careful. And about the accountant, Robert Feather: The FBI can't find him either. He's gone missing."

"Yes," said Dimitri. "So now is just old man is problem."

The air hostess brought Dimitri a big glass of iced vodka and some beluga caviar. He decided the movies were all crap. In ten hours he would change planes in Moscow; in less than twelve he would be back in Chelyabinsk with no progress to report. The money was as gone as it had ever been.

Dimitri gazed out at the night sky. The full moon shone on the shield of clouds passing beneath them. This Morgon guy was definitely on the list of people to be dealt with. First Usher, then Morgon, then Larrimer. He needed them alive until he got Larrimer's money. Maybe Morgon would lead him there. He just had to figure out how to play the guy. Just the thought of Larrimer stealing his money put Dimitri in a rage all over again. "Fucking crook!" he said and slammed his fist on the armrest.

The woman in the seat across the aisle from Dimitri jumped.

"Sorry," he said. "Is business. Bad business." Dimitri was sure he would feel better once he was home.

Chelyabinsk was far to the east of Moscow and protected by the Ural Mountains to the west, which is why, during the buildup to the Second World War, it became a center of weapons manufacturing. Chelyabinsk produced so many Katyusha rocket launchers and T-34 tanks that the city came to be known as Tankograd. After the war, Chelyabinsk and the surrounding area became a nuclear weapons production center, and as the Cold War heated up, so did the manufacture of atomic bombs in and around Chelyabinsk.

Sergei and Irina Adropov had grown up in Kasli, a small town near Chelyabinsk. Like most of their neighbors, they worked in the Mayak nuclear fuel processing plant. Weapons were built with a great sense of urgency and a minimal regard for safety, so a disaster was all but inevitable. The explosion of a nuclear waste facility, when it came, propelled massive amounts of radioactive waste into the atmosphere, which then rained down on the surrounding country. A large region, including the villages of Kasli and Mayak, were rendered uninhabitable.

The area was evacuated, but it was too late to make a difference for many. Hundreds had died in the explosion and in the following days, and now the slow and agonizing death of many others from radiation poisoning commenced. Sergei was among the afflicted. He was moved to the hospital in Chelyabinsk, and Irina moved with him. The region around Chelyabinsk was shut off from visitors, and a veil of official secrecy fell over the area and was not lifted until nearly fifty years later.

Sergei lay in bed in the hospital, dozing or hallucinating from the drugs he was given. "I smell death on myself," he said. He held his arm against his nose and inhaled deeply. "Can you smell it?" He stretched his bluish, thin arm toward Irina. Or he said, "I am glowing. Turn out the light and see." Irina switched off the light. "Do you see?" he said. "See the green glow?"

"I don't see anything, Sergei," she said. But she knew he was dying. Irina was three months pregnant at the time.

The doctors at the Lenin Hospital Clinic were not hopeful about the condition of the child. "Radiation sickness is in your blood and bones," they told her, "and it will be in your child's bones too." Irina prayed to the Blessed Virgin. And when her baby boy was born, he was not only healthy, but large and strong and strapping, with a full head of black hair and a voice like a bugle. He did not cry so much as shout, and when Irina gave him her breast, despite the doctors' objections—"your milk is radioactive," they said—it was as though little Dimitri wanted to swallow her breasts, first one, then the other.

Dimitri turned two the day his father died, but he remained robust and healthy. In fact, his health was so overwhelming that it seemed contagious. Irina had been showered by radioactive debris and then breathed the poisoned air and had shown early signs of radiation poisoning. By all rights she should have been dead. But instead she flourished, and little Dimitri—who was never really little—flourished as well. It was as if he shared his life spirit with his mother, and she took it in.

Irina worked on the assembly line in a metal stamping factory. Dimitri joined her there when he was sixteen. At the same time, he did what anyone did who wanted to get ahead: He joined the Communist Party. By the time he was twenty, he had advanced off the factory floor and onto the administrative committee. By the time he was thirty, he had been named one of the factory's managing directors. His salary was nominal, but the opportunities for graft were almost unlimited, and Dimitri took full advantage of them, extracting kickbacks from suppliers, substituting cheap alloys when steel was called for, and banishing rivals, all in the name of the Communist Revolution.

When the Soviet Union collapsed in 1991, Dimitri sought, and was given, the assignment to oversee the disbanding and disposal of the factories around Chelyabinsk. If you wanted to buy a factory in Chelyabinsk—and there were plenty to be bought—Dimitri Adropov was the man to see.

Valery Grushin, a former KGB operative, was the first to show up with a suitcase full of dollars, and Dimitri allowed Valery to purchase the metal stamping factory and several nearby pipe rolling facilities at an extremely advantageous price. For his efforts Dimitri was granted an enormous commission, which Valery gladly paid. Soon other buyers showed up, and Dimitri gave them such extraordinary deals that his commission often exceeded the price they paid for the factories.

In a matter of months, Dimitri was a wealthy man. He used his gains to buy several small oil and gas production and transport companies. (He had held the best factories back for himself.) These companies made up the core of what eventually became Gazneft, which he then sold to a consortium of businessmen.

Dimitri had two qualities that made him a formidable opponent and a danger to anyone operating at cross purposes with him. Having been a communist one day and a capitalist the next, Dimitri mistrusted all ideologies and all organizations that subscribed to them. He saw ideologies, and in fact all beliefs, as false and stupid and, above all, a distraction from the main business of life.

He believed mainly in force. He remained the principal director on the Gazneft board, but he had others serve as president, chairman, treasurer. He directed things from the shadows. He did not have to trust these others because he owned them. He could harm them, and they knew he would, so they pretty much did his bidding.

Dimitri's second dangerous quality was that he preferred to do his own dirty work. Other men with his means hired it done. But Dimitri derived a measure of satisfaction from doing what needed to be done. He was not a sadist; he did not enjoy the suffering of others. But he didn't shy away from it either, if he thought it necessary. And when it had been done, what gave him satisfaction was knowing that an unpleasant job had been expeditiously and expertly carried out. He thought of himself as a craftsman whose specialty was mayhem.

Dimitri was not a man without tenderness. He had a lover with whom he was generous and kind. But his greatest love was reserved for Irina, his mother, who lived in a small apartment in a less than fashionable part of Chelyabinsk. Dimitri had bought her a large, luxurious apartment across town, but she had refused to move in. She found the size and the luxury oppressive. "It is too big," she said. "What am I to do in all this space? How will I even keep it clean?"

"You will have a cleaning lady, Mamochka."

She looked at her son with horror. "Then why did we even have the revolution?" she said.

"Look, Mamochka," he said, trying to drum up her enthusiasm. "The faucets are gold." He turned on the hot water.

"Like the tsar's," she said, and went back to the small flat she had lived in since coming to Chelyabinsk in 1957. He bought her other gifts—clothing, a car—and of course she rejected them as well. Even the appliances he had delivered to her old apartment were refused. "My old stove is fine."

"Mamochka, I just want you to have a better life. Things have gone well for me, and I want to share my good fortune with you. I owe you everything. I love you, Mamochka."

Irina reached up with her plump, wrinkled hand and caressed Dimitri's cheek. "I know, Dima, my little Dimka. I know. You have worked very, very hard, and hard work always succeeds." It was true. In his way, Dimitri *had* worked very hard. Over the years, as the money had rolled in, he had put it in banks in Liechtenstein, Mexico, the Caymans, and Switzerland, including the unfortunate EisenerBank.

XXVIII

A HARD FREEZE HAD TURNED Louis's garden into a ruin and driven him indoors. He pulled up the bean poles and scaped away the vines. He pulled out the tomato cages and put them away. He dug up the last of the sweet potatoes, gathered the few squash he hadn't already taken in, and spread them on the cement floor at the back of his painting studio. He spread compost across the garden. The days were short and relentlessly gloomy.

Louis fed the wood stove in the studio. He stretched a dozen canvases, squeezed some color on the sheet of glass that served as his palette, and began to paint. He stood at the easel with art books open around him. He leafed through the books, painted, then went back to the books again and again. He stared at the canvas for a long while before he scraped away much of what he had done, and started again.

Early in the new year, Pauline came from Paris, and together she and Louis made a dinner party. The Renards, Isabelle and Jean, were there. Their son, Jean-Marie, came from Paris, where he worked for the customs service in its telecommunications division. Louis had known Jean-Marie since he was a small boy. Marianne was there along with Paolo, her artist friend, and a few other friends too. Jean-Michel Aubert came. He brought the wine. Luc and Isabelle Delaroche, Jean Maussion, Thierry Juge, Louis and Dominique

Lansade, their daughter Lea, and her husband and new baby, Lisane. Over twenty guests in all, so that Louis had to put an old door on sawhorses to make a second table.

Louis made an enormous stew in multiple pots: shrimp and monkfish and merguez sausages and oranges and potatoes and flageolets in a curry sauce with tomatoes, onions, and red peppers. There were huge pots of couscous and slabs of bread and bottles of red. The improvised table sagged under the weight of it all. Everyone served themselves over and over, finally mopping up the last sauce with hunks of baguette. There was a green salad. A platter of cheeses went around.

An animated debate erupted as to whether Louis had improperly placed a wedge of Camembert on top of a fresh round of the cheese. "It would be impolite," said Louis, "to present a round of cheese that hadn't been started. So you cut out a wedge and place it on top to give others permission to cut into that wheel of cheese. Or at least so I've been told."

"That's right," said Isabelle Renard. It was she who had told him.

"But no," said Thierry Juge. "No, no, no, it's impossible. It can't be done. One opens the cheese, but one removes the wedge from the tray entirely. It can't be placed there like . . . like a trophy. On top of the cheese, it is too . . . too . . . well, no, it can't be done." Others chimed in with their opinions, and before long, the debate had spread to the other table, interrupted by laughter and derision.

Thierry stood up and gave an impassioned dissertation on the importance of maintaining traditional etiquette. "It is *not* about manners," he said. "Manners are bourgeois and stupid. It is principle, it is tradition, it is how things are done." He pulled out his cell phone and punched in a number. Everyone quieted down to hear what he was doing. "François," said Thierry into the phone and posed the question of the cheese. The room erupted in laughter.

"He is the chief of protocol at Élysée," Thierry said in a stage whisper. "He will know." Thierry left the room to be able to hear François's ruling, which Thierry proudly announced on returning.

Placing the wedge of Camembert on top of the round was a gross violation, comparable to, say, using a steak knife to eat fish, or burning the crème caramel. Everyone laughed until tears ran down their cheeks. Fortunately Louis had not burned the crème caramel. And the coffee was hot and delicious.

People got up and began carrying dishes to the sink and stacking them wherever they could find space. "Stop," said Louis. "Leave everything. I want you all to see some new paintings." He led the way across the terrace to the barn. He opened the door, threw a switch, and the studio was bathed in a blaze of light. Everyone stepped inside and went silent.

Next to the squashes and sweet potatoes, Louis had leaned ten canvases against the wall. Everyone knew Louis's work, or thought they did. They were familiar with his careful and expressive and—even Renard had to admit—beautiful landscapes. He represented the surrounding countryside again and again in swaths of color layered over other colors, brushed here in fury and then elsewhere using the most delicate strokes, all in pursuit of that shimmering quality of the light here in the Dême Valley and the trembling impermanence of all things. But these appeared to be twentieth-century masterpieces by France's greatest painters.

Paolo, the avant-garde iconoclast sculptor, was the first to break the silence. "But, Louis," he said with a laugh. "Where did you find all this old crap?" The room erupted, and Paolo was shouted down. Then everyone went silent again.

Pauline stepped forward and looked closely at the first canvas in line. "I thought I knew Matisse."

"I made it up," said Louis.

"You didn't copy something? You made up a Matisse?"

"I know *what* he liked to paint, *how* he liked to paint. I made up the painting."

"And a Picasso," said Thierry Juge, pointing.

"Three of them, actually," said Louis, pointing at the other two at the end of the row. "All late works."

"Actually, they're better than Picasso's Picassos," said Paolo.

"No, they're not," said Louis. "And the Matisses. They're medio-cre. And the Cézanne." There were two more Matisses, two Derains, a Cézanne—yet another view of Mont Sainte-Victoire—and a Bonnard. "The Bonnard is an utter failure, I'm afraid. Like a burned crème caramel."

XXIX

"You *know* that I'm your friend."

Louis hated it when Renard started conversations this way. Especially when they were in the police station, as they were now. It sounded a little too much like an official conversation. "Yes. I know you're my friend."

"But you're going to make this difficult, aren't you?" said Renard.

"If I can."

"Okay. Those paintings you made are forgeries."

"I like to think of them as fakes. But in a sense, yes, they're forgeries."

"In a sense?"

"Well, they're original paintings."

"Under the law they're forgeries."

"Well, that depends, doesn't it? On what I do with them."

"And what are you going to do with them?"

"I don't know—"

"Stop it."

"It's true; I don't know. It depends on how other things play out. St. John Larrimer—"

"The investor?"

"The thief. He's an art collector as it turns out—Picassos,

Bonnards, others. I'm trying to figure out how to get to him. I'm exploring the banking avenue too. In fact I'm exploring every avenue, and one of the avenues is painting. So I thought I'd do these. They may come in handy, although I can't yet say how."

Renard took out a cigarette and stuck it in his mouth. He almost lit the filter but turned it around in time. Once it was lit, he blew out a great cloud of smoke. "You're going to try to sell him your forgeries?"

"He'd see right through them. They're on brand-new canvas; the paint is new. Even if he didn't recognize that the painting is fake, he'd know from the canvas, the stretchers, the paint. Besides, even if he bought every one of them at a huge price, it would be only a fraction of the money he stole. Anyway, I don't want to get the money from him by selling him paintings, if that's what you're thinking."

"What *do* you want?" said Renard. He repeated the question to be certain Louis understood his exasperation. *"What do you want?"*

"I want him to make restitution and answer for his crimes."

"Then leave it to the authorities."

"We've been over that."

Renard stood up from his desk and walked to the window. "How are we friends? I sometimes wonder."

This surprised Louis. "Because we like each other," he said.

"If I uphold the law and you break it, how can we be friends?"

"Well," said Louis, "think of how much we have in common."

"Like what?"

"Well, for one thing, we both think we're right. And for another, we're probably both wrong."

"Jesus!" Renard was so exasperated that he ground out his cigarette on the windowsill. "Now look what you made me do."

XXX

THERE WERE A NUMBER of rich people Hamilton Jones (né Joseph Hamilton) thought of as his clients. They went with him to art exhibitions, where he told them what was good and what wasn't, what would make an important addition to their collection and what wouldn't. He guided them through the labyrinthine byways of the art world in hopes of making a sale. But too often, when it came time to make actual purchases, the "clients" turned to auction houses or other dealers where they could arrange favorable payment terms or negotiate price reductions.

Unless Hamilton managed to scare up something extremely unusual and exactly to their liking, he often found himself going without a fee, getting nothing more than a fancy dinner and a gratuity for his troubles. Four years earlier he had managed to arrange a deal that had netted him a $270,000 fee for a Whistler that had gone for over eight million. But since then, nothing much.

Hamilton Jones lived in a small, rent-controlled apartment in an old building on East Ninety-third Street. He had some excellent paintings by excellent, but entirely unknown painters hanging on his walls. And where there were not paintings, there were bookshelves filled to overflowing with art books. A small closet contained his meager wardrobe of two suits, a few slacks, two blue blazers, some dress shirts and striped ties.

Thanks to his expertise, Hamilton regularly got invited to fancy dinner parties. For this he was grateful, since it not only gave him the chance to give a client useful advice about his collection, but it also got him a free meal. He had accepted Louis Morgon's invitation more for the dinner than for the prospect of having him as a client.

He had had his doubts about Louis from the beginning. First of all there was the supposed quality of the collection. He would have to have heard of the guy, no matter how secretive and reclusive he was, if he really had a collection half as good as he claimed. Hamilton had asked around, and nobody, but *nobody*, had ever heard of Louis Morgon. By the time several months had passed, Hamilton Jones had all but forgotten about Louis. Then one day a thick manila envelope arrived in the mail.

Hamilton sat down by the window. He slit open the end of the envelope and peered inside. There was a letter with some photos attached. He let everything slide out onto his lap and laid the letter aside. "Jesus!" he said looking at the top photo. He lifted his glasses onto his nose. "Holy Christ!" Hamilton turned the photos over one by one—a Cézanne, a Picasso, another Picasso, *another* Picasso, Matisse, Matisse, Matisse, Derain, Derain—nine paintings in all, none of which he had ever seen before.

Hamilton switched on the lamp. He leaned toward the window and studied the Cézanne. Mont Sainte-Victoire. He reached for his loupe and went over the photo more carefully. It was an amateur photo, but it was good enough to reveal a beautiful if somewhat eccentric Cézanne.

Hamilton went to the wall of books and pulled down a large volume on Cézanne. He took it back to his chair and leafed through it. He laid the photo beside a similar painting in the book. The color was right—the oranges and greens and lavenders. It looked like a view from the Bibémus quarry. The brushwork was superb. The perspective was odd. An 1897 painting, he thought.

After two hours studying the photos, leafing through his books, making comparisons to photos, he could only conclude that he had before him evidence of a collection of what looked to be exquisite paintings whose value appeared to be beyond estimation. Of course there was no way to tell without seeing the paintings in person. One of the Picassos looked like a companion to *The Lovers*, which Sotheby's had just offered in November for nine million. It hadn't met the minimum, even with the house's ringers bidding, but had they set a more reasonable five million, it would have gone right away.

Hamilton could think of perfect clients for *three* of the paintings right off the bat. And six percent in commissions—three from the buyer, three from the seller—would be . . . he simply could not imagine it. The thought made him dizzy. He picked up Louis's letter. It was handwritten on ordinary paper.

> *January 5, 2009*
> *Dear Mr. Jones,*
> *You may recall that I spoke with you about your helping me to dispose of my collection of paintings and drawings. But things have intervened—family matters, business—and that is why it has taken me so long to write.*
> *I have enclosed photos of the best paintings in my collection. I think you will recognize that these are works of the highest quality. It is my impression that they should command excellent prices even in a depressed market such as we are experiencing now.*
> *I expect to be in the United States again in the near future. I hope we can meet then to discuss exactly how I might best proceed. In the meantime please feel free to call if you have any questions.*
> *Sincerely,*
> *Louis Morgon*

That night Hamilton Jones tossed and turned in his bed and dreamed of a life in which money and gorgeous paintings and ruin were inextricably tangled together. He woke up thinking he had no choice but to go to France and then woke up an hour later, being absolutely certain he was being taken for a ride. There was no reason to go to France. The paintings were fakes—good fakes, but fakes nonetheless.

A good painter had only to study a great painter's work to come up with a decent facsimile of his methods. Hamilton and Louis Morgon had discussed that very proposition. In fact Hamilton believed that the greats were easier to imitate than the less-than-great because their style and vision came through consistently in all their work, while lesser painters had lapses of style and ability. It was these lapses that were all but impossible to imitate.

To "do" a good painter, you started by mixing colors, especially the odd and signature combinations your painter used. You used linseed oil or turps as he did. You learned to pick the paint up off the palette or out of cups or however your painter did it and then swing the brush across the canvas or push it or scrub with it the way he did. Then you invented an image in your head and you painted it. If you had internalized your painter's vocabulary—his use of color, his strokes, his tremors and hesitations, the accidents he fixed, the others he let stand, if you had made all that your own, then the result would be more than satisfactory. It was difficult to do, but by no means impossible.

It would never look like his best work—nobody but Picasso could do a great Picasso, because his best work contained the rich accumulation of his entire experience. But it would pass easily for a half-baked Picasso, of which there were many, painted in moments of weakness or inattention or laziness or indifference by the master himself—*The Lovers,* for instance.

These lesser works sold for extravagant prices, just like the great works did. The differences between the great and the less-than-great—

and the fake—were obliterated by the obscurantist noise of the marketplace, as the critics and the experts fumed and fussed and disagreed.

Hamilton Jones picked up the telephone and called Louis Morgon in France.

"Mr. Jones. I take it you got my package?"

"I did, Mr. Morgon. It arrived yesterday."

"I'm sorry it took me so long to get back to you."

"I have to say, Mr. Morgon, it is the most extraordinary collection of paintings I have seen in private hands in quite some time."

"Thank you. I am very proud of the collection. I worked hard to put it together."

"How did you come to acquire it, may I ask?"

"Are you asking because you doubt the provenance, Mr. Jones?"

"I do not doubt it, Mr. Morgon. I simply do not know it."

"If you come see the work, Mr. Jones, I will make the provenance quite clear. You will see that it is clean and irrefutable."

"I would like nothing better than to come see your paintings, Mr. Morgon. But to be completely honest with you, sir, I am . . . thanks to the current economic situation . . . I find myself . . . in difficult circumstances, so I feel that I need to know more just to reassure myself, you understand, that the trip will be worthwhile."

There was silence from Louis's end.

Hamilton continued. "I can't afford to make the trip without knowing a bit more about these paintings and, quite frankly, about you, Mr. Morgon. You have been secretive with me about pretty much everything. With me, and apparently the entire world. I have asked around a good bit and learned nothing. You declined even to tell me how you found me."

"If it will help things along," said Louis, "I'm willing to tell you how I got your name. I got it from St. John Larrimer."

Now it was Hamilton Jones's turn to be silent. And he remained silent for a long time. "Larrimer," he said finally. "He told you about me?" Hamilton Jones was trying to put things together in his mind and not having an easy time of it.

"He didn't exactly tell me about you. Lorraine Usher, his secretary—"

"Mr. Morgon," said Hamilton. "This may seem an impudent question, and yet as I consider it, it seems like the most important question, in fact the *only* one, I can ask. Who painted those paintings?"

Louis hesitated only briefly. "I did."

"You did. The Picassos?"

"Yes. The Picassos."

"The Cézanne?"

"Yes, that was the most difficult one. Except for the Bonnard, which failed altogether and which I didn't send you."

"All of them?"

"All of them."

"And why did you contact me? Is this your idea of a joke? Yours and Larrimer's?"

"It is not a joke, Mr. Jones. I was trying to find a way to Larrimer when I learned he was a collector and that he used your—"

"That son of a bitch used me to collect paintings and then he stole my life savings," said Hamilton Jones.

Louis had been unprepared for this turn. "Your name is not on the list of his clients," he said.

"I used . . . another name—Joseph Hamilton. I had to work it out so that he didn't know it was me. I thought he would refuse to take me on if he knew. If only he had refused."

Louis had not known going in whether there was any use to be made of Jones's connection to Larrimer, but he had led the man to believe that he, Louis, was a genuine collector of paintings and that there was money to be earned. Louis now regretted having done so; he explained all this to Jones.

"And have I been of use to you?" said Hamilton Jones.

"Yes, I am certain you have," said Louis.

"What is it you want?" Jones was getting angry all over again.

"More or less the same thing you want, Mr. Jones, if I understand you correctly: to bring Larrimer to account. To see him brought to trial. To see his assets attached and—"

"Did you lose money to him?"

"A small amount," said Louis. "That's not my reason."

"Not your reason?"

"No."

"I see." Jones thought for a long moment. "And you have a plan."

"One is . . . evolving."

"Using your fake paintings."

"Perhaps."

Hamilton went silent. "As bait?" he said finally.

"I had thought of that. To draw him out."

"You know where he is?"

"I have an idea where he is. But it doesn't matter. If my paintings are interesting to him, I'm thinking he'll show his face."

"Oh, he'll be interested all right. He's a big collector who wants to be bigger. It's not about the art."

"Does he know art?"

"He knows what he should own, but he doesn't know art. I know art. . . . That is, I *used to* know art for him."

"He'll be fooled by my art?"

"I was," said Hamilton.

"But we don't just need him. We need to find his money. To *get* to his money, his assets, whatever's left."

"Is there a 'we'?"

"I hope so," said Louis. "It depends on you."

Hamilton remained silent for a while and Louis waited. Finally Hamilton said, "Larrimer had an assistant, a young Brit named Jeremy . . . something."

"Jeremy Gutentag," said Louis. "He's gone, I don't know where."

"I think he was from London."

"He may have been, but he's disappeared completely. Without a trace, either here or in London, as far as I've been able to tell."

"Disappeared?"

"For the moment," said Louis.

"For the moment?"

"I hope we can find him when we need him," said Louis. "Larrimer also had an accountant."

"I met him once," said Hamilton. "Robert Feather."

"If we could find him—"

"Oh, it's too late for that," said Hamilton. "They found him. It was in the papers."

"They found him?"

"Floating in the East River. He had a bullet in the back of his head."

XXXI

THERE WAS NOTHING CONNECTING Jeremy Gutentag, the former Oxford whiz and head of the Larrimer trading desk, to Charanjeet Kapoor of Lahore, Pakistan. Charanjeet had made certain of that. Jeremy Gutentag had been the son of British shopkeepers, had spent his entire life in London and New York, and now he was gone. Charanjeet Kapoor was a Pakistani who lived in Lahore and worked in the family business. Secure in the conviction that he would never be found out, he settled into life in Lahore as though he had never left.

Charanjeet had a suite of rooms in one wing of his parents' villa, looking out on the wonderful gardens that surrounded the complex. He awoke each morning to the sound of birds singing and splashing in the fountain beneath his bedroom window. He had breakfast most mornings with his father before accompanying him on his ten-minute walk to the office.

There Mohan introduced Charanjeet to the arcane culture of running a business enterprise in Lahore, Pakistan. He enrolled him in the Chamber of Commerce, and they went to meetings together, where Charanjeet met other businessmen. Mohan also introduced him to suppliers and shippers and accountants as they came through the office.

He made sure Charanjeet met the civil servants he needed to

know, the health and safety inspectors, the tax assessors, those who issued the various permits and licenses necessary to run a thriving enterprise and to whom baksheesh would be owed at the appropriate moment. "These are the people we most depend upon," said Mohan. "They are lowly bureaucrats, but without their help and permission, we could not be in business. I'm certain it is not how things are done in New York or London, but in Lahore it is necessary." In general, though, there was no better training for running a business in Lahore than a stint in one of the top New York investment banks. Charanjeet took to it like a duck to water.

Mohan and Charanjeet walked to the office together most mornings. One day a little rain had fallen and they had run a few steps. Mohan sighed and sat down heavily at his desk. He was sixty and overweight. "I am getting old," he said.

"No, Daddy," Charanjeet protested. "Not you." But he had already noticed a slight hesitation in his father's step.

"Yes. Oh, yes, I am. Anyway," said Mohan, "I have built this business for you. And for your children, when they come along, God willing." He rose with difficulty, just to show that he was not dead yet, and kissed Charanjeet's cheek.

"Thank you, Daddy. I want nothing more than to live up to your expectations."

"I have no doubt that you will, my boy." Mohan made him the head of the Fine Fabric Works. FFW was a small operation with a long-serving and loyal staff, so that the transition from Mohan to Charanjeet should come about with a minimum of disruption. Mohan assigned Hashinur Chakmani to guide Charanjeet through the process.

Hashinur was a tiny, wizened man of indeterminate age. He had dark, shriveled skin, a pointed white beard, and large black eyes that swam behind thick glasses. He wore the same thing, day in and day out—a white turban, a short-sleeve shirt with a pocket full of yellow pencils, a *lungi* (the traditional wraparound skirt), and large, battered leather sandals.

Hashinur had been at the Fine Fabric Works since even before Mohan had bought the company, longer than anyone could remember. When he had arrived, the muslin that was their specialty had been manufactured on a dozen ancient hand looms by weavers passing a shuttle back and forth, working the clacking treadles with their bare feet. As Mohan modernized and expanded the company, Hashinur rose through the ranks from sweeper to weaver to carter to supervisor and finally to senior foreman in charge of the entire FFW manufacturing operation.

If Hashinur had stood erect, which he did not, the top of his turban might have reached Charanjeet's chest. "The first time I saw him," said Mohan, "he looked pretty much as he does now." On Charanjeet's first day, Hashinur bowed deeply. Then he took Charanjeet by the hand and led him out of the office and onto the factory floor. They stopped in front of one of the new electronic looms and watched while the operator performed the regular maintenance. He did so with great concentration and care, removing, disassembling, and cleaning the bobbins, using a fine brush to remove the lint from beneath the bobbin posts and behind the shuttles. He used electronic gauges to check the alignment of this part and that one and made fine adjustments on the control console. Hashinur had not let go of Charanjeet's hand the entire time, and he now used his own hand to raise Charanjeet's and aim it in this and that direction like a pointer as he explained what they were watching in a high, nasal voice.

Hashinur had come to Lahore as a young boy from a village in the farthest northwest corner of the country, and his Punjabi was heavily colored by his native dialect. It was also delivered with great rapidity, so that it was all but incomprehensible. Hashinur did not speak either English or Urdu. He spoke only his version of Punjabi and some words and phrases of a peculiar language no one could identify and everyone thought must be of his own devising. And since he often fell back on these strange gurglings and warblings, which had come to be known as "Hashinurian," those he worked with had little choice but to learn this language too.

At first Charanjeet could hardly understand Hashinur. And yet, after being led around by the hand for a number of days and pointed in this direction or that, he found that he was learning the fine fabric manufacturing business from the ground up. And he was learning Hashinurian at the same time.

One day a delegation of customers arrived at the Fine Fabric Works from Stockholm. They were the first customers who had ever come from Sweden. Charanjeet was by then sufficiently versed in the factory's operations that he could show them around the floor, pointing out the particular operational details that made FFW fabrics the finest in the world.

The Swedes spoke excellent English. But they were exacting in their inquiries, and at one point a question arose about production methods that Charanjeet could not quite grasp. He could comprehend their words, but not the operation being referred to. The Swedes conferred in Swedish among themselves, searching presumably for another way to phrase the question.

Hashinur had been standing by in case he was needed. Suddenly he stepped up to the Swedes and began speaking Hashinurian, which turned out to be Swedish, heavily accented, to be sure, but grammatically correct and entirely comprehensible. He went on at some length in his high-pitched, rapid-fire way. The astonished Swedes responded with a dozen questions to which Hashinur responded to their apparent satisfaction. Everyone else, including Charanjeet, stood in stunned silence.

As soon as the Swedes had left—after placing a substantial order—Hashinur was bombarded with a hundred questions: How did he know Swedish? *Why* did he know Swedish? Had he lived in Sweden once long ago? Had he had a Swedish lover? Hashinur smiled or scowled depending on the question. But he did not answer.

XXXII

WHENEVER MOHAN CAME to the FFW factory, as he occasionally did, it was only to see whether there was any way he could be of use—some aspect of the operation that needed explaining, some quirk in the bookkeeping perhaps, some balky supplier. But Charanjeet now knew the operation well enough to deal with any contingency.

"We had some balky bobbins replaced not long before you got here," said Mohan.

"I know. And two of the replacement bobbins were still breaking thread. I insisted Shabilan Bobbins replace them immediately and check their milling tolerances. I am in touch with Baenbal in Germany—"

"They are excellent, but pricey," said Mohan.

"They have agreed to match Shabilan's prices and offer a longer warranty," said Charanjeet.

This made Mohan both happy and melancholy. "I have become entirely superfluous," he said.

Hashinur confirmed what Mohan already knew: Charanjeet was doing an excellent job. Hashinur led Mohan around the factory floor to show him a new piece of sorting equipment and the most recent production samples. Mohan had become a visitor in his own factory.

"How is it, Daddy, that Hashinur speaks Swedish?" said Charanjeet, trying to cheer him up.

"He speaks Swedish?"

"What everyone called Hashinurian turns out to be Swedish."

"Really?" Mohan laughed. "Then we all speak a little Swedish, don't we?" The thought of it made him laugh again.

Charanjeet and Mohan met for lunch every week at Bistro 77, and at one such lunch, Mohan proposed that Charanjeet might soon take over the entire Kapoor Industries operation. "I think it is time," said Mohan.

"Are you all right, Daddy?" said Charanjeet.

"Oh, yes. For an old man, Charanjeet, I am quite well. True, my blood pressure is higher than it should be. And I am too fat. Dr. Burgati wants to put me on a diet." He sadly moved the chunks of curried lamb around on his plate.

Two weeks later at lunch, Mohan clutched suddenly at his chest. His face went white, and he began to sweat. "I don't feel good," he said. His head lolled back. He slumped in his chair, his hand dropped onto his plate with a crash. Charanjeet watched in horror as brown sauce seeped across the white cuff. "An ambulance!" he cried.

Mohan was loaded onto a stretcher and wheeled out of the restaurant into the ambulance. A paramedic strapped him down, hooked him up to oxygen, then worked over him, checking his vital signs and starting an intravenous line. Nurses met the ambulance at the hospital door and wheeled the stretcher into the emergency room. They drew a blood sample. The doctor on duty injected a "clot-buster" medicine into the port in his arm. Mohan was hooked up to an electrocardiogram machine, which began whirring and clicking. A second port was inserted into his other arm through which nitroglycerine was injected. He was given a handful of pills to swallow. "You have had a heart attack," said the doctor.

"A mild one?" said Mohan hopefully.

"We shall see," said the doctor as she studied the EKG readout.

Charanjeet had arranged for a private room. Mohan's stretcher was wheeled through the wards to his room. Charanjeet met him there and then sat holding his hand. Before long, Golapi arrived, accompanied by Dr. Burgati. The doctor scowled as he looked through Mohan's file. "There can't be much in there yet," said Mohan. Dr. Burgati looked up from his reading but didn't say anything.

The next morning Mohan was scheduled to have an exploratory catheterization. An attendant shaved his groin. "That is where we will insert the catheter." Two hours later Mohan woke up back in his room. Dr. Burgati was there.

"Nothing too serious, I hope," said Mohan.

"It is too late for such wishful thinking, Mohan. You now have two new body parts. Stents have been placed in two arteries." He showed Mohan the pictures, pointed out where the vessels where dangerously narrowed, and then showed him the picture with the stents. Mohan felt his eyes fill with tears. Golapi wept beside him. "What does this mean?" said Charanjeet.

"It means your father dodged a bullet," said Dr. Burgati. "For now. You will be in hospital for three or four more days at least. You should hire an attendant."

"We can take care of him," said Charanjeet.

"Can you? Can you bathe him? Feed him? Shave him? Help him to the toilet? Wipe his behind? No, I thought not. Hire someone. There are servants trained to do these things. You will especially need someone once you are home."

"We have—"

"I know what you're thinking. But your maid will not do such work. Nor should she. She knows nothing about sanitation. She is not trained in these things. And once you are home, Mohan, you must change your ways—a healthy diet, exercise, less stress, no cigars—your habits will kill you."

"But I eat a healthy diet."

"No, you do not. Ghee and oil and lamb and chicken are not

healthy, certainly not in the quantities you eat them. Vegetables and fruits, brown rice and beans—that's what you must eat."

"I know you're a fanatic about food," said Mohan.

"Look at yourself, Mohan," said the doctor, and reached over and patted Mohan's belly in a not entirely friendly manner. "Now look at me." Dr. Burgati was proud of his trim form. He held open his white coat and turned this way and that. He patted his own flat belly. "You see, Mohan? We are the same age. And yet you weigh as much as two of me. I can do thirty pushups." Mohan was afraid Dr. Burgati might actually get down on the floor and do the push-ups. He felt old and sick and pathetic, and finally pulled the covers up over his belly and looked to Golapi for help. But she remained silent.

"You will have pills to take that will lower your cholesterol, others to lower your blood pressure, and others to thin your blood so that it flows easily past the stents." He held up each little bottle as he named the contents. "The pills are important, but they cannot save your life. That is up to you."

When he thought about it, Mohan had to admit that he had known this was coming. He had noticed that he was short of breath after climbing a flight of stairs or running a few steps to get out of the rain. And there had been moments of a thick heaviness in his chest that he had dismissed as he was wont to dismiss any disagreeable news. So here he was on the other side of a heart attack.

Life would be different now, for him, of course, but also for Charanjeet and Golapi. She was fat too, now that he thought about it. "We must change the way we eat," he said. "Cook will have to change the way she cooks." Golapi looked at him in horror. She knew he meant it. Charanjeet had been contemplating his father's bedpan. "And we must find an attendant," he said.

Lahore was a city of seven million people. It would not be hard to find someone willing to do the work. Finding someone who was competent was another matter altogether. The hospital administrator suggested that Charanjeet contact Caritas, an agency affiliated

with a Roman Catholic order of nuns. They agreed to send several
candidates to the hospital.

The first three women who showed up were impossible. The first
seemed on death's door herself, the second was doltish, the third confessed she was terrified to be around sick people. Charanjeet could
not imagine why the agency had sent them.

"But, Mr. Kapoor," said the agency representative, "this is difficult
work for very little pay, and for most people the work is hateful. For
a woman to touch a man in the way that attendants must sometimes touch their clients is sinful and forbidden in most people's
minds. We have to hire the desperate."

"All right, if not a woman, then a man" said Charanjeet.

"But a man won't do it. Men are unwilling to do such work."

Charanjeet sighed. "What are we to do, then?"

"We will send you more candidates." And so they did. Over the
next two days, there was a steady parade of women of every age, all
from the lower social castes of course, and all uneducated. "Well,"
said Mohan despondently after one particularly sorry candidate had
fled in tears. "We will just have to do the best we can without an
aide." He was still too weak to stand or walk without a walker, and
he still had an oxygen line in his nose. But he was eager to leave the
hospital and sleep in his own bed.

At that moment a girl limped into the room. She looked to be no
more than fourteen. She was thin and didn't appear strong enough
to do much of anything. The left side of her face had a raw looking
scar that went from her ear to her chin. She walked with a curious
twisting gait, owing to a deformed right leg. She wore Western
clothes—pale cotton pants and a threadbare men's shirt buttoned up
to her neck. Her black hair was tucked under a scarf.

Charanjeet was shocked at the sight of her, and at first he didn't
know why. There was nothing in her person that was particularly
shocking, and he had never laid eyes on her before. Then he realized
it was the scarf wrapped around her head that had shocked him.
Every well-to-do New Yorker would have recognized it.

"*Insouciante!*" he cried.

On hearing Charanjeet's incantation, or what sounded like one, Abinaash—for it was she—took a step backward, ready to flee if necessary. She wore this tattered headscarf rescued from the ashes of the Kavreen Style factory as a kind of totem, a reminder of the terrible fire and of the windings and turnings her short life had already taken. Wearing the scarf reminded her of her own courage.

"I have come for the interview for the position of medical aide," she said.

After taking a few moments to pull himself together, Charanjeet managed to interview Abinaash and, to his surprise, found her to be well qualified. She could read and write, and she knew some English, all of which was highly unusual. And she was not afraid of hard work. She had some hospital training and work experience. "I have been learning to be a nurse's aide," she said proudly, "at the Caritas Hospital."

"And how will you have time to do your studies *and* take care of my father?" said Charanjeet.

"I will take care of Mr. Kapoor," said Abinaash. "Then I will study."

"You do not look terribly strong," said Mohan. He could not imagine her hoisting his bulk out of bed.

"My strength does not show," said Abinaash.

"Are you an invalid?" said Mohan.

"I am not. I was injured in a fire. This"—she touched the scar—"will fade, I am told. I can walk, but I will always limp."

"We will need you to stay with us, of course. Are you willing to live in our house?" said Mohan.

"Of course. It is part of the job. If I am to be your aide, I will have to be there."

"You will have to shave and bathe my father, and feed him," said Charanjeet. "Then there are . . . the bedpans." He watched for her reaction.

"It is part of the job," she said. "It is to be expected."

XXXIII

ABINAASH CHANDHA HAD REMAINED in the Caritas Hospital in Lahore, not very far from the burned up Kavreen Style factory, for three months. Her shattered leg had required four surgeries. Every morning in hospital, when the nun on duty brought her breakfast of spiced rice, onions, and mangoes, with yogurt *lassi* and sweet tea, Abinaash would say, "I cannot pay for this. I must leave and go back to my village. I have no money."

And every morning the nun on duty would smile at her and say "Abinaash, you are not expected to pay. The word *Caritas* means that you do not have to pay."

"But I want to," she said. "I have to." Her insistence was unceasing and relentless.

"So, Abinaash," said the mother superior one day, "I will tell you how you can pay. You get around well enough now. The doctors and nurses say it is good for you to walk, to exercise your leg. It is what we call physical therapy. You can help take the meals around to the other patients."

"But I want to pay with money," said Abinaash.

"Well," said the mother superior, "we will pay you for your work, and then you can pay for your care."

The next day Abinaash accompanied the nun delivering patient meals, and she did so every day after that. She would be waiting by the kitchen door each morning when the assigned nun came downstairs. Abinaash spooned the rice into bowls, scooped up the yogurt, dished up the fruit. She pushed the cart from ward to ward. Abinaash needed time to recover after each surgery, but she was always impatient to return to her rounds.

"Soon you will have repaid all the surgeries," said Sister Hildegard, a German nurse. Hildegard had taken a special liking to Abinaash.

"I can never repay all that. The care. The food. Never," said Abinaash. "How could I?"

Sometimes, after she had changed Abinaash's dressings, Hildegard sat and read to her.

"I can read," said Abinaash.

"But can you read German?" Of course Abinaash could not, so Hildegard read to her from a German book. Abinaash sometimes fell asleep to the sound of Hildegard's voice.

One day Hildegard told Abinaash that she was ready to be discharged from the hospital. Abinaash went around to the sewing factories, but when the managers looked at her, they saw a cripple and turned her away. "I am an excellent seamstress," she explained. "I was on the sixth floor of the Kavreen Style factory. On the sixth floor we did the fine stitching."

They looked her up and down. "Go away. Cripples are depressing to look at. You can do better on the street begging. With that scar and that leg." Walking through the teeming markets and busy streets of the city, Abinaash thought maybe that was true.

One morning, the mother superior at the Caritas convent came downstairs and found Abinaash sitting in front of her office door. "I want to work here, sister. I can help. You know I am good at it."

"But Abinaash, you are an experienced seamstress and an excellent worker."

"No one will hire me. They don't want to look at a cripple."

It was true that Abinaash had performed valuable service while she was still a patient, and they could certainly use the help. "But how can we pay you, Abinaash? We don't have the money to pay you."

"If I can live here," said Abinaash, "you don't have to pay me." After consulting with her colleagues and checking the budget, the mother superior offered Abinaash a job with room and board and the small sum of six thousand rupees a month. Since her room and board were taken care of, she could send all the money home. She sent a letter with the first month's pay.

"I am paid the same as when I was sewing, but I don't have to spend anything. And I have a bed in a dormitory and excellent food every day. I am happy to send you this money to help with expenses." Her brother read the letter to the family sitting on straw mats in their hut. Abinaash's mother clutched the bills to her heart with tears in her eyes. Her father just stared at his hands, chafed and callused, the ragged nails caked with dirt.

Abinaash was energetic and curious. When she was not serving meals or cleaning up, she followed Hildegard on her rounds. Hildegard explained what she was doing, how you changed a dressing, how you took someone's temperature or measured their blood pressure, and why. "Your body has a temperature, like the air or water. If it is too warm, it tells us you are sick. We can measure your temperature by putting this thermometer under your arm. And blood always flows through your body like water through a pipe. If the pressure is too high, it is also an indication the patient is sick."

Abinaash watched in astonishment each time Hildegard drew blood, tying off the blood vessel, thumping it with her finger, then sliding the needle in easily, right through the skin as if by magic. The ruby-colored blood rose in the syringe. She pulled the needle out and pressed a piece of cotton over the spot where the needle had been.

"How does one become a nurse?" said Abinaash.

"There is a lot of schooling involved," said Hildegard. "It takes a long time."

"I have time," said Abinaash.

The next day Hildegard showed Abinaash a brochure for a nurses' training program at the Mayo Hospital in Lahore. "It is our sister hospital," she said.

"But I have never been to school," said Abinaash.

"You're smart, and you can read," said Hildegard. "Nothing is impossible."

Sister Hildegard could be forgiven for being an incorrigible optimist. Her father, a private in the German army, had disappeared into the freezing Russian mud in 1943. Five years later, despite all odds, he had showed up alive in Würzburg on his parents' doorstep. He had spent four years in a Soviet prison camp, but he picked up his life as though nothing bad had happened. He married his child-hood sweetheart. They had three children, and he began a success-ful business career.

He often told his children his story with its grim beginning and hopeful outcome, and he always ended with the words that Hilde-gard spoke now. "Nothing is impossible." Despite twenty years of experience in the squalor and poverty and despair of Pakistan, Hil-degard continued to believe in improbable dreams. Even in the face of overwhelming evidence to the contrary, she could not abandon hope. Worse yet, she could not stop dispensing it.

Abinaash lay awake on her narrow cot that night, trying to imag-ine what going to school might be like. And what would it be like to be a nurse? She leafed through the brochure over and over, studying the pictures of people in white coats doing various medical things. Even being a nurse's aide exceeded anything she had ever imagined for herself.

Abinaash had never known ambition, never dreamed of being anything besides what she already was and always had been. But something had been awakened in her. Hildegard had given her a cast-off stethoscope. Abinaash listened to her own heart pound with excitement. She tried to talk herself out of it. *Who do you think you are, Abinaash? You are nobody. Your father is a tenant farmer in a small village. You are a girl. You have nothing, you have no money, you have never been to school. You know nothing about the world, about hospitals, about nurses. You are just dreaming.* But the dream had planted itself in her thoughts, and it would not be uprooted.

XXXIV

THE CIA HAD HAD AN interest in currency fraud ever since the money operations behind al Qaeda had come to light, and Peter Sanchez was in charge of the CIA's fraud unit. He had been watching St. John Larrimer since Larrimer, Ltd.'s collapse, and the Eisener-Bank in Zurich for even longer than that. He knew all about Dimitri Adropov and Gazneft, and in fact had been responsible for gathering the evidence that resulted in the earlier charges against Adropov.

Peter did not quite know what to do now that Louis Morgon had come into the picture. Louis was smart and inventive and extraordinarily enterprising. He had outmaneuvered Peter more than once. But he also had a fanciful understanding of the law and only a vague loyalty to it. He seemed to value what he called "the truth" above American national interests.

Peter did not think Louis could be connected to the Russian mob, although Louis had previously associated with unsavory types—gangbangers, various criminals, Muslim fanatics. So with Louis, anything was possible. Peter picked up the phone. "Tell me what you think Adropov is up to," he said when Louis answered.

"We're eating lunch," said Louis.

"It's after two," said Peter.

"That's when we eat here," said Louis. "Call me back in an hour."

Peter did.

"We had cassoulet, in case you're interested. Sausages, duck, white beans. And a 2006 Bourgeuil. It was delicious."

"Sounds good." Peter tried not to sound impatient. "And Adropov: What's he up to?"

"He's trying to find Larrimer. He must have seen me at Lorraine Usher's house—she was Larrimer's secretary—and must have followed me to my hotel. I didn't see him after that, but he may just have gotten more careful after running into me.

"By the way," Louis said, "where's this Jeremy Gutentag? Have you talked to him? I'm guessing he would be an extremely useful source."

"We're waiting until we've got more information."

"So you don't know where he is either?"

"We know he left for London in a hurry. That's where he'll be when it's time to find him."

"All right." Louis decided to let it drop. "Who killed Feather?"

Peter pretended to answer. "Adropov."

"Maybe," said Louis. "Except he's *looking* for leads, not *killing* them. At least at the moment."

"So you tell me," said Peter.

"Larrimer. Or maybe someone he hired. Like Gutentag."

Peter tried to change the subject. "Adropov's back in New York."

"Well, you don't come back to town right after you kill someone, do you?"

Peter was silent.

"So what keeps bringing him back? He must know Larrimer's out of the country."

"Larrimer's money," said Peter.

"It's out of the country too."

"Maybe the means to get at it aren't."

"By the means, you mean what?"

"The means to hijack Larrimer's money. That's what Adropov's after. I'm convinced he's got a banking connection in the US. Maybe he's a decent hacker himself, if only he can get some of the bank's computer codes."

"You've lost me," said Louis. "I'm afraid I still write checks and put them in the mail."

Peter explained that all bank accounts could be accessed by computer. Of course accounts were well protected by a series of firewalls, encryption, and other electronic security measures, as well as internal banking controls. One needed a whole series of passwords and access codes to get through. And having a collaborator inside the bank wouldn't hurt, since the codes and passwords changed regularly and required entry by at least two different entities. "But the vulnerable point is always the banker. All you really need is a banker with access. A decent understanding of computer algorithms would be a bonus. Get your own banker, and you can get right in."

"Can you really?" said Louis.

Peter didn't like the sound of that.

XXXV

ONE REASON ADROPOV was in the US had to be the bank angle. But another was certainly to get to Larrimer. One path to Larrimer started with Jeremy Gutentag. But he wasn't in New York, and he wasn't in London either, as far as Louis could tell. He had vanished completely.

Another path to Larrimer started with Lorraine Usher. Unfortunately for her, Adropov had seen Louis at her house, which meant that she was at considerable risk. Louis knew that Adropov would not stay away from the United States for very long. And now that he was back, it was almost certain that he would turn his attention to Lorraine. Of course Lorraine resisted the idea of leaving, especially when Louis explained what he had in mind. "Newark?!" she said. "You must be kidding. Have you ever been to Newark?"

"It's only for a short period of time, I promise. You'll be with friends of mine."

"What about Arthur? Do they like animals?"

"They have a dog."

"No. I'm sorry. That won't work."

"Ask your lawyer what he thinks."

Bruno thought it was a *very* good idea, given what Lorraine had told him about her Russian visitor. "I'll look in on you," he said. "If it doesn't work out, we'll figure out something else. I promise."

"Now, Lorraine, listen carefully," said Louis when she got back in touch the next day. "What you're doing is crucial to what I'm going to be doing. You're not just hiding out. You're laying down a false trail for Adropov. Sooner or later, he'll come to your house and go inside."

"You mean he'll break in?"

"He needs information that he thinks you've got. So you're going to give it to him. Here's what you do: write Larrimer's Guadeloupe address on a tablet and leave it by the telephone. Write the phone number too. On another page, write down an airline itinerary that takes you to Terre-de-Haut—you can get one on the Internet or from a travel agent. It should look like you've written down notes from talking to a travel agent. In fact, dial up a travel agent as the last call you make. That's important. Adropov will probably check your phone to see who you've called. Pack some things and—"

"So the Russian will find the notes—"

"Right. That's what we want. We're trying to divert him. And we want to know where he is and what he's doing. So if you have Bruno check your house regularly, we'll know when he breaks in. We can then report the break-in and report who did it, which should also bring some heat to bear on the Russian."

"Maybe I should write down the travel info and tear off the top sheet. Then he can rub the pad with a pencil and find the number." She had seen that done in the movies.

"He may not have seen those movies," said Louis. "In any case, meanwhile you'll be in a car on your way to Newark." Which was how Lorraine found herself waiting one evening at JFK Terminal Four, Departures Level, as Louis had instructed. She had taken a cab with Arthur's carrier and her small valise to the airport. She stood watching the passing cars, wondering what to look for, whom to expect, whether anyone would even show up. Whether the Russian might have seen through their ruse. Oh, dear. It was too transparent, too easy, she thought to herself.

"Are you Lorraine?"

She turned to see who had spoken. He was enormous. He wore work boots, black jeans, and a black sleeveless T-shirt despite the fact that it was only forty-five degrees.

His skin was black, his head was shaved, his arms bulged, and one was encircled by a tattoo. His eyes were covered by wraparound sunglasses. His nose was broad and flat and had been broken at least once. He had a gold stud in one ear and a gold tooth that made his smile, when it finally came, seem even more radiant than it was. She had no choice but to smile back.

"I'm Bobby." Bobby leaned forward and took her astonished hand in his.

"I'm Lorraine."

"How ya doin', Lorraine? Let me take that for you." He took Arthur's carrier in one hand and her valise in the other. The valise looked like a toy as he carried it carefully between his thumb and two fingers. When they got to his Cadillac—he always referred to it as his Cadillac, never his car—he gave the passenger door a hard yank. "It sticks," he said. "You got to kick it to get out." Once she was in the car, he put the valise and Arthur on the backseat.

They rolled out of the airport and onto the Van Wyck Expressway. "The Van Wyck is always a rough ride," said Bobby. "Damn potholes. You okay, Lorraine?" They took 495 to 278, then went over the Williamsburg Bridge to Delancey Street and across Manhattan. There was only a short wait into the tunnel. Finally they bounced along the battered streets of Newark past the Bergen Industrial Canal and the Filipo Testaverde Public Housing Project. Halfway down Keyser Street, Bobby swung in and parked by a fire hydrant. He got out and yanked open the passenger door and helped Lorraine out. He picked up the valise and Arthur's carrier from the backseat. He lifted the carrier to his face, to get a good look at Arthur, and saw Arthur looking back at him.

"Damn! That cat's got some eyes on him."

At that moment the door to the house burst open and a large dog came bounding out, barking and jumping and panting, happy beyond all reckoning to see Bobby and whomever he had brought with him. "Stay down, Junior!" Junior rushed up to Lorraine and stuck his snout under her skirt. "He don't mean nothing by it," said Bobby. Junior sniffed her valise and the cat carrier. He peered in at Arthur, and Arthur looked back. Junior barked once—which Arthur likely took to mean "Welcome, Your Majesty. I am and will always remain your obedient servant"—and bounded up the front stairs and back into the house.

Bobby and Lillian had been together for twenty-five years and married for five. "Lorraine? That's a pretty name. You come in here, honey." Lillian carried the valise into a bedroom just off the living room. "You stay in Felicia's room. Felicia's up in Patterson, and she never stays here no more. We're glad you're here. You'll be safe here."

"Louis said—"

"That Louis!" cried Lillian. "Ain't he a sweetie? And Pauline. Have you met Pauline? Well, you will, honey. You will. She's a wonderful person. They're both good people." Lillian wrapped Lorraine in a warm embrace. "Everything's going to be fine. You'll be fine here with us."

"It's only for a little while—"

"Don't you worry about that, honey. As long as you need."

Bobby had recently had his hours cut back at the Newark Airport long-term parking. Lillian still had her beauty shop. "But people don't have the money anymore. Beauty. That's always the first thing people give up when times are hard, don't you know?" Louis had arranged to pay Lillian two hundred dollars a week for Lorraine's room. Lillian had protested mightily, but Louis had prevailed. And Lorraine also insisted that she would do some cooking and some housekeeping besides.

"Bobby's awful particular about what he eats," said Lillian.

The first time Lorraine made her artichoke quiche, Bobby sniffed and poked at it with his fork as though it might jump off the plate and go straight for his jugular.

"What's *this*?" he said.

"Bobby, it's delicious," said Lillian. "And if you don't take at least one taste, then you're a bigger fool than I thought."

Bobby gave Lillian a look. He took a tiny morsel on his fork and, after studying it closely, then sniffing it, he put it in his mouth. He held it there gingerly, right at the front, so he could spit it out if he had to. Which he fully expected to do.

Bobby took tiny chews. He waited after each chew for the horror to set in. But it didn't. Bobby got a studied look on his face and swallowed hard. He picked up another small piece of the quiche and put that in his mouth. This time he chewed less hesitantly, more courageously. He allowed the food to make contact with his taste buds. His eyes looked up to the right and then up to the left. He swallowed.

"Damn!" he said. Bobby stared down at his plate in astonishment. Then he lit into the remainder of his slice of quiche with such gusto that it was gone in a minute. He held his empty plate toward Lorraine.

"What do you say, Bobby?" said Lillian with a scowl.

Bobby's face fell into a huge grin. "Please!"

Lorraine's brother-in-law, Bruno, was surprised to get a telephone call from France from Louis Morgon. He knew of Louis of course, but was surprised that Louis knew of him. Bruno expressed gratitude for Louis's concern for Lorraine's safety. He had been going by her house every evening, but no one had gone in yet.

"Are you certain?" said Louis.

"Yeah, I'm certain. No jimmied windows, and the front door hasn't been opened. I'll let you know as soon as it happens." Bruno asked whether there was anything else he could do to help.

"Maybe there is," said Louis. "I'm on my way to New York. Can I see you while I'm there?"

Bruno suggested that he pick Louis up at the airport. They could have dinner together—he knew a nice little Italian place—and talk things over. "How I might possibly assist with your project," was how Bruno put it.

When Louis emerged from customs, he picked Bruno out immediately. Bruno was maybe fifty, not very tall, balding, wearing a cheap suit and tie and a trench coat. They shook hands. "I just came from work," he said. "New York City Housing Authority."

"Lorraine told me. She said you're a financial analyst and an attorney."

"Yeah. My job is finding housing and tax cheats."

"Is it?" said Louis with interest.

"She likes you," said Bruno. "She said you live in France?"

"That's right."

"Okay," said Bruno. "Good enough. Let's go eat." He took Louis's suitcase.

Guido Ristorante was not very far from the airport. The place was dimly lit, and the tables with their red checkered cloths were far enough apart so that conversations would not be easily overheard. Each table had a lit candle in a Chianti bottle in the center.

"Hey, Bruno! Welcome." The waiter shook Bruno's hand and showed them to a table.

"Renee and I come here all the time. It's good, and it's not too far from home. And actually my dad started the place." Both men had lasagna. They drank a Montepulciano, which Louis found very good. They had tortoni for dessert and a wonderful espresso. The waiter brought them a glass of *limoncello*. "Compliments of the house, Bruno."

"That was good," said Bruno. Louis had to agree that it was good. He set the little glass on the table with a contented sigh. "So, Louis," said Bruno, "how come you live in France?"

"I like it there. I've been there almost forty years now. I can't imagine living anywhere else after all this time."

"I don't mean to pry, Louis, but Renee and I, we're both concerned about Lorraine. She's told me about what you're trying to do."

"It's natural that you'd be concerned."

"And you're not connected with the SEC or law enforcement or anything."

"If that makes you uncomfortable, Bruno, I would understand if you don't want to get mixed up in this—"

"Well, let's just say I'm concerned. I want to help, but I'm a lawyer, and I don't want to do anything that could, you know, get me or Lorraine in trouble. So I'd like to know what you have in mind."

Louis explained again, as he had to others, that it was his intention to bring St. John Larrimer to justice and to separate him from his ill-gotten gains.

"But you're working on your own. . . ."

"I am," said Louis. "And I'm guessing most law enforcement types won't like that."

"Well, most isn't all," said Bruno. "Still, forgive me for being blunt, but what do you get out of this?"

"Satisfaction, mostly."

Bruno studied Louis. "Satisfaction. It's not the kind of thing people do these days. You know, the Lone Ranger thing . . ."

"No, it's not. And that's probably just as well. I have to confess those closest to me don't like my doing it. If it makes you uncomfortable, Bruno, as I say—"

"So far, I'm okay. So, what did you want from me?"

Louis explained that what would be useful was some angle on the Russian. "Who he is, his business dealings here and in Russia, his whereabouts, any information you might be able to get on him."

Bruno looked at his hands while he considered how to respond. "I thought you might ask about him," he said, turning his hands palms up and then palms down on the checkered tablecloth. "Given where we are and all." He gestured with his head to indicate that he was talking about the restaurant. "As I said, my dad, Guido Gramicci, started the place back in the fifties. And my brother, Emilio, runs the place now." While none of the Gramiccis were mobsters or associated with mobsters, some of Guido's regular customers were. Which gave both Emilio and Bruno what Bruno called "particular insights into the goings-on about town." Bruno did not have any knowledge of Adropov. "But I know some people who know some people who might."

The very next day Bruno called. "The Russian, Adropov, he stays in Brooklyn, Brighton Beach. In Russia, he's in the oil and gas business, on the board of some mobbed-up companies. He comes here, supposedly, to do oil and gas business, but he seems to have other stuff going on too. My source doesn't know what.

"Anyway, when he's in the US, which he is right now, he hangs out at the Odessa Grill. He stays with a cousin, Stanislav Borgoi— 1077 Ocean View Avenue. The cousin owns a clothing store. The cousin seems legit. Adropov likes to keep a low profile, which isn't easy for a guy his size. He's big. And mean looking. Have you seen him?"

"Yes," said Louis. "He is big."

"You think he's dangerous?" said Bruno.

"He could be," said Louis.

"I'm not asking for myself, but Lorraine . . ."

XXXVI

Dimitri Adropov lived in plain sight. The FBI knew where he was, the CIA too. Dimitri knew about their "hidden" cameras above the bar and in the men's room in the Odessa Grill, where he spent his afternoons drinking Turkish coffee and playing dominoes. There were cameras in Cousin Slava's apartment too. Good old Slava, he didn't have a clue. Dimitri was pleased to have the camera surveillance; he acted as though he didn't know it was there. Being watched afforded him a kind of liberty, as long as he did nothing illicit on camera. The surveillance tapes and recordings offered him ready-made alibis and certified his innocence.

They couldn't watch him all the time, of course. He was not that high on anyone's interest list at the moment, and he wanted to keep it that way. Nobody followed him when he left the Odessa or his cousin's apartment. He had checked with his FBI sources. So when it came time to engage in activities the authorities might frown on, Dimitri conducted his business on the move—usually walking—using stolen cell phones, which he discarded frequently.

Dimitri had tracked down a former EisenerBank trader right here in New York. He had not only promised to allow the guy to go on living, but he now paid him a monthly retainer. And while the ex-banker had managed to get the computer codes and routing numbers for Larrimer's old accounts, and for Jeremy Gutentag's London accounts too, the numbers were all essentially useless. Larrimer had moved his money around to banks whose expertise, presumably, was hiding money. He had surrounded his millions with an apparently impenetrable layer of firewalls and passcodes. Dimitri was no closer to Larrimer's money than he had ever been. And it was a small comfort that nobody else was either.

"But how is this possible?" Dimitri hissed into the phone. "How he can hide so much money?" He had just come out of the Q train's Sheepshead Bay station and was walking east.

"If you get me Larrimer's personal codes—" said the banker.

"And Gutentag, where he has money?"

"You get me his codes—"

"How I can get codes? I pay you lots of money for what?" Dimitri closed the phone.

He turned south on Nineteenth Street. He opened the phone again and poked in the number of his FBI contact. "FBI has Larrimer's bank codes? I need bank codes."

"They're not available to me *if* we have them, which I doubt."

"What good is FBI then?"

"I *have* got something for you, though," said the FBI man. "Louis Morgon, the old guy that ran into you? He's definitely *not* CIA. He was, but then he was dismissed from the CIA back in the seventies. And he was charged as a terrorist just a few years back."

"So, now you telling me, old man is terrorist? This is bullshit."

"No, that's not what I'm telling you. The charges were dismissed and his file was sealed."

"Sealed?"

"I can't get it," said the FBI man. "By the way, he lives in France." He gave Dimitri the address.

Dimitri stopped and turned around. "Where he is now?"

"I don't know. But he's after the money like you. He tried to wire money to Larrimer's old account. I'm guessing he hoped it would be forwarded and he'd get his account number. It didn't work."

"Why in fuck he mess with me, this old man!" Without waiting for the answer, Dimitri jammed the phone shut. He looked around once more before letting the phone slide into a trash can as he hurried past.

Louis watched him walk a good three blocks before retrieving the phone.

XXXVII

LOUIS HAD CALLED WITH THE news that he would be in Washington the next day, and Peter had agreed to meet him. But now as they sat opposite each other in a little Georgetown restaurant waiting for their salads, Peter wondered why. They were even, he owed Louis nothing, and the guy was a pain in the ass. Peter scowled at the cell phone Louis had just handed him. "This is the little present you mentioned? You came all the way to Washington to give me this?"

"No, I came to Washington to visit my children," said Louis.

"So why is this interesting?" He waved the phone in front of Louis's face.

"It was thrown away by Dimitri Adropov."

"Who?"

"The Russian. It's how he's doing business these days. Do you know where he is?"

"We have him under surveillance. Of course we know where he is."

"And you know who he's talking to?"

"Cell phones make that a little tricky."

"That's the reason for my little present. The last call he made before he ditched *that* phone was to someone inside the US government. The FBI, I think. And the call before that was to a banker. He also called some numbers in London, looking for Gutentag, I'm guessing. He's trying to get to Larrimer's money."

"Like you."

"Like me," said Louis.

"And you know this how?"

"I was tailing him. I saw him make the calls, then ditch the phone. I tried the numbers in the phone. He got some interesting calls too."

Peter looked skeptical. "And how did you find him?"

Louis was not inclined to bring Bruno or Emilio Gramicci into the conversation. "He's easy to find. It should be easy to find out who he was talking to. I'd do it if I were you. You've got a traitor in your midst." Their lunch did not go any better after that. Both men were happy when the check came. They split it.

Michael and Rosita got up from the porch swing as Louis pulled the rental car into the driveway. Louis and Michael embraced and clapped each other on the back. Louis kissed Rosita. "And the baby?" he said.

She smiled and held her belly between her hands.

"Jenny's in the house," said Michael.

The table was set for five. Jennifer came out of the kitchen and embraced her father. "Thanks, Dad, for all your support." She kissed his cheek.

"Any news on the clinic?"

"Soon, I hope. Mr. Cohen has a building he owns where a ground-floor space just opened up. He's been great. The rent will actually be less than the old place. And he's helping with renovations. We're working out the last details. It's in a rougher neighborhood, but that's where our clients live. If everything comes together, we can open in a month. And look who's here, Dad."

Jennifer stepped aside, and there was Zaharia. He had gotten tall. He had to lean down a bit to receive Louis's kisses on one cheek and then the other. "I hear your English is perfect."

"Pretty good," said Zaharia.

The house filled with wonderful smells, and Michael urged everyone toward the dining table. Rosita had made what she called weeping stew, since the recipe called for chopping up six large onions. Michael had done the weeping, she said. When the onions were soft, you added rice, chicken stock, chunks of lamb, cilantro, and a few mild chilies and let it cook on a low flame. And there were braised Brussels sprouts with slivers of almonds and chestnuts in a buttery mustard sauce. It was almost midnight before Louis left for his hotel.

He was back the next morning right after breakfast. "Let's go for a walk, Dad," said Michael. It was a crisp day. The sky was streaked with narrow clouds whose shadows passed swiftly across the city. Louis had thought he would remember his way around Washington, but he didn't. They walked through Rock Creek Park then climbed the hill onto Connecticut Avenue and then walked all the way down to Lafayette Square. Louis stopped and gazed at the White House. "I was inside many years ago," he said to no one in particular.

"Jenny said you're trying to do something about that guy . . . not Madoff," said Michael.

"Larrimer," said Louis.

"That's him. So what are you trying to do?"

Louis tried to give his usual vague evasion about justice and retribution.

Michael stopped walking. "What does *that* mean?"

The question made Louis uncomfortable. Dealing with a swindler had already drawn him into swindles of his own. This was nothing new for Louis, but the uncomfortable feeling was new. The doubts and uncertainty were new. Louis was a few years into his seventies now. He was more careful going up and down stairs. He had always driven slowly, but now he drove slower still. He held himself to one glass of his beloved Médard Chinon a day. He went to bed earlier and slept longer. Despite his walking and gardening and other exercise, frailty and caution had infiltrated his daily habits. And, not surprisingly, caution had infiltrated his thinking too. He tried to resist, but it was inevitable.

Louis was more aware than he had ever been of unintended consequences, of what military types were fond of calling "collateral damage." He knew there were those entirely innocent of whatever misdeeds he was intent on punishing who, their innocence notwithstanding, might be caught in the line of his fire. Said a different way, he recognized that no matter how virtuous his intentions, the stones he cast into the pool sent ripples outward in all directions, and somewhere scattered here and there were people barely able to keep their noses above the surface. Without having played any part in what had gone before, they would be swamped by those spreading ripples. Louis knew nothing of Abinaash Chandha or Mohan and Golapi Kapoor or Irina Adropov. In fact, even the villains like Adropov and Jeremy Gutentag and even Larrimer were essentially unknown to him. But he knew they were not just villains, they were human beings, with aspects of innocence alongside their guilt.

When Louis had been in fifth grade, he had been required to memorize population numbers, and while nothing else from the fifth grade had stayed with him, for some reason the numbers had. The United States: one hundred fifty million. Russia: one hundred million. China: five hundred fifty million. The earth: two and a half billion. There had been space between people then. But now much of the space seemed to have disappeared. There was global this and global that. Sneezing here caused a breakout of disease there. There was an epidemic of interconnectedness that seemed sometimes, at least to the seventy-plus Louis Morgon, to render the concept of individual and autonomous action a thing of the past.

"Dad, what does that mean?" said Michael again.

Louis turned and looked at his son as though he had only just noticed he was there.

Michael repeated himself. "What do you mean when you talk about retribution and justice?"

"For now it means nothing, Michael. I don't know what I mean.

I can't find a way to him. I mean, I think I can get to *him*, but I don't think I can get to his money. And even if I could—"

Michael did not have Louis's reservations. "Well, you can find out *where* the money is, can't you?"

"I don't know."

"And if you can find it, you can probably get it."

"I don't think I could."

"All you need is someone to get through all the firewalls and that sort of thing. Someone who can move the money without Larrimer even realizing it's being moved."

"You're talking about fraud, Michael."

"Only in the legal sense," said Michael. He laughed, and when Louis didn't laugh with him, he added, "That's what you would say, Dad."

"The real question is, is it possible?" said Louis, ignoring Michael's implication.

"Of course it's possible," said Michael.

"What do you mean?"

"It's just computer stuff, Dad. Software, breaking codes, that kind of thing."

"You don't do that sort of thing, do you, Michael?"

"Dad, you're so thick sometimes." Michael put his arm across Zaharia's shoulders.

"Zaharia?"

"Do you remember what Zaharia studies and where he goes to school?"

"Of course I do," said Louis, beaming proudly. "Computer science at MIT."

XXXVIII

ZAHARIA HAD BEEN LIVING IN his grandmother's house overlooking the port of Algiers when his teacher had said to him, "Read books, Zaharia. Everything worth knowing is in books." The teacher probably did not remember in the next minute what he had said, but the words were as if branded in Zaharia's brain. He had been searching for an explanation of his miserable life, and he took the teacher's words literally. If he read books, he would discover why his mother was a drug addict and prostitute, he would learn why his father had scraped along as a petty criminal and then been murdered before his eyes.

Ali, an elderly man, opened his door to see the neighbor boy looking at him. "You have books," said Zaharia. "I see them through the window on my way to school."

"Yes," said Ali. "I have books."

"My teacher says everything is in books."

"Your teacher is right." After a moment's hesitation, Ali invited Zaharia inside.

His apartment was small. But every centimeter of every wall was covered, floor to ceiling, with bookshelves. Even in the kitchen and above the door and the windows there were shelves packed with books. And where there were no shelves, there were stacks of books.

Ali explained to the boy that he was a bibliophile. "It's Greek," Zaharia explained to his grandmother later that afternoon. "It means a lover of books. *I'm* a bibliophile."

Ali showed Zaharia where the house key was hidden under the geranium pot. "Come anytime," he said. "Take any books that interest you. It is a shame to see them dying on the shelf. And a joy to see them used."

Zaharia came after school and on weekends and read and read and read, book after book. *Consumed* would have been the better word for it. He did not exactly find answers to the questions he had about his mother and father. But he found bits of understanding of life that promised, someday, taken together with other bits of understanding, to lead him to answers. By the time Zaharia finished with a book, it looked limp and depleted, like an exhausted lover. History, geography, religion, literature, art, and mathematics. Especially mathematics.

Zaharia read mathematics the way others read the newspaper. Mathematics, it turned out, was his natural tongue; it spoke directly to him, unmediated, unfiltered, needing no translation. Ali watched all this with growing astonishment and joy. One day he took Zaharia to see a friend, a university mathematician named Mafouz, who immediately recognized Zaharia's gifts.

Mafouz pressed Zaharia into the chair in front of his computer, the first Zaharia had ever seen up close. At first the boy watched the screen and poked gingerly at this key and then that. In a matter of hours, the entire theory and structure of artificial intelligence had become apparent to him. He doped out the machine's language and began programming it. Soon he was designing simple programs, then more and more difficult ones. He posited problems that needed solving and created the algorithms to solve them.

The next time Mafouz saw Ali, he pronounced Zaharia a computer genius. "I have never seen anything like it," he said. "He must go to America, and in America he must go to Boston, to MIT." Mafouz wrote to a former student who was now a professor at MIT.

A scholarship offer for the fall semester came by return mail. Prodded by Mafouz and Ali and also Louis, who had been his earliest benefactor, Zaharia accepted the MIT scholarship.

The fall semester was still months away. Zaharia had by now read every book on mathematics in Ali's library. And Mafouz had taught Zaharia everything he could without the resources of a university.

"What you need now is a real-life computer problem," said Mafouz. "Something that tests all your skills."

"And," Ali added, "something that will make you think on your feet."

It so happened, that the news just then was full of the ferment and upheaval that two and a half years later would explode into the Arab Spring. Tunisia and Egypt were already having regular strikes and sit-ins. And Iran was seeing larger and larger street demonstrations against the regime's oppressive control. Even in Algeria there were demonstrations and protests. They were quickly suppressed, and rarely got into the papers, but everybody knew.

All these various uprisings were uncoordinated, and so their suppression could easily be accomplished by a handful of police waving batons or firing tear gas. But why, Zaharia wondered, couldn't they be coordinated? Why could tyrannical governments so easily control the flow of information?

He saw that others had been asking themselves the same questions on the Internet. Before long he found himself looking for digital paths around the Algerian government's Internet restrictions and firewalls. He began using his computer—by now he had his own laptop—to disrupt the censorship and repression organized by the regime against the people. He shared his methods with others, and they shared theirs with him. Of course he could not tell Ali or Mafouz anything about his project. They would have been horrified.

"I'll explain what I'm doing, once I get results," he told them, and they were wise enough not to inquire further.

"And were you able to disrupt government censorship and help organize protests?" said Louis. The very idea amazed him. They were sitting on a bench in front of the Capitol Building looking down the great expanse of the National Mall.

"It wasn't just me. There were a lot of people involved. There still are."

Louis looked at Michael. Michael shrugged. "Don't ask me."

"But a bank?" said Louis.

"A bank might be harder." Zaharia smiled.

Zaharia had a light and energetic way of walking, rolling off his toes and almost bouncing. Sometimes he jumped or skipped or ran ahead and waited. He was twenty now and a head taller than Louis, but in some ways, he was still a boy. "I can't ask you to do this," said Louis.

"To do what?" said Zaharia.

"Break into a bank."

"I'm not interested in breaking into anything. I'm interested in constructing and then solving computer problems."

"That's sophistry. Do you know what sophistry is?"

Zaharia gave him a look.

"Besides," said Louis, "it could be dangerous. You could get in serious trouble."

"Why? We want to move money that a thief has stolen back where it belongs."

"It would be against the law."

"Would it be wrong?"

"It would be wrong *because* it is against the law."

"*That's* sophistry," said Zaharia. "Do *you* know what sophistry is?"

"And how exactly would you do it?" said Louis.

"It always begins with an exact formulation of the problem, which has to include a precise exploration of the engineering of that which we are seeking to penetrate. Codes, firewalls, encryption—you've heard of those things? They're really all the same thing as everything else on a computer, electronic impulses assembled differently to do different things. So I explore the engineering by bumping up against it again and again, the way you might test any fortification. What I want to do is reduce it to its basic electronics, find how it's made, its grammar, its logic.

"It's never a matter of penetrating anything, compromising anything, although that's the way a lot of people think of it. I think of it as trying to join an exclusive community. Once you're part of it, they do not see you as an intruder. They recognize you only as part of the family."

XXXIX

On his way back to France, Louis called Carolyne Bushwick. "It's Louis Coburn, Ms. Bushwick. You showed me some Greenwich properties a while back. I'd like to bring my wife up to see them."

There was a brief silence at the other end of the line. "Oh, yes, Mr. Coburn. I remember. We've been very busy since you were here. As I told you, properties in the range you were looking at are moving fast. Let me see whether anything I showed you is still available." Louis heard some papers rattling. "I'm sorry, Mr. Coburn. Three of those properties have sold. The fourth one, the one on Midgen Lane, is awaiting an offer. We're expecting it at any moment."

"In fact, I liked that one best of the four," said Louis. "So I'd still like to bring Mrs. Coburn up for a look."

"You'll have to move quickly, Mr. Coburn. As I say, there may be an offer any day now."

"I understand," said Louis. "We'll rearrange our schedule and see whether we can get up in the next couple of days."

"Call first," said Carolyne. "Just to make sure."

"And in the meantime, could you put me in touch with the bank you mentioned? It would help speed things up to know what kind of terms we can get."

"It's the Charter Island National Bank, Mr. Coburn."

"Charter Island National Bank. And the phone number?"

"They are an online bank, Mr. Coburn. They're in the Cayman Islands. I also deal in Caribbean properties. I've worked with Charter Island for a number of years and have found them very reliable. They generally offer favorable rates. I know it sounds a bit unusual to have a mortgage with an offshore bank, but Charter Island has charters in the United States, England, and France. Go to Charterisland-nationalbank.com, and you'll find everything you need to know about them—who they are, mortgage banking, private banking, and so on. And you'll find loan application forms you can download."

Next Louis called Zaharia. "Where are you?" said Zaharia. He could hear a loudspeaker making announcements in the background.

"Kennedy airport," said Louis. "It was wonderful to see you, Zaharia. Pauline will be jealous. Will you visit us in France?"

"I'm going home to Granny for spring break. I could stop on my way. Would you mind?"

"You have money for the flight?"

"I've been robbing banks."

Louis didn't laugh. He felt uneasy about involving Zaharia in his shenanigans. That's what Renard called it. Shenanigans.

"I've been writing programs for the university," said Zaharia. "A part-time job. It's easy, and it pays well."

"Please come. We'd love to see you. And here's a bank—Charter Island National Bank—that might be useful to look into. In the Cayman Islands. They have a Web site—"

"Charter Island National. I'll find it." Louis heard a keyboard clicking in the background.

"Just find out a bit about them for the moment, all right? Who they are, what they do. Nothing else. Don't do anything else. You promise?"

"I promise," said Zaharia.

When Louis got home late the next morning, there was a telephone message from Zaharia. "Call me."

"Have you found something interesting?"

"Yes. I didn't take anything or change anything, I promise. They know someone's been there looking because they have tracking software. But I set up a phantom ISP, so they don't know who or where I am."

"You're speaking a language I don't understand."

"I know," said Zaharia. "Charter Island is a bank that exists entirely online. Their Web site lists them as being chartered in Switzerland, the United States, the United Kingdom, France, and several other countries, including the Cayman Islands, where their headquarters are located. And their name is misleading, because they're not anybody's national bank, and they never have been. They say they're affiliated with UBS, a giant Swiss bank, but I don't find any connections."

"*Affiliated* can mean almost anything."

"They say they offer traditional banking services, commercial banking, private banking. What is private banking?"

"Private banking is for rich clients. That's the part of the business that interests us, I suspect."

"Well, that's where the highest security seems to be," said Zaharia. "So that's where I went. The site seems straightforward and normal. It's when you get behind the site that things get kind of messy and interesting. In the private banking pages, there are links that shuffle you through other intermediate links, like going through boxes inside boxes. It's not something you'd notice if you just clicked on the link. The security isn't especially remarkable, but having lots of layers makes it hard to get through if you're trying to follow a trail. That's one interesting thing."

"What makes that interesting?" Louis wondered.

"Well, it's more than just a security measure. It means that the site engineer wanted to prevent anyone from following a trail. They wanted to keep the destination secret." Zaharia was reading from notes. "Okay. Another interesting thing—not a computer thing—is that their physical address in the Caymans is only a drop box. It's not even at a post office. I didn't know banks could do that."

"It means," said Louis, "without court orders, it's impossible to know who rents the lockbox and who gets the mail. In fact, I bet it gets forwarded somewhere else."

"And this is also interesting," said Zaharia. "While they list the US and other countries as where they do business, nowhere on the site do they mention where they do *most* of their business."

"Ah," said Louis. "And where is that?"

"Nigeria, Pakistan, Saudi Arabia, Andorra, and the Netherland Antilles. Most of their traffic goes back and forth between the Caymans and those places."

"My guess is they're laundering money, Zaharia. They take stolen money and filter it into legitimate businesses—bonds, mortgages, and loans. Maybe real estate. Can you tell who sends and receives the traffic?"

"No, I can't tell any of that. The Caymans IPO is a cover address that hides the real one. It could be anyone anywhere. All electronic addresses are like that."

"So, somebody has built a kind of maze behind the scenes that goes beyond normal bank security?"

"That's a good way of saying it."

"Is there some way to check the bank sites and subsidiary sites or the correspondence between those sites to see if certain names come up?"

"Names?"

"People. Either in the body of e-mails or the headings or . . . wherever else there might be names."

"That would mean breaking their encryption." Louis could tell Zaharia was eager to try. He gave him a list of names to check.

Zaharia called back an hour later. "There's only one hit from the names you gave me. Smythe, Richard J. You want his e-mail address?"

XL

PAULINE WAS UNHAPPY THAT LOUIS was using Zaharia—*using* was her word, not his—to advance his investigation. She agreed to listen to his explanation if he promised not to give her a lecture about truth and virtue and the obligations of citizenship. And if he peeled the onions. They had decided to make Rosita's weeping stew. Louis got his swim goggles from the cabinet above the stove. He wore them whenever he peeled onions.

First, Louis said, he was fairly sure that Larrimer's former wife was up to no good, and if she was not complicit in the actual theft of the three billion dollars, then she was at least complicit in concealing it and profiting from it, spiriting it out of the country and helping launder it. And thanks to Zaharia, Louis had a pretty good idea where that money was going and how it was being laundered.

"Then you should turn your findings over to your CIA contact."

"You mean Peter Sanchez? And what will he do? As far as he's concerned, my 'findings' are tainted because of how I got them."

"Well, he's right, isn't he? They are tainted," said Pauline.

"*In a sense* he's right. But only in a sense. They violate procedures. They skirt the law. In a law court everything I've discovered would be thrown out and there'd be no case. And I would probably be indicted for fraud, conspiracy, that sort of thing." In his agitation Louis had taken off the goggles, but he started to cry so he put them on again.

"That's because they are crimes and a society depends on its citizens not taking the law into their own hands."

"That's the theory: that we live in a world ruled by laws. But the laws are almost constantly sidestepped and abused by the rich and the powerful to their own advantage."

"So what makes you think that at some point there *won't* be a case against you and there *will* be a case against Larrimer?"

"Honestly, I can't be sure. But sometimes—not often, but sometimes—that's how things work. Once the government has the money and they have Larrimer in shackles, then how all that came about won't seem as important as it does now. Having a case might be too tempting to resist; maybe they'll even turn a blind eye to how it was acquired."

"Maybe," said Pauline. "Maybe, maybe, maybe. That's a lot of maybes."

"At that point they can avoid looking at everything they'd rather not see. But not now; not yet."

"And what about Zaharia? He's a boy."

"He's twenty."

"Louis, *he's a boy.*"

"Yes, I know." Louis stopped and remained silent for a long time. He peered past Pauline through his goggles, like an explorer from elsewhere in a poisonous atmosphere. "He's a boy," he said again. "Did you know he helped protestors get the word out about Algerian government corruption? He did. On his own. From Algiers, using his little laptop computer, he penetrated government computer security and helped shine a light on the government's goons and thugs. Remember those images on television? Well, we saw that because Zaharia and others were operating outside the law. And the Algerian government never even knew he existed. They still don't."

"What you're doing is different."

"He tells me this can be exactly the same kind of operation. No one will ever know who he is or what he's done unless he tells them."

"But you'll know. And he will know."

Louis did not have an answer. He peeled and chopped, and Pauline browned the lamb in a sizzling skillet.

"These aren't fanatics and thugs," said Pauline.

"Maybe not fanatics. But thugs. And thieves. Abetting terrorists and outlaw regimes. Their bank is laundering money from Nigeria and Pakistan. Drug money. Terrorist money. Human trafficking money. The fact that Larrimer and his banker don't traffic in drugs or women doesn't mean he's innocent of that trafficking. If he's involved in a money laundering enterprise, he's part of it."

"You're not God," said Pauline.

"I wish the world were an orderly place," said Louis, ignoring her implication. "I wish it were a place where those in power go after wrongdoers, bring them to justice, and then restore what was stolen to its rightful owners. But it isn't. You know that. The strong and the rich rule, and the billions—the poor and the vulnerable—get trampled underfoot. I guess some powers are better than others when it comes to justice. But every nation—even the US, even France—are constrained by the worst among them, because nations are sovereign. We all have to treat North Korea as though it had rights. But it doesn't."

"But it does," said Pauline.

"In my mind it doesn't," said Louis. "The North Korean people have rights, but North Korea doesn't. As far as I can tell, it's no different than any other criminal enterprise, except maybe in its scale and the scale of its evil. How can any country claim rights for itself greater than the rights it gives its own citizens?"

"You are like an Old Testament prophet," said Pauline. "With goggles." She laughed and took his head between her hands and kissed him. The onions were finally in the pot, and the goggles came off.

"I don't see why everyone doesn't use goggles to peel onions," said Louis.

The stew was delicious, Pauline agreed.

"I'm glad to be home," said Louis. He reached across the table for her hand.

"Are you?" she said.

"My children are there. And when I'm there, I admit, there are moments when it's almost as though I had never left. I can feel an odd yearning."

"I can imagine," she said. "But I'm glad you're here."

"Those moments pass. They get crowded out by the culture. That strange, superficial, juvenile culture takes hold again, where forward motion is everything. Life in America doesn't just advance. It surges forward on waves of money and fashion and celebrity and narcissism. The next big thing is all that matters. That seems to breed the Larrimers and the Madoffs. And nothing really stops them."

"But *you* will," said Pauline, unwilling to surrender her sense of the absurdity of the entire enterprise. At that moment Louis glimpsed his reflection in a cabinet door, obscured and distorted by the old glass and the stacks of cups and saucers behind the glass. There was something ghostly about the face. His eyes were lost in dark shadow, his neck thin and insubstantial, his hair all but invisible. It was as though he was seeing the very preposterousness of his pursuit in those glass panes.

"What is it?" said Pauline.

"It's this world. I don't like it; I'm an alien here."

"Well, you're old. Old people are aliens everywhere."

XLI

CHARANJEET KAPOOR DID NOT BELIEVE in omens or other such hocus-pocus; he was an Oxford and London School of Economics graduate, after all. He believed in charts and statistics and capital and markets. But when Abinaash appeared suddenly in his father's hospital room wearing the *Insouciante* scarf around her head, it was like a sign from the gods. She seemed an oracle, the bearer, Charanjeet was certain, of bad news and ominous implications. Jeremy, Charanjeet's almost forgotten alter ego, was suddenly front and center, summoned back from the subconscious oblivion into which Charanjeet had banished him. Jeremy's misdeeds loomed large, his culpability even larger, and the prospect of just punishment—which Abinaash and the scarf represented—caused Charanjeet to tremble and perspire.

Mohan noticed. "Is something the matter, my boy?"

"It's nothing," Charanjeet snapped. "I'm fine." After a moment he was able to steady himself enough to conduct the interview of Abinaash and test her qualifications. To his dismay, she met all the criteria Charanjeet and his parents had agreed upon. He could not easily send her away. Still, when he looked at her, he saw only the scarf. She was an oracle, and the scarf was his downfall.

Charanjeet turned to his parents. "She will not do at all. She is too young and too small and extremely insolent."

Mohan and Golapi looked at him in astonishment. "What are you saying, Charanjeet? She seems highly qualified to me," said Mohan. "And as for insolence, well, I see no such thing." Abinaash stood watching the back and forth with interest.

"I'm sorry, Daddy, but you are not seeing things clearly," said Charanjeet.

"I think I am seeing things quite clearly," said Mohan. "And since I am the one who will pay her wages, the decision is mine." Charanjeet had no choice but to make the offer. "We can pay you fifty dollars a month plus your room and board." He was rattled, so he spoke in dollars.

"How much money is that?" Abinaash wanted to know.

"That is thirty-five hundred rupees," said Charanjeet.

"But that is not what we agreed upon, Charanjeet," said Mohan. "It is to be seven thousand rupees."

Charanjeet continued as though he had not heard. "There will be a one-month trial to make sure your service is satisfactory. You must move in next Monday. The cook will show you where you will sleep." Charanjeet sought refuge in the ways of old Pakistan. Because Abinaash was of a lower caste, he spoke to her in a patronizing manner. He took no note of her name, nor did he inquire after her origins. And yet he could not help but notice when she turned her head and the scar was out of view, that she was strikingly pretty, with coffee-colored skin slightly darker than his own and large dark eyes, a narrow nose, and beautiful teeth. And she was not diffident or retiring either, as he might have expected, but inappropriately proud and confident. It made him angry all over again that she did not cast her eyes downward when he looked at her. Instead her eyes met his and held them.

"Have you been in service before?" he demanded. Now that they had agreed on terms, other things he should have asked occurred to him.

"No, I have never been in service. I am a nurse's aide." She might as well have said, "I am the president of a major company," the way she pronounced the words.

"Of course you will wear a sari when you are on duty," he said.

"A sari is neither appropriate or practical for this work. I have a uniform that consists of slacks and a tunic. And a headscarf," she said as an afterthought, and touched her head. "I assure you, sir, my appearance will always be correct."

The next Monday Abinaash moved into the Kapoor house, a large colonial structure surrounded by a walled garden filled with bougainvillea, hibiscus, date palms, and fig trees and with fountains at each end of the house. She was given a narrow bed in the cook's room on the fourth floor where the servants lived.

The cook had had the room all to herself until now, so of course she resented Abinaash's presence. Abinaash arranged her meager belongings in the bottom drawer of the small dresser. She put her books on the room's only bookshelf.

"Don't hog all the space," said the cook. "Half of that shelf is mine, you know."

"Do you have books too?" said Abinaash.

"I might," said the cook, who could not read. "It doesn't matter: The space is mine."

Abinaash left half the shelf empty. She did not mind. She had never lived in such luxury.

XLII

Hamilton Jones had urged that Louis send photos of his fake paintings to Christie's and Sotheby's and to several prominent galleries. "Gagosian and Zwirner, for certain. We need to get some buzz going. Gavin Brown, maybe. Pace, Metro Pictures."

"Buzz?" said Louis.

"We need people talking about this extraordinary and mysterious cache of masterpieces. Remember, Louis, nothing moves a collector like envy. Collectors will want your Picassos not because they appear to be great paintings. They will want them so no one else can have them. For the rich, being a collector almost always comes down to the joy of claiming something unique and precious as their own. By the way, that goes for museums too. The Met, MOMA, Chicago Art Institute, the Getty, the Louvre, they'll all be trying to find you."

"Should we send them the photos too?"

"I think the auctions and galleries will do the trick. The story will get told to *The New York Times* and then everybody will know."

Finally Hamilton Jones sent photos to St. John Larrimer's Cap d'Antibes address. They would be forwarded to Larrimer wherever he was, and St. John's sense that he was well hidden from the world would not be compromised.

Hamilton wrote a letter to introduce the paintings.

Dear Mr. Larrimer,

Your situation may dictate that you not add to your art collection at this time. But the masterworks in the enclosed photos have just come to light. You will recognize that they are of extraordinary quality. I thought you should at least know of their existence and availability.

An elderly and secretive French collector has just decided to liquidate his collection, including these exceptional late Picassos and the eccentric but wonderful Cézanne. The provenance of all these works seems impeccable. Some were apparently acquired by this gentleman from Picasso himself. The fact that they have never been seen before makes their appearance at this late date a unique event in the entire history of modern art. I haven't yet seen them in person, but judging from the photos, I believe the Picassos would easily bring six or eight million dollars each—probably more—in a strong auction, and the Cézanne at least twenty.

As it happens, this collector prefers to sell as he bought—privately and not at auction—which means the paintings will sell for something less than their full value. This gentleman approached me thanks to a friend of his who is a longtime client of mine. I have spoken with the gentleman on two occasions and have made plans to go to France as soon as I can to see the paintings.

I must inform you that I have two other clients to whom I am also sending these photos. My usual arrangement for finding paintings of this value—a three-percent-of-purchase-price fee—applies. Please let me know whether I can be of service.

Sincerely yours,

Hamilton Jones

At first St. John was amused by Jones's letter and by the enclosed photos. He looked at them and smiled and shook his head at each one. St. John was not an idiot. He knew that various forces would stop at nothing to get their hands on him. They would not be above using his passion for collecting to ensnare him. He put the photos aside and went to bed. But at four in the morning, he was suddenly wide awake and suffering under the constraints he had brought down upon himself. The agony was almost physical. He felt like Gulliver, held immobile by a thousand silken threads. He was lying on silk sheets, living as luxuriously as he ever had, and yet he was a prisoner. He tore himself from his bed, as though he were breaking free from the Lilliputians' tiny ropes. He strode to the kitchen. He poured himself a glass of milk and drank it so greedily that drops ran down his cheeks and onto his pajama top.

The photos lay on the table where he had left them. He spread them out in front of him and was overcome by their beauty and, simultaneously, by the sense that acquiring them, especially in his circumstances, would be a coup of unparalleled proportions. And what was the risk, after all? He could see them in France without fear of arrest and make certain they were what they appeared to be. Jones would have to be there too. Maybe St. John would invite his friend, the French president, to come along. Maybe he would offer them as a permanent loan to the Louvre or the Pompidou Center in exchange for a seat on their board or governing council or whatever they called it in France.

The acquisition of these paintings would represent the return of normalcy to his life. It struck him suddenly how terribly he missed this normalcy, the serenity and calm. And the power! He would renew his sense of power and show the world that it was undiminished, that he was as big as he had ever been. No one should own these paintings but him.

He arranged the photos on the table as though he were planning how they might be arranged on his walls (in case the Louvre thing didn't work out). He stood over them and gazed down at them, while the desire and avarice Hamilton Jones had so skillfully summoned surged through his being. The sight of these paintings made him ache.

St. John sat down with a deep sigh. No. No! There was no way he could buy these paintings. To see them meant leaving his seclusion and, despite the French president's protection, that meant putting his liberty at risk. Besides that, he would have to move large sums of money. He would have to reveal his whereabouts, raise his profile. No, no. It was impossible. He simply could not afford to take the chance.

St. John slid the letter and photos back into the envelope. He looked out onto the Caribbean Sea. The day was dawning. Little whitecaps danced on the gray water. An albatross passed slowly in the distance. A cormorant sat on a rock with spread wings while another dived for a fish. What was life without risks? Everything St. John had ever accomplished had been done *despite* the risk, even *because* of it. Risk was his motivator and the piquant spice of his life.

Without thinking what time it was, St. John picked up the phone and dialed.

"Jones? Hamilton Jones? . . . Larrimer here."

XLIII

A Sotheby's assistant opened the packet Louis had sent. The assistant did not quite realize what she was looking at until she read the letter. She took the packet to her boss, who gave the pictures one look and ran up three flights of stairs to the Impressionist and Modern Art Department. It was the first time he had run anywhere in years. He passed the photos to a modern painting specialist as he fought to catch his breath.

"Just came . . . in the . . . mail," he panted.

The specialist let out a cry. Other specialists crowded around. They too let out cries of amazement and adoration. They passed around the accompanying letter, but it was not informative. There was no return address. The postmark was Paris.

> *To Whom It May Concern:*
> *I have enclosed photos of the best paintings in my collection. I think you will recognize that these are works of the highest quality. They have never been exhibited or seen publicly.*
> *It is my impression that they should command excellent prices even in a depressed market such as we are experiencing now.*
> *I expect to be in the United States in the near future. I hope we*

*can meet then to discuss exactly how I might best proceed to liqui-
date my collection.*

The letter closed with an illegible signature.

"How do you know it's not a hoax?" said a voice from the back of
the scrum. Everyone turned to glare at Melanie Witkowski. She was
an intern of course.

"Collectors of this caliber are secretive by nature," explained one
of the specialists as patiently as he could manage. "Besides: look at
the paintings, dear girl."

The reactions at Christie's and at the galleries Hamilton Jones had
chosen were similar. And just as he had predicted, an article appeared
in *The New York Times* a few days later. It began on the front page
and jumped to the Arts pages, where there was a half page of photos
showing the Cézanne, the Derain, and two of the Picassos. The story
told how a trove of never-before-seen modern masterpieces had been
discovered in France. An investigation by *The New York Times* had
revealed that the paintings belonged to a reclusive and secretive
French collector, believed to be either an arms manufacturer or a steel
magnate whose wife had recently died and left him despondent. He
lived in Paris and Morocco and kept his collection at a secret location in a specially designed climate-controlled vault. The story included quotes from various experts on the quality and value and the
apparently extraordinary condition of the paintings.

The New York Times could not exactly be blamed for getting nearly
everything wrong. It was a concocted story to begin with, and when
the writer sought to check his facts with other sources, they confirmed them as true to the best of their knowledge. But in fact they
had no actual knowledge either.

The Times had found itself on the horns of an all too common
journalistic dilemma. "How do we know this is true?" said Clementine Horn, the editor in chief. "How do we know these are real?" She
gathered the photos and passed them back to the arts editor and the

features editor, who sat across the table facing her. "Do we have un-impeachable sources?"

"We've got Sotheby's and Christie's assessments," said the features editor, "which are admittedly tentative and based on unprofessional photos. But they seem pretty convinced." He glanced at the arts editor, who nodded agreement.

Clementine Horn was suspicious of art. All art. It wasn't earth-changing, the way politics and catastrophes were. And they had run stories on forgeries and fakes before where the experts had been bamboozled. She imagined it would be easy enough to fake paintings. Still, she had joined *The Times* the week the Pentagon Papers were published and had watched in astonishment as that story had divided the Supreme Court and the country and elevated *The New York Times* into the journalistic stratosphere. The paper was roundly praised for its courage, good judgment, and perspicacity. Other papers, most notably *The Washington Post*, followed suit, but *The Times* had been first with the story. There had been nothing like it since. In fact, various missteps during the Iraq and Afghanistan wars had tarnished the paper's reputation. This was not the Pentagon Papers, but it was still a big story, and if *The Times* missed it . . .

"We need another source," said Clementine. "Someone completely reliable."

"Colin Smallwood at the Met, Whitehead Drucker at the Whitney, and Simon Sadaway at MOMA are all looking at the photos as we speak."

"When will we hear back?"

"They promised within the hour."

Dicky Restin looked up from his iPhone. "They've got the story at *The Washington Post*."

Clementine Horn took it upstairs to the Sulzbergers. They had to choose between missing one of the biggest arts stories in a very long time or possibly getting some facts wrong. What choice did they really have?

Within hours of the *Times* article, the entire art world was agog.

The Internet was awash with theories of every sort. Speculation about the collector and his collection was rampant—who he might be, where he might live, where the paintings might be, where the specially designed climate-controlled vault might be found. In a matter of days, museum curators and directors were swarming across France in search of the paintings and their reclusive owner. Known modern art collectors were interviewed to determine whether they were the mysterious collector or, if not, whether they knew who he was.

Hamilton Jones made certain that St. John Larrimer got a clipping of the *New York Times* article and a link to the juiciest Internet sites. Larrimer called him. "Goddamn it, Jones, when can I see those paintings?"

"I'm working on it," said Hamilton Jones. "The owner won't let me near him. But nobody else knows where he is either. Give me some time."

"Is he a nutcase or something? Goddamn it, Jones, push him. Mention my name if you have to."

"I did."

St. John hadn't figured on how lonely it would be out of the limelight. Six months after the discovery of his theft, the newspapers had forgotten him. The boards he had served on had stricken his name from their letterheads and found replacements. His friendships had evaporated almost entirely.

"Almost. But not entirely," said Richard J. Smythe and clinked St. John's crystal tumbler with his own.

"Thank you, Richard. You don't know how much I appreciate your friendship right now."

"Be happy to be forgotten, St. John."

"You're right," said St. John. Then in the next breath: "Why is Madoff still in the news?" Bernard Madoff had just pleaded guilty to various felony charges. His wife's money had been confiscated. The feds were trying to figure out how to compensate Madoff's victims, while the victims were squabbling over which of them was the most aggrieved. Some had never withdrawn any of their earnings and were left with nothing. But others who had withdrawn some or even all they had put in, believed nonetheless that they were entitled to the full sum Madoff was supposed to have earned for them. No one seemed daunted by the fact that only a small fraction of Madoff's loot remained to be divided up. They all insisted on their fair share, and hired lawyers and filed suits against one another.

"If you want attention, get yourself arrested," said Richard.

St. John was not to be diverted from his misery. "It's as we've always said, Richard, human beings are hardly different from the baser species. Yes, we reason and they don't, but that becomes important only because we define intelligence and reason to our advantage, in order to place ourselves at the top of the heap. An animal that uses a twig to dig for termites: Shouldn't one say he has reasoned, since all the components of reason and intelligence are at play in the way he figures out how to dig for termites?"

Richard was skeptical. "Wait a minute. Doesn't the fact that he's still digging for termites while we're sipping cocktails beside your pool suggest who's smart and who's not? He's still digging for termites after hundreds of generations because he hasn't figured out how to get beyond digging for termites. And we have."

St. John was inconsolable. "Look at these." The photos of Louis's Picassos were now mounted on heavy black stock and in plastic sleeves in a black vinyl binder.

"Oh, are these the paintings you told me about?" He gave the photos a glance. Richard had recently acquired manuscripts of all of Shakespeare's tragedies, with a signature supposedly in the playwright's own hand. They had been part of the British royal collection for four hundred years, but had only recently been deacquisitioned because doubts had arisen as to their authenticity. Richard had planted a story causing the authenticity questions to linger. By the time the doubts were finally and definitively laid to rest, it was too late. The royals had gone ahead with the sale, and Richard had bought the precious pages at a fraction of their real value. "A triumph," he said, taking a sip and gazing at the vast green ocean. "No termites here."

"I intend to get those paintings," said St. John.

"Oh?" said Richard. "How?"

"I'll need to move some money."

"It's risky, St. John. When you move large sums by wire, it doesn't go unnoticed."

"Does it matter, really? When I buy those paintings, everybody will know anyway."

"True. And by then the wire transfers will have been completed and the transfer records will have been purged. No one will know where the money came from or where it went. Still, there is risk during those brief periods while the money is moving."

"I'm counting on you, Richard."

"I'm not trying to alarm you. I just think you should know. You're talking about moving a large sum of money—how much?"

"I figure a hundred million."

"That much? Movements of sums like that show up on the system. They register and can be read from anywhere. So, as I say, there's serious risk involved."

"Goddamn it, Richard, I want those paintings. Nobody else should have them."

"You know, St. John, maybe it's not reason after all that makes us human." Richard smiled.

Richard would have preferred that St. John use other money, that he move money from somewhere else besides his Charter Island account. He had a billion in that account, but he also had at least a billion with UBS. Why not move some of that?

No, no. St. John wanted to take the money out of Charter Island.

Richard wondered whether St. John might want to lighten his Charter Island account. He hoped not.

St. John assured Richard everything was fine. He was pleased with things as they were.

The trouble for Richard was that, for several years now, he had been siphoning money from St. John's account. Before St. John could transfer the money from Charter Island, Richard would have to replenish the account with money from elsewhere. It wasn't a problem, but anyone watching the transfer would be able to see several very large transactions—money going out of St. John's account, and other monies going into it. There would be a moment when an alert auditor would at least be able to see the finagling going on and would, at worst, figure out what was happening.

"I'll give you plenty of notice to arrange the transfer," said St. John.

XLIV

Bruno Gramicci was at his desk in the office he shared with two other housing department lawyers when the receptionist called to say there was a Mr. Smith to see him. "Send him in," said Bruno, even though he didn't think he knew any Mr. Smith. It was the Russian; Bruno recognized him from Lorraine's description.

"What can I do for you, Mr. Smith?"

"We can talk outside?" said Dimitri.

"I don't see why not," said Bruno. "Follow me." They went out to the parking lot.

"Where is Lorraine Usher?" said Dimitri. He stood facing Bruno with his feet apart and his huge fists planted on his hips.

"She left," said Bruno.

"I know she left," said Dimitri. "Where she go?"

"How do you know she left?"

"I knock on her door many times. I call. She was not there. Where did she go?"

"She didn't say," said Bruno.

"Where did she go?" Dimitri demanded. "Is important."

"I don't know."

"Is important," said Dimitri. He let his jacket slide open so Bruno could see the gun in the holster under his arm.

Bruno thought for a moment. "Mr. Smith, you realize—don't you?—that this parking lot where we are standing belongs to the United States Post Office over there." Bruno pointed, and Dimitri turned to look. "Which means this is federal property. Do you see that camera up there?"

Dimitri raised his hands. "Not to get excited," he said. He showed a smile that he meant to be reassuring. "I only want to talk with her."

Bruno smiled back. "If you give me your telephone number . . ."

Dimitri took out his wallet and withdrew a business card. "She can call me here. It is important."

Bruno watched him leave the parking lot and went back inside. He found the slip of paper in his wallet with Louis's phone number.

"Mr. Morgon? This is Bruno Gramicci."

"Yes, Bruno. Is everything all right?"

"I think so," said Bruno. "Lorraine's fine. But I just had a visit at work from the Russian. He said he wanted to talk to her. He gave me a card with his number. The card actually says Mr. Smith."

"And the number?"

"It's the Odessa Grill."

"And she's safe in Newark?"

"Yes. She seems pretty happy down there, but I'm worried."

Lorraine was not happy. That very afternoon, after three weeks in Newark, she had decided it was time to go home. "Are you sure, sugar?" said Lillian. "You think it over. Maybe you should check with Louis."

"You have both been very kind to me," said Lorraine. "You've made me feel really welcome. But I want to be in my own house." She had enjoyed her time with Bobby and Lillian more than she would ever have thought possible. Even the cat and the dog, Arthur and Junior, had reached a reasonable accommodation. They were not exactly pals, but they happily shared things—even Bobby. Arthur slept on Bobby's lap when he watched television, and Junior lay at his feet. Sometimes Junior stuck his nose up wistfully. Then Bobby patted him and he sighed a doggy sigh and lay back down.

As for Bobby, he had learned to enjoy a variety of exotic dishes he would never have looked at if Lillian had made them. "Have you got all her recipes?" said Bobby.

"I've got them," said Lillian.

"That artichoke pie?" He couldn't quite bring himself to pronounce the word, *quiche*.

"I've got them all," she said.

"That sausage–sweet potato thing?"

"I've got every single one, Bobby." She waved the sheets of paper in front of his face. He still felt compelled to go down the list of his favorites one by one.

On Sunday afternoon, Bruno pulled up out front and got out of his car. Junior rushed out to greet him. Bobby came out carrying Arthur's carrier, and the two men shook hands. Then Lorraine came out. She embraced Lillian and then Bobby. She scratched Junior behind the ears, and he let out a tremendous bark. Then she and Bruno got in the car and drove away.

"Do you think this is a good idea?"

"We've been over this, Bruno. I need to be in my own home. I can't live like this. I just can't."

"Have you talked with Louis Morgon?"

"No. But he can't change my mind."

"That Russian Adropov is looking for you."

"What am I supposed to do, Bruno? I can't keep hiding forever."

"He knows where you live. He'll show up one day. You're alone there. Who knows what he'll do."

Lorraine thought about that for a moment. "What if I weren't alone when we met?"

"Lorraine, I love you, but I can't be with you all the time—"

"I'm not talking about you, Bruno, and I'm not talking about at home. What if I met him somewhere where there are other people around?"

"Where?

"In his office? I don't know—wherever he spends his days."

Even though they had just come off the bridge and the emergency lane was especially narrow, Bruno pulled the car over and stopped. Trucks roared past shaking the pavement, their wash rocking the car from side to side. "Lorraine." Bruno tried to stay calm. "His office is a club in Brighton Beach, a Russian mob hangout. You can't just walk in there like that."

"He won't expect it," she said.

"He certainly won't. You're right about that. But where would you even get an idea like that?"

"What if I give him everything I've got, everything he wants— Mr. Larrimer's address, old bank account numbers, everything."

"He's still going to want to . . . You're still a witness to what he's doing."

"But what if I become an accomplice? That would change things, wouldn't it?"

Bruno gripped the steering wheel and leaned his head on his hands. Lorraine reached over and touched his arm. "I can take care of myself, Bruno. Really, I can."

Bruno turned his head and looked at Lorraine—small, pear-shaped, gray-haired, her wide eyes peering at him through over-large glasses. She clutched her purse with both hands. "How? Lorraine. Jesus, *how?* You can't just go meet him. Will you take your little baseball bat? What are you thinking?"

Lorraine held her purse toward Bruno and opened it. Bruno looked down into the purse. Despite having a nodding relationship with some members of the Italian mob, thanks to his brother Emilio and the Guido Ristorante, Bruno had seen very few firearms in his life. Which is why it seemed to him that the pistol in Lorraine's purse—squared off, cold blue steel, a Glock .45 in fact—was the largest gun he had ever seen.

"Don't tell Louis Morgon about this until after I meet the Russian, okay? And don't tell Renee. It would make her crazy."

XLV

THE ODESSA GRILL WAS ONE of those places that never look open. No fixed hours were displayed outside. The small, white neon sign announcing the name of the place flickered off and on, apparently at will. There was a makeshift bench that was never used outside the entrance. The entrance itself was a heavy wooden door with a small, diamond-shaped window that revealed only the darkness inside. Lorraine looked up and down the street. Bruno had wanted to come along. "I'll stay out of sight," he promised.

"No," she had said. Now she regretted having been so insistent. She hoped he had come anyway, that he was somewhere nearby. Just in case. But in case of what? What could Bruno do, or anyone she might have brought along, for that matter? Lorraine took a deep breath, and just as the Odessa Grill sign flickered off, she pushed hard on the door and stepped inside. She held the door open to allow her eyes to get used to the darkness. A man walked toward her out of the shadows. "Yes, ma'am?" he said. Lorraine let go of the door, and it closed behind her.

When Lorraine emerged from the Odessa Grill a half hour later, Bruno waited impatiently while she walked down the block. Finally he stepped out of the doorway where he had been waiting. He tried to hurry her away.

"Calm down, Bruno. It's all right. Mr. Smith and I have an arrangement."

Dimitri Adropov had been there, just as Bruno had suggested he would be. And, knowing he was on a surveillance camera, he had mostly been on his best behavior. He was extremely solicitous and polite. He called her Miss Usher. He offered her a chair at one of the tables nearest the door. He brought her tea with lemon. "I want," he said, "like everyone, to recover what belongs to me, what was taken from me."

Lorraine offered to tell Adropov what she knew in exchange for being left alone. Adropov interrupted her before she could finish, saying there was no need to exchange anything. He wanted nothing from her. He suggested they had to wait for the authorities to find Larrimer, impound his ill-gotten gains, and return the money to its rightful owners. Lorraine agreed and said she had lost money too. She assured him that they would all recover their money in time.

"It went on like that for a while," she explained to Louis. It was the next afternoon and she had called him with the news of her departure from Newark and her meeting with Adropov.

"It went on like what?" said Louis.

"The back and forth for the cameras and microphones."

"You knew about the cameras?"

"Not at first, but then I could tell he was playing to an audience that wasn't there. So he'd insist that we abide by the law, and I'd agree that that was what we should do. There had to be cameras.

"There was one tricky moment when he said—rather insistently—that he'd like to see me elsewhere. I said that might be possible. I suggested my house. 'Do you know it?' I said. I said the address. When I did that, he backed off right away. He didn't like it that I gave my address. Who's watching him? Whose cameras and microphones are they?"

"I'm guessing the FBI," said Louis. "They'll probably rush to plant cameras in your house now, if they haven't already. In any case, that was clever of you. It's no longer safe for him to go there. But he still doesn't know where Larrimer is."

"He didn't like my playing to the cameras that way. I think he knew where they were exactly. Anyway, at one point he leaned forward a bit and opened his jacket so that I saw his gun."

"And what did you do?"

"Well, I looked astonished, I'm sure. I wasn't expecting that. Then I remembered my purse was on my lap and, I'm pretty sure, out of sight of the camera too. So I opened it and took out an envelope with Larrimer's address and all the other information in it and I passed it to him."

"Under the table?"

"No. Right across the tabletop. It made him nervous, and he grabbed it and slid it into his jacket pocket. I scared him, I think."

"You think *you* scared *him*."

"No, no. Not with the envelope. I left my purse open, and he saw my gun."

"Your gun?"

"Bruno didn't tell you? A Glock. I know you probably don't like me having a gun. I don't like it either. When this is over . . . But for now—"

"You're enjoying this, aren't you?"

"I admit it, Louis. I am."

XLVI

Lorraine was more or less correct in her assessment of her Russian adventure. She had not exactly scared Dimitri, but she had momentarily stymied him. He hadn't broken into her house and so had missed the false trail—the notes by the phone—that she had left. And he was certainly not about to break into her house now. The FBI, however, had been inside to place cameras and, while doing so, had found the notes she had left with St. John's Guadeloupe address and phone number, as well as airline information.

"Hey, Sal, look at this."

"What is it?" said Agent Morconi.

"Airline information and a phone number."

"I knew it. And I'll bet you anything that's a flight to Guadeloupe. And the number will be Larrimer's." They put the slip of paper in a plastic bag and labeled it. A quick search back at the office proved Agent Morconi correct. "Now we've got her," he said.

Lorraine was radioactive; Dimitri had judged correctly. And Louis, with his CIA connections, whatever they might be, wasn't much better. They were both to be avoided for the moment. All Dimitri needed was another run-in with the American law. And Feather, the accountant, was dead, which left only Larrimer himself and Gutentag, the vanished trader.

"I save Larrimer for last," said Dimitri. Mixed in with his volatile murderous inclinations, Dimitri also had a sense of order that was almost aesthetic. He arranged his various tasks, murder included, like flowers in a bouquet, like the courses of a meal. Killing Larrimer would be the rose among lesser flowers, a big piece of Sacher torte after a sumptuous meal.

There was also a secret, tender aspect to Dimitri's personality that gave the hunt for Jeremy Gutentag its own enticements. Dimitri was not married, and no one ever saw him with a woman. "Dimitri is all business," said his associates. "He is married to business." But Dimitri was not all business. Whenever he had the time, he flew to Vienna to be with his lover, a pastry chef named Jürgen. Given the way Dimitri conducted business, one could be forgiven for assuming that he would be a brutish and demanding lover. But with Jürgen, Dimitri was as if transformed. His eyes glowed, he smiled, and his entire countenance softened into angelic sweetness. With Jürgen, Dimitri was tender and patient, generous and kind.

Jürgen, for his part, a handsome dark-skinned boy of thirty-four, adored Dimitri right back, but as a younger man will, with a lingering yearning for the next adventure. Jürgen oversaw pastry production in one of Vienna's most celebrated coffee house/bakeries. While Jürgen was at work, Dimitri shopped for groceries with which Jürgen produced exquisite meals each evening. Of course every meal ended with the most sumptuous cream-filled pastries or sometimes a Linzer torte or a Sacher torte or some other Viennese confection. Jürgen had recently opened a pastry shop in Paris with Dimitri's generous support. A New York branch was in the offing. Dimitri and Jürgen were happy together.

Until they weren't. Dimitri's work kept him away from Vienna for longer and longer periods. And Jürgen found someone else. Dimitri was heartbroken, but oddly enough, he was not bitter. He had loved Jürgen unreservedly, and now he wished him well. Instead of vengeance and recrimination toward Jürgen, Dimitri turned his attention to Jeremy Gutentag. He had never met or seen Jeremy.

He knew nothing about him. But he had managed to find his picture on the Internet on a site devoted to publicizing the crimes and
misdemeanors of Larrimer, Ltd., and on seeing the photo, had been
struck dumb. Jeremy, standing with some of his trading room colleagues and smiling at the camera, bore such a striking resemblance
to his beloved Jürgen that they might have been twins. Jürgen,
whose grandparents had indeed come from Pakistan, assured Dimitri that there was no connection between them.

Dimitri was now more determined than ever to find Jeremy.
Whether to kill him or love him, he did not yet know. Dimitri tried
the London School of Economics. The school records were online,
and though they were confidential and password protected, that did
not pose a problem. He found Jeremy's application for admissions, his
progress reports and grades, his graduation certificate and letters of
recommendation and reference. Of course none of these documents
revealed anything about his present whereabouts. They were strangely
opaque about his past as well, which Dimitri found noteworthy.

There was also a personal history with the names of Jeremy's parents, James and Sophie Gutentag, and the dates of their deaths. Sophie's maiden name was given as Parker. The reference to their home
and shop was vague. No name or street address was given for either.
The original application had been made from the Trinity School in
Tronklin and that address was given as Jeremy's home address. An
academic counselor, James Wyatt Cheswich, had signed the application alongside the signature of Jeremy Gutentag.

Armed with only that information, Dimitri set off for London
and from London by rental car for Tronklin-on-Wye. It was a rainy
day. Fog rose from the fields and woods and cast the Vale of Leadon
in silver shrouds. The first thing you saw when you entered the village
of Tronklin from the south was the arrangement of timbered buildings that made up the Trinity School. Normally the school would
have been crowded with students and teachers, but it was a holiday
weekend and the place was mostly deserted.

The school offices were closed. But Dimitri rang the bell anyway, and when no one came to the door, he rang it again and again. He had come this far, and he was not going away without answers to his many questions. Finally he managed to raise a watchman who, at Dimitri's insistence, summoned the headmaster.

It turned out that James Wyatt Cheswich, the counselor who had signed Jeremy's application, was now the Trinity headmaster. He greeted the visitor who called himself Mr. Smith with some trepidation. Mr. Smith was a powerfully built man with cold, narrow eyes and a chilly smile. He seemed indifferent to the rain soaking through his expensive suit. Sensing the headmaster's discomfort, Dimitri smiled harder and assured Mr. Chasswick, as he pronounced it, that his purpose in coming was entirely benevolent. He was there, he said, to establish a scholarship fund so that two deserving underprivileged boys might be able to attend the Trinity School every year. Mr. Cheswich had no choice but to invite him inside.

They walked down the hall to the headmaster's office, Mr. Smith making a squishing sound and leaving wet tracks on the stone floor with each step. Once in his office, the headmaster pointed to a chair and Dimitri sat down. "Please, Mr. Smith, may I offer you a drink?"

"Yes, thank you," said Dimitri. "Scotch."

The headmaster poured the drink and took a seat opposite the Russian. Dimitri withdrew a Barclays Bank draft from his inside pocket and handed it to the headmaster. It was for a hundred thousand pounds and was made out to Trinity School. The fund, as Dimitri explained, was to be named the Jeremy Gutentag Scholarship Fund in honor of one of the school's most illustrious graduates.

"I don't quite know what to say," said the astonished headmaster.

"You knew Jeremy?" said Dimitri.

"I did indeed," said James Wyatt Cheswich.

"And you personally taught him?" said Dimitri, wondering to himself whether stealing other people's money had been part of the lesson.

"I taught him literature. He was perhaps the most gifted student I have ever taught."

"He was very good student."

"He was indeed. His papers were brilliant analyses of various literary classics, and I believe any one of them could have been published in any of the leading literary journals. They were simply brilliant. I am very pleased that you are honoring Jeremy, but may I ask, Mr. Smith, how it is that you are endowing this scholarship in his name? This really is most astonishing." Cheswich shook his head in wonderment.

"Jeremy is my colleague," said Dimitri, "who has helped make my company very successful. It is my company endowing the scholarship." He pointed to the check that Mr. Cheswich continued to stare at.

"That is extremely generous. I truly don't know what to say."

"It is the least we can do. All people in my company are very proud of Jeremy."

"Well, we are very proud too, of Jeremy, and of the education we provided him. And are certainly grateful to you."

"Is big surprise, yes?"

"It certainly is," said the headmaster still shaking his head in wonder.

"Will be surprise for Jeremy too. We want to have dinner to honor him, make a speech. Have a toast. Maybe you can tell me about Jeremy as young man. About his home, his family?"

James Wyatt Cheswich rubbed his chin thoughtfully and paused as he tried to recollect the details. "His parents were shopkeepers, I think. From London, as I recall."

"Not from India, then?"

"India?" He laughed. "Oh, dear, no. He spoke the King's English, you know. I guess he still does." He laughed again.

"Yes," said Dimitri, "the King's English."

"No, not from India," Cheswich continued, "although he looks the part, doesn't he? No, his parents were shopkeepers. In London. I'm quite sure."

"And you have information on shop, what kind of shop, where it was?"

"I will have to check for you," said the headmaster.

"Did he have scholarship to go to school here? Trinity was very expensive even then. No?"

"Yes, it was. You know, I don't recall whether he had a scholarship. I don't think so. No, I'm quite sure he didn't have a scholarship."

Now it was Dimitri's turn to rub his chin. "Hmm. I think he said he had scholarship, because his parents were dead."

"No, I don't think so. I think he was a full tuition student."

"I want to get information correct for presentation."

"Of course," said the headmaster. "Let me check." He went to a bank of filing cabinets and searched briefly. "Aha. Here we are." He pulled his chair next to Dimitri's so they could both look in the file. "Here, you see? A record of tuition payments."

"I am surprised. But his parents were already dead, yes? So who paid? Who we have to thank for his excellent education?"

"Here's the notation," said Cheswich, pointing. "You see? Full payment, wire transfer."

"From Lahore," said Dimitri.

"Yes, I see."

"Oh, yes, he has uncle in Lahore," Dimitri suddenly remembered. "That must be it."

"He definitely has uncle in Lahore," said Dimitri. "He often says how grateful he is to his uncle. See here? Mohan Kapoor. In India after all."

"Um . . . Pakistan, Mr. Smith."

"What?"

"Pakistan. Lahore is in Pakistan."

XLVII

Louis heard from Hamilton Jones. Larrimer insisted on seeing the paintings. "He wants to come here, to Saint-Léon?"

"He does," said Hamilton. "He's flying me to Terre-de-Haut, and we'll all fly from there to Tours and drive to you. How far is it?"

"Forty kilometers."

"I have to say, Louis, I'm eager to see these paintings too, to see how good a painter you are."

"I'm as curious about that as you are."

"You better be damned good."

"When does he want to come?"

"June fourteenth."

"Tell him the eighteenth," said Louis. "And before I agree, he needs to present proof that he's opened an escrow account for fifty million dollars. Does that seem too odd, Hamilton?"

"It's a little odd. But he knows you're an eccentric, so he should buy it. At least as long as it's in his own bank. Is that all right?"

"Absolutely fine," said Louis. "It just has to have my name on it. We just want to see the money move. He should send me evidence of the escrow account."

Nothing happened for several days, until suddenly the new account materialized online. A short while later five million dollars moved from one account to the new account. Then another five million, and another, until fifty million had been moved.

"Now we know which are his accounts," said Zaharia.

"Why five million at a time?" Louis wondered.

"Maybe he's just being cautious," said Zaharia. "Or maybe it wasn't Larrimer who decided to do it that way at all. There's something else, something more interesting going on at the same time, which could be the reason. The bank is loading money *into* Larrimer's account from its own reserves."

"Really? Why?"

"I don't know. Let me watch it for a while and see if I can figure it out."

A few days later Louis got an envelope in the mail. Inside was a Charter Island National Bank statement for a numbered escrow account containing fifty million dollars.

Louis had never exhibited his paintings. He had never had any desire to do so.

"Well, you're going to show them now," said Pauline.

"Yes," he said. "But not as paintings. As bait."

"So Larrimer's got to believe that they're the masterpieces they resemble."

"Yes," said Louis. "At least for a little while."

"Then you're going to need them in fancy frames."

"I know. I've been getting them ready. Come see." Louis had been visiting rummage sales and junk shops, and had managed to find a good number of large, old frames. They were mostly battered and chipped, and he had gotten them cheaply.

Louis's neighbor, Étienne Dubois, a cabinetmaker, mostly made doors and shutters and heavy kitchen tables. He squinted at the frames and at the canvases standing side by side. He took a small notebook from his pocket. "What about repair?"

"Cut out the damaged parts where you can. Otherwise just a little cosmetic repair. Nothing too fine," said Louis. "Nicks and cracks are good. These are supposed to be old frames on old canvases."

Étienne smelled intrigue; his eyes sparkled. He walked up and down looking at each frame, making notes as he did. Louis opened a bottle of Muscadet and poured two glasses. Étienne did a little figuring in his notebook. "Four hundred eighty euros," he said.

"If you get them done by next Friday, I'll make it six hundred," said Louis. "And not a word to anyone." He raised his glass, and Étienne raised his.

"To art," said Étienne. He loaded the frames and canvases in his truck and drove down the hill. He disassembled the frames, cut them to size and mitered new corners. After he had reassembled them, Etienne filled the worst chips and dulled the fill and finish. He mounted the canvases in the frames and drove them back up the hill.

Louis's Cézanne was now in an ebony frame with dented and worn gilt edges. One Picasso was in a silver frame that had once surrounded a mirror. A Derain was in a Rococo gilt frame. Each painting was in the frame that suited it best.

"The frame on the Cézanne is almost too perfect," said Pauline. She looked around the studio, admiring the paintings all over again. "What a difference a frame makes."

"It does, doesn't it? You can put a frame on almost anything and elevate it into the realm of art. And in addition—in this case—the frame hides the stretcher. He won't notice how new they are. Not right away, anyway; not until he turns a painting around."

"Will he do that?"

"I think he probably will. He certainly should. He's contemplating paying millions. He must know enough to look at the backs."

Pauline still had her reservations about Louis's tightrope walk along the edge of illegality. But she could not deny that the paintings were exciting to look at. "And where are you going to show them? Where is Larrimer going to see them? It can't be here. He'd know right away you made them. It has to be someplace more . . . imposing, someplace grand."

Renard had not changed his opinion about Louis's project. How could he? He had sworn to uphold the law, and here was Louis, his best friend, concocting a rather elaborate confidence game. The fact that it was being directed against a criminal, with the objective of recovering the money he had stolen and turning him over to the appropriate legal authorities, did nothing, in Renard's opinion, to mitigate that larger fact of its illegality.

"I understand that," said Louis. "Your dilemma has a solution, though. All you have to do is be there to see that nothing illegal transpires. If it does, you can arrest the perpetrator. Whoever it might be." He lifted his coffee cup to his lips.

"Don't be ridiculous," said Renard.

"Excuse me?" said Louis. "If you think a crime is about to occur and you know where it will occur, isn't it your duty to be there to make certain it does not occur?"

Renard narrowed his eyes at Louis.

A man opened the door and a gust of wind seemed to sweep him and his wife into the bar. "It's raining!" they both said at the same time. Everyone turned to look as the first large drops splashed against the window. It had not rained for nearly two months. The hay had stopped growing and could not be cut. The wheat too appeared stunted. And the grape vines were covered with dust. But now it was raining.

It was lunchtime, and most of the booths were full. Some people were already eating their lunch. And yet everyone got up and filed out to look, as though something miraculous were happening. Christoph cranked down the awning, and they all stood there looking at the rain in wonder as it hammered on the awning above them and filled the air with its sweet ozone smell. Even Louis got up to take it in.

It came down hard enough that you could not see the fields above town, only the silver sheets of water slanting down. Small rivulets ran between the cobblestones. A car drove slowly across the square. The driver had his windows open and was smiling. He waved and everyone waved back. Then they went back inside.

It is odd, but a moment like that, an unexpected moment, can sometimes change things in the most mysterious ways, things over which it should have no effect at all. "All right," said Renard. He did not know why he suddenly agreed. "Where? Where are you going to show him the paintings? I'll be there."

XLVIII

It was the eighteenth, and it was raining again. A black limousine sped up the gravel drive. The driveway curved around two huge stone barns before the Beaumont château came into view, first its brick tower above the trees, then as the trees thinned out, the main building: three stories of brick and stone with a steep slate mansard roof, surrounded by broad stone terraces and a low balustrade. The main house had been built in the sixteenth century; the rear wing and the tower were more recent, but the whole ensemble—house, barns, garden—seemed perfectly harmonious, if a bit neglected. The car came to a stop by the front stairs.

Nigel stepped out and opened the rear door for St. John. Hamilton Jones had ridden up front with Nigel. Nigel reached inside his jacket and adjusted the pistol in its holster. St. John stood looking at the building as though the house might reveal what kind of man lived there all by himself surrounded by a secret collection of unknown masterpieces. The three men climbed the stairs to the terrace and walked to the door. Nigel lifted the heavy iron knocker and let it drop.

The door opened, and a man—St. John would have called him old—stood there with an expectant look on his face. He was not tall; he had blue eyes and a cloud of unruly white hair wafting about his

head. He was dressed in baggy corduroy slacks and a sweater and battered leather boots.

"Yes?"

"Mr. Larrimer to see Mr. Morgon," said Nigel.

"Yes," said Louis, stepping aside. "Please come in."

"Mr. Morgon is expecting us," said Nigel.

"I'm Louis Morgon." Louis offered his hand to Larrimer, then to
Nigel and Hamilton Jones. "Mr. Jones, I've been looking forward to
meeting you."

"Likewise," said Hamilton Jones. "The pleasure is mine." His English accent had gotten stronger again since they had last spoken.
"What a lovely house you have."

In the 1970s, not long after moving to Saint-Léon, Louis had
become acquainted with the Comte de Beaumont, the proprietor of
a number of properties throughout France, including the château
Louis was now pretending was his own. The occasion had been
Louis's interest in the French Resistance and his involvement in
sorting out a long-unresolved and festering crime from the era of
the Nazi occupation.

For many French men and women, those years had been a time
of extreme moral ambiguity and inconvenience, but not for Maurice
de Beaumont. He and his wife, Alexandre, were heroes of the Resistance. They had put their lives and their entire wealth, happiness,
and well-being at risk in order to fight against what they both knew
to be evil. That fight had cost Alexandre her life.

The count was more than ninety now and frail. He was not often
in residence in Saint-Léon—he mostly stayed in Paris. When he was
in Saint-Léon however, Louis made a point of visiting. Otherwise
the two men carried on their friendship by correspondence. They had
two things in common—their sense of moral clarity and their love
of art.

The moral aspect gave their relationship its solidity, but they
talked and wrote mostly about art. The count had an extraordinary
collection of paintings—Titian, Tintoretto, Ingres, including old

family portraits by some of these masters. Louis always felt a surge of pleasure when he found a letter from Maurice in his mail.

> *Hôtel Valmont, Paris*
> *June 3, 2009*
> *My dear Louis,*
> *What a delight it was—as it always is—to get your letter. Who writes letters anymore? Sometimes I imagine it is just we two, although I don't see how that could be true. My grandchildren want me to e-mail or "text" (I understand that is now a verb), but I steadfastly resist their entreaties. They have no choice but to put up with my handwriting, which is starting to wobble.*
> *I have of course read in the newspapers about St. John Larrimer and all the devastation he has brought about. The sad news about Pauline's brother was especially lamentable. You know that I loathe this sort of thing and admire your wanting to do something about it.*
> *I do not expect to be in Saint-Léon anytime soon, so I am unable to help you get the house ready for what you have in mind. I think, however, it should be in pretty good order. Ghislaine looks in once a week to tidy up; I'll tell her to turn up the heat and get everything ready.*
> *Please get the key from Laurent. He will help you clear things away to make room for your paintings, which, by the way, I am eager to see. I am also eager to hear how this all comes out. Please be careful.*
> *Yours with admiration and friendship,*
> *Maurice*

"Follow me, please," said Louis and closed the door. They passed into a tall corridor lined with portraits. Louis stopped halfway. "Tintoretto," he said pointing. Hamilton Jones lifted his glasses and peered at the painting. "Yes, it is," he said. "And a fine one." St. John gave the painting a perfunctory glance.

The corridor led into a large kitchen with an enormous fireplace.

A long table in front of the fireplace was draped with a tablecloth and set with dessert plates and wineglasses.

Louis poured wine in four glasses. It was a white Chinon, a rarity that Louis had recently discovered. The three visitors sat at the table while Louis sliced up a tarte tatin and slid pieces onto four plates.

"You made this?" said St. John.

"I did," said Louis. "Do you like it?"

"It's very good," said St. John and took another bite.

"Very good," said Nigel.

"Excellent," said Hamilton. The men ate in silence.

"You're American," said St. John. "I wonder how an American comes to live in France."

"Well," said Louis, "I could ask you the same thing."

St. John tried another tack. "How did you acquire your collection?"

"Over time," said Louis. Hamilton Jones had warned St. John that Louis Morgon's long list of peculiarities included extreme reticence and a prickly secretiveness about his life and art collection. Morgon had agreed to show his collection to St. John, which was a near miracle. It was best just to sit and wait until he was ready. This was exactly the kind of negotiation—long, slow, and mostly silent—that St. John detested.

"Do you live here alone?"

"As you can see."

There was nothing St. John could do. The pauses grew longer until the four men lapsed into what seemed like eternal silence interrupted only by the occasional scrape of Nigel's fork on his plate getting up a last crumb of tarte tatin he had somehow missed. Louis got Nigel another piece.

The rain had stopped without amounting to much. It was nearly seven o'clock, and the sun came out. "Follow me," said Louis. He was suddenly on his feet and out into the hallway, walking fast. The other three scrambled to catch up.

They turned off the hallway and through a door and found themselves in a large salon filled with antique furnishings and worn oriental rugs. One wall was floor-to-ceiling windows that opened onto the rear terrace. The wind was chasing a few dead leaves about in frantic little eddies. The wall opposite the terrace held Louis's paintings. They were hung high, each one between bookshelves, each advantageously illuminated. The three visitors stopped in their tracks and stared. Hamilton Jones was the first to step forward. He stood under the Cézanne, looking up at it. He turned and looked at Louis.

"This is as astonishing as I hoped it would be," he said.

"I am glad you think so."

Larrimer stepped up to the painting and then moved from one to the next. He leaned in close to each painting and then took a step back. He reached up and touched the surface of one of the Matisses. He knew that touching a painting was not allowed, which was why he allowed himself to do it. He was going to own this painting, after all, and he would damn well touch it if he wanted to.

"I'd like to take it down," he said.

"Why?" said Louis.

"I want to examine it out of the frame. The back isn't sealed, I hope?" Hamilton Jones sincerely regretted ever teaching St. John to ask these questions.

"It isn't sealed."

"Let's take it down, then," said St. John. "Give me a hand, Jones."

"I don't want you to take it down," said Louis. "Why do you need to take it down?"

"I'm concerned about the provenance," said St. John.

"We should look at them on the wall first, Mr. Larrimer." Hamilton tried to sound congenial and relaxed. "The provenance question will resolve itself. But let's see what we've got here purely in the way of paintings. Their condition, how good are they, that sort of thing."

But St. John's appetite had been whetted to the point of his coming undone—first by the photos, then by all the waiting, then by the travel and the pie and this crazy old coot of a collector. Besides, what was this sudden great reluctance? He and Nigel exchanged glances. Nigel nodded slightly. Something funny was going on.

"I want to see those paintings off the wall," said St. John. "Or we're leaving."

"If you insist." Louis shrugged. He walked toward the Derain at the end of the room.

"Not that one. This one." St. John pointed at the Cézanne.

"Of course," said Louis. "Would you help me?" Nigel stepped forward and helped Louis lift the painting from the wall. They set it down against a bookshelf.

"Turn it around," said St. John.

He stepped forward to examine it. Louis had done the paintings on pale brown linen that could, at first glance, be taken for old canvas. St. John was momentarily uncertain. He stared at the back of the canvas before he summoned Hamilton Jones to his side. He pointed and Hamilton got down on hands and knees with his nose very close to the painting. He touched the inside corner of the stretcher. The two men whispered back and forth a few times. Hamilton continued to examine the painting as he spoke. "Have these paintings been remounted?"

"No," said Louis. "Certainly not."

Hamilton stood. "We need to see the other paintings off the wall," he said.

"Which ones?"

"All of them."

All the paintings were on new linen canvas. The stretchers were constructed of new wood in the new manner, with mortise-and-tenon joints and without shims. There was no mistake about that. And when Hamilton Jones stuck his nose up next to each painting, he smelled linseed oil. There were no fissures in the pigment, even where it was thick. The colors were vivid; the whites were white; there was no yellowing. No cleaning in the world could have restored paintings to this pristine condition. "These paintings are new," Hamilton declared with great indignation in his voice.

"Yes," said Louis. "They are. I did them this past winter."

St. John Larrimer was unfamiliar with disappointment. And he was certainly unused to being thwarted. When he wanted something, by God, he got it, or somebody paid. Uncharacteristically, he had allowed himself to be enticed into believing there were lost masterpieces to be had and that he could have them. And now these supposed masterpieces turned out to be fakes. To add insult to injury, St. John Larrimer—himself the master of manipulation—had been manipulated. He had been royally conned.

"What the fuck are you playing at?" He turned on Hamilton Jones. "Any idiot can tell these are fakes!" St. John jumped at Hamilton Jones and threw a punch with sufficient force to knock him off his feet and onto the Cézanne. The painting popped out of its frame.

"Apparently not *any* idiot," said Louis, with the intention of turning St. John's wrath in his direction. He succeeded in his purpose. Nobody, but *nobody*, ever spoke to St. John Larrimer like that. St. John's face went crimson. *"What did you say?"* It was of course a rhetorical question, and Louis did not feel compelled to repeat himself. St. John launched himself at Louis.

Louis sidestepped barely in time, and St. John crashed into one of the Matisses, bringing a bookcase down on top of himself. When Nigel pulled out his pistol, Renard emerged from his hiding place and put both Nigel and St. John under arrest for destruction of property, aggravated assault, assault with a deadly weapon, and illegal possession of a firearm.

It was an excellent story, and Louis told it so well that Maurice de Beaumont insisted on hearing it again. "Never mind about the bookcase."

"No, no. I will see that it is repaired. And a chair and carpet may have been damaged."

"And were you hurt?"

"I strained my shoulder and neck somehow, but otherwise I'm fine."

"Well, if you do this again, you'll have to let me know so that I can be there."

Renard was less amused than the Comte de Beaumont. He summoned Louis to his office to take a statement. "You knew what I intended," said Louis.

"I knew no such thing. I knew you were meeting with a fugitive from justice—an *American* fugitive from justice for whom no warrant exists in France—but I did not know that you meant for it to get violent. You could have been killed. Nigel, as it turns out, is wanted in France—"

"So you can hold him."

"We can. He's in Tours while Larrimer arranges for his bond. But—"

"And will he be released?"

"That remains to be seen. He shouldn't be; he has a record. And he's a definite flight risk. But at the same time, I am getting calls on Larrimer's behalf."

"Lawyers?"

"Are you kidding? Paris. Ministries of this and that."

"So he's played the system." This was good news as far as Louis was concerned. If anything was certain to get Renard's back up, it was some minister in Paris or his own police captain in Château-du-Loir, for that matter, interfering in his business.

Louis tested the waters. "Maybe I should go to Tours and pay Nigel a visit."

Renard gave Louis a baleful look.

Louis wrote Nigel a note asking to meet, but he got no response.

XLIX

LOUIS HEARD FROM PETER SANCHEZ. The telephone call came on a Saturday morning. Although it did not come at mealtime, it was not a friendly call. This pleased Louis. Long experience had taught him that angry and unhappy witnesses were most likely to give something away, even a professional like Peter.

Louis considered Peter to be a witness in the case he was building. Without much effort on Louis's part—in fact Peter had done all the work—Louis had been registering his whereabouts with Peter, in one way or another, every step of the way so that eventually, if it ever came to that, he would have Peter Sanchez as an alibi witness, albeit an unfriendly one. From the moment the Russian had turned up, Peter had people keeping a watch on Louis, hoping to use him to find Larrimer and to discover the money trail.

While Peter was not at all in agreement with Louis's methods, he was not above making use of whatever Louis turned up. He had long ago resigned himself to Louis's loose ways when it came to laws and treaties and other legal niceties. Peter thought of himself as "running" Louis, as he had run agents and double agents throughout his career. Except now Louis had gone off the rails, forging paintings, trying to sell them to Larrimer, and alerting Larrimer to the fact that the law was closing in. Peter suddenly found himself with what amounted to a renegade agent.

"Oh, really?" Louis was astonished. "Is the law closing in? I hadn't noticed."

"That you haven't noticed means nothing."

"So your people were in Saint-Léon? And you followed Larrimer home to Terre-de-Haut?"

Peter did not answer.

"And you've been watching him moving money around?"

Again Peter was silent.

"And Nigel?"

"We saw your message to him."

"And the Russian?"

"What about him?" said Peter.

"Did you know he's here in Saint-Léon?" said Louis.

Peter did not answer. He was certain the Russian was not there, or rather he had been certain until Louis had suggested that he was. As soon as he got off the phone with Louis, he would check. Peter had called to discover what Louis was up to and to admonish him to cease his bizarre activities. But he realized in the middle of their conversation that he should not have called. He was not learning anything, while Louis was learning a great deal.

There was nothing Peter could do to constrain Louis, short of having him arrested. And Peter wondered whether arresting Louis might not play right into his hands. Their conversation had gotten away from him, and Peter could not figure out how to get out of it without giving that fact away. All he could think to do was to warn Louis again to back off and leave things to the professionals. "Or you will find yourself in serious trouble all over again." Peter regretted the words as soon as he said them. He knew it was an empty threat, and he knew that Louis knew it too. And worse yet: Nothing quite motivated Louis like an ultimatum.

Louis could sense Peter's frustration, so he decided to give him a gift. "A lot of Larrimer's money is with a Caribbean bank—Charter Island National Bank. Charter Island is run by an old friend of Larrimer's, a man named Richard Smythe. It looks like Smythe is stealing from Larrimer."

Peter surrendered entirely. "Charter Island?"

"National Bank. And Larrimer's ex is helping him launder the money. Oh, and the Russian is *not* in Saint-Léon."

"I knew that," said Peter.

Of course St. John did not abandon Nigel to his fate. He could not risk leaving Nigel where he was sure to be questioned and perhaps turned against him. St. John made a few phone calls, delivered some favors, and Nigel was released and allowed to return home. St. John sent the jet to pick him up.

Another of St. John's bodyguards met Nigel at the airport and drove him home. Nigel gave St. John a complete account of what had happened to him, including Louis's message, but St. John barely listened. He sat staring out to sea as though he expected a ship to suddenly appear. He was preoccupied with his narrow escape from Louis's con game. "Was Jones in on it?" he wondered.

"He had to be," said Nigel.

"But why? Why would he do it?"

"Why? A hundred million dollars! That's why," said Nigel. This was not like St. John, these second thoughts. He should have been figuring out how to get even. Now all he seemed able to do was wonder about why and how. He should stop wondering. "Pay attention, sir," said Nigel. "Think of all those other suckers. You were almost a sucker yourself."

St. John looked at Nigel sharply, then turned his gaze back on the sea. He sat uneasily on the edge of his chair, his arms on his thighs, his fingers interlocked. The breeze rippled through his hair. He unlocked his fingers to sweep the hair back out of his face. He did this again and again without noticing. His drink, the ice melting, sat forgotten on the glass table beside him. Finally Nigel left him alone.

After a while St. John picked up the portable telephone. He looked in the phone's directory and found Carolyne's number. He pressed the Talk button and then pressed it again to stop the call. He did the same thing with Richard Smythe. He laid the phone aside but soon picked it up again. He pressed the Talk button and heard Nigel's voice talking to someone else. Before St. John could get off, Nigel said, "Sorry, Mr. Larrimer. I was just checking on—"

"No, no, don't bother. It's all right, Nigel." St. John hung up.

What Nigel had said was true. In fact he *had* been suckered. He had gone all the way to that godforsaken place to see a bunch of fake paintings. He ought to be planning the destruction of that fucking weasel, Louis Morgon, and Hamilton Jones, that traitor. And how many others had been involved? He ought to set about finding out. Morgon and Jones couldn't have done it alone. Yet when St. John thought about bringing them all to ruin, he found he had no appetite for it. He had none of the white heat he needed to make his revenge happen. Where was his rage? Where was his hatred?

St. John opened the computer lying on the table beside the forgotten drink. He clicked to the Charter Island Web site, then to private banking. After a few seconds the log-in page came up. He punched in his username, his PIN, and the security codes and went into his accounts. He studied the most recent cash movements into and out of the accounts. He went back a month and studied the numbers there, then a month before that. He peered hard at the screen as though he might be able to see bundles of thousand-dollar bills moving from somewhere to somewhere else. Not moving, but *being* moved.

Were the numbers right? What was that large withdrawal? That large deposit? Why had he not paid closer attention to those transactions? He had entrusted the safekeeping and movement of hundreds of millions of dollars to Richard Smythe, a fellow thief. He closed the computer and pushed it away.

St. John stayed out on the deck the rest of the day. Nigel brought him supper on a tray, but he had no appetite. Night fell. He lay on the bare wooden decking with only a chair cushion under his head. He gazed straight up into the darkening sky. The house was dark; the floodlights along the security fence were out of sight on the other side of the house. Soon he lay in total darkness. The new moon—a thin, lightless sliver—hung above him surrounded by a million stars.

St. John awoke with a start, still lying spread-eagle on the deck. The moon had moved elsewhere, and St. John thought it had taken something of his spirit with it. He felt a lightness, no, an emptiness. He felt as though his body might float up off the deck, or maybe it would collapse into a heap of dust. He wondered whether he was going mad.

1

St. John was not going mad. He was merely experiencing an entirely unfamiliar set of feelings and sensations. The rage and fury he had expected had never even showed themselves. But something else, something he did not recognize, had. He did not feel doubt or hesitancy exactly, although those two things played a part. It took a while before he was able to give the new feeling its true name. Regret. That was it. He was feeling regret.

But regret for what? Knowing—suddenly and viscerally—what it felt like to be the sucker, feeling what all the suckers he had stolen all that money from must have felt. Feeling loss and the sense of betrayal had knocked him off track. His assurance that the world was a sucker-tree ripe for the plucking, that he was smarter and more deserving and superior to his victims, was suddenly in question. His sense of his own cleverness lay in shambles. His self-certainty, which had seemed indestructible one minute, had collapsed into rubble the next.

Of course St. John's sense of regret was as tiny and malleable as his senses of entitlement and self-justification were gargantuan. And he immediately set about doing battle with what he feared might be a nascent conscience. Would regret lead to remorse? And would remorse lead to his ultimate ruination? He shuddered to think of it.

Nigel came out onto the deck the following morning and found St. John talking to himself. After listening for a moment, Nigel stole from the scene. St. John spoke into the morning breeze. "I'm not going to be complicit in making the world seem like a better place than it is. Thomas Hobbes had it right: nasty, brutish, and short. Those are the cards we've been dealt, and we're powerless to change them. I am going to live in the world I've been given. I'll play by its rules. People suffer, that's true. Some at my hand." He made a stab at honesty. "*Many* at my hand. Many lives have been ruined by . . . what I did. I don't deny that. But I was acting as life's instrument in accordance with life's rules. I feel no regret," he said as a wave of regret swept over him.

"I'm no Ebenezer Scrooge," he said, trying to push the regret away. His was not going to be a Dickensian tale, where cold, hard practicality somehow magically metamorphosed into charity, thanks to a few visiting ghosts. St. John's main regret was that he had not gotten away scot-free with his fraud, and furthermore, that he was now allowing empathy to cloud his vision. He vowed that the "rot of conscience," as he called it, would never inhabit and weaken his soul. He promised to keep his regret in check and see to his own survival. And well-being. And prosperity.

Marlies, the masseuse, came at her usual hour and spent forty minutes working on St. John's back and neck. "You're a bundle of tension," she said. She held the small cotton sheet in place while he turned onto his back. She draped it over his midsection and smiled down at him while he settled in. Some music he had not heard before—she brought her own music—was playing lightly in the background.

St. John was startled for a moment and looked around as though he didn't know where he was. They were on the terrace near where he had been sleeping. The sound of the sea and the gulls, and the sight of his own house, the curtains billowing in the soft breeze, reassured him. He closed his eyes.

He heard Marlies rub oil into her hands, a voluptuous slurping noise. Then he smelled vanilla as Marlies began working on his chest. She pressed deeply with the heels of her hands and moved out toward his arms as though she were separating his muscles into discrete bundles to be worked on later.

He opened his eyes. She stood above him, her face directly over his as she worked. She held the tip of her tongue pressed between her lips in concentration. There were little beads of sweat on her forearms and wrists, and she breathed strongly from the exertion. Her pulse flickered at her throat. She noticed St. John looking.

"How is that?" she said.

St. John smiled.

"Good," she said.

She slid her arms under his shoulders and used his weight to work the shoulders. She took his left upper arm in her strong hands and squeezed and released and squeezed and released it. St. John watched as her body bobbed above him in time with the work her hands were doing. She wore a loose white T-shirt. He could plainly see the contour of her body beneath it. She saw him looking and smiled. St. John smiled back. St. John liked for a massage to merge into sex. And Marlies was generally willing to comply. He closed his eyes.

The music she had brought was a seductive melding of orchestra and female voices, with the voices sometimes taking instrumental parts and the instruments, including cellos and accordions, singing as human voices might. The song was a long one in a major key with a rising, uplifting melody. It alluded to folk songs, and then suddenly to Mozart or Bach; St. John didn't know enough about Bach or Mozart to know which one it might be. Still, he found himself listening with more interest than music normally elicited, trying to discern why it seemed familiar—he felt sure he had never heard it before.

St. John looked straight up, past Marlies, into the cloudless sky. Here in the Caribbean the water often reflected the sky, echoing its violet or turquoise tones. But on rare occasions it was as though the water emanated its own particular colors, and the sky then reflected the water, picking up its blue first of all, but then its liquid shimmering green layers and its blue-black depths. It made St. John dizzy since he was looking up but had the sense that he was looking down into the ocean.

Although these layers of color were not clouds—there were no clouds—the layers he saw took on the quality of clouds, faintly at first, then becoming increasingly opaque and yet vague at the same time, drifting past and across and over one another in different directions, massing and dispersing in unexpected ways. There were so many layers that there was no way to see past them all, and yet suddenly they configured themselves in such a way, one above the other, that there was a clear aperture through them to clarity, a hole that was, as St. John experienced it, nothing less than a hole through time, which afforded him, without his having sought or desired it, an unmitigated, unrefracted view of his own distant past.

Through the hole in the sky or ocean or whatever it was, St. John saw himself in front of the small house where he had grown up on Kenawa Street on the far outskirts of Milwaukee between the Little Menomonee River and the Spooner Farm. He stood beside the red-bud tree he and his father had dug up in the woods and planted in the grassy strip between the sidewalk and the street.

He was eight. His sister stood beside him, and they peered intently into their hands, which were cupped and joined, examining something. St. John was intensely aware that this moment was leaving as quickly as it had arrived; he rushed to gather up as much as he could of the riches he somehow was certain it held.

He was a boy again. Not as we all become our younger selves from time to time, finding a forgotten moment presenting itself vividly in our present. No, he was a boy as if for the first time—purely, entirely, and with only the dimmest, most vague sense that that boy had a future he had already lived through. He felt the absence of a future that a child feels, the sense that the moment is everything and that what comes after is unimportant. He stood there without memory or a sense of his own experience and peered into his and his sister's hands. He could not see what they held, did not know what they were examining, but knew at the same time that it was everything, it was the universe.

If there had been a magnifying glass between their gaze and its object, the object and their hands would have burst into flame, so intense and complete was their scrutiny. St. John felt things, long-forgotten things, sensations and feelings that he had known intensely as a boy, but that had disappeared slowly and imperceptibly on the long meandering journey to adulthood and now middle age. Along the way these things had been sloughed off because they had no value. Until they were gone. Then, once they had disappeared, it was as if they had never been there, had never been the most important part of who he was or how he felt.

At twelve St. John had felt safe, for instance, safe meaning unassailable, invulnerable, and immortal, because he knew with absolute certainty—he could not imagine that it was or would ever be otherwise—that his father and mother were watching over him as God was watching over his creation. Their love was presumed, taken for granted as were all the laws of nature. All St. John had to do was run up the stairs and into the house calling "Mom!" and his mother would rush to see what was the matter.

"Are you all right, Sinjy? What's wrong, sweetheart?"

His father worked long hours at a tiresome job so that St. John could have a better life than he had had. The twelve-year-old was not aware of any of this. He knew only the moment in which he found himself. And though he had a slowly awakening sense of time, it was of an endless continuum of minutes that could last an eternity. Latin class was fifty-five minutes long, but it might as well have been a year. He could look at the clock and then look again an hour later, and the clock would not have advanced a single minute. When the school year ended, the summer stretched before him like endless territory, golden and immense, its proportions so great that its sides and end and eventually even its beginning lay far beneath the most distant horizon.

The hole closed; the layers slid past and closed over one another;

the sky became the sky again. St. John came back to himself with a rush. He felt a great loss, the death of everyone and everything, including himself. They all now lay behind interminable doors. Doors after doors upon doors. If he could somehow open one, if that impossible power to move back through time, as he just had, could magically be granted again, there would be another door, and behind that another, and another, and another. The past was gone, done and sealed forever. None of it belonged to him. His mother and father were dead and had been for a long time. He had avoided them during their last years, and they had been relieved that he had. He never saw his sisters or even spoke to them.

He should have realized it before, but he hadn't: His past was by now the far greater part of his life. His future was a small, insufficient slice of the pie. Even if St. John lived out the remainder of a natural life expectancy and died in relative old age, what remained to be lived was a short time, shorter than a single Latin class, certainly shorter than a twelve-year-old's summer. St. John felt his eyes fill with tears. It was not self-pity; it was genuine loss.

"Are you all right, honey?" said Marlies.

St. John sent her away.

LI

Zaharia had monitored St. John's bank accounts on a daily basis for weeks now, and so was the first to notice that something big was amiss. A flood of money was leaving the accounts. In a matter of days, the various accounts together now contained not hundreds of millions of dollars but a few thousand.

"A grand total of fourteen thousand six hundred and fifty dollars."

"Fourteen thousand . . . ?" Louis was astounded.

"And six hundred and fifty."

"Where did it all go?" Louis had been working on a new painting. A Louis Morgon, and he was having trouble getting the other painters—Picasso, Derain, Cézanne—off his palette and out of his hand.

"I don't know," said Zaharia. "All the transaction and routing information has been scrubbed clean. All the history. And no Charter Island accounts, including the bank's own reserves, seem to have grown by any amount that would account for the missing money."

"So he's taken it out of the bank."

"I guess he has." Zaharia was crestfallen. "He or someone else. But where should I look for it?"

"I don't know. Wouldn't a transfer that big show up?"

"It might if the money stayed together and I knew where to look.

But if he divided it up into odd, smaller amounts and wired it in all different directions . . . I'm sorry, Louis."

"No, *I'm* sorry, Zaharia. I shouldn't have mixed you up in this whole affair in the first place."

The Russian, Dimitri Adropov, and his banker had an analogous conversation in a small office in midtown Manhattan. "Hundreds of millions cannot just disappear." Dimitri pulled back his coat so his man could see the gun. "You moved money and now you not tell me."

"I swear," said the man. He was sweating. "I swear I didn't. Where could I move it?"

Against his better judgment, Dimitri believed him.

At about the same time, Richard Smythe stared at the bank of computers on his desk. He looked from one screen to the next. He could not believe his eyes. Not only had St. John emptied his accounts, but he had done it while the accounts were flush with assets from proprietary Charter Island accounts, assets Richard had been stuffing into St. John's accounts to make up for the money he—Richard—had been stealing. Not only had St. John withdrawn his millions, he had also—unwittingly this time—made off with a lot of Richard's money.

Richard looked at the routing information—information Zaharia had not yet found—and groaned. St. John had used the money to buy industrial and government bonds and various countries' treasury bills. Some of the money had gone into Swiss and other offshore accounts. Richard picked up the phone and called St. John.

"Did you get the paintings, my friend?" Richard heard the cry of gulls in the background.

"Hey, Richard, how are you?"

"Excellent, excellent, Sinj."

"Still in Bali?"

"No, I'm home," said Richard. "Things to attend to. Always upgrading our security. You know." He laughed.

"Did you sell the yacht?" said St. John.

"You know, I was going to. But then I've just spent the loveliest four weeks on it, so I'm going to hang on to it for now. And you? What about those Picassos you were going to buy?"

"No, that didn't work out. They were of lesser quality than the photos showed. Picasso did some real crap, you know? Most people don't know that. They would have diminished the collection. Let someone else have them."

"I see you moved your money."

"I did. It was a bit sudden, I know."

"How, without . . . ?"

"Impulsive, I know. I used drafts and checks and wire transfers. What with the paintings falling through and . . . It seemed prudent to divide it up, have it more places. A lot of people are looking for it, you know."

"Yes. One can't be too careful; no argument from me there. No dissatisfaction with our service, then? I know Citi, Bank of America, some of the big guys are offering the same services, but—"

"No, no, no, Richard. Don't even think it. No dissatisfaction whatsoever. I owe you big time."

"You know, you can always move it back, Sinj. The way you moved it out; move it back in pieces. If you decide you prefer a banker who . . . someone on your wavelength after all. We could revisit our arrangement if that would help. But hiding money, avoiding scrutiny—it's what Charter Island does. Better than anyone. We're structured with that in mind. Bonds don't hide anything. And they're negotiable, St. John; remember that. They're pretty much like cash. If anyone gets hold of them, they're gone. I'm sure you know the Swiss banks are under pressure from the Americans to reveal their account holders, and I expect they'll cave. Think about it, St. John. I say it as your oldest friend. For your own sake. I'm always ready to help, Sinj. You know that."

"I know, Richard. I know."

Peter Sanchez was certain that *he* knew what had happened as soon as he heard from the forensic banking guy that the Larrimer money was gone. He didn't know how he had done it, but Peter was certain Louis had it.

LII

SINCE HIS DISCHARGE FROM THE HOSPITAL, Mohan ate breakfast with his son every morning on the broad veranda. Charanjeet waited at the table laid with a gay tablecloth and bouquets of flowers and bowls of fresh fruit. He watched anxiously as Abinaash walked Mohan to his chair. Mohan would have preferred to remain in his pajamas, but Abinaash insisted that he dress. "You must greet the day as everyone else does," she said, "ready for your work."

"I have no work," said Mohan mournfully.

"Your work is to get well," said Abinaash. "It is a very important job."

Mohan seemed unsteady on his feet. "We could use the wheelchair," he said hopefully.

"Dr. Burgati says you must walk and not ride," said Abinaash.

Once Mohan was seated at the table, Charanjeet rose and went over and kissed him. They ate porridge with fresh mango, banana, and berries. There were some sweet buns and tea.

"I would like eggs and bacon," said Mohan, but Abinaash had already gone inside, so there was no one to contradict him. He sighed. "She would not allow it anyway."

"I do not like the way she talks to you," said Charanjeet.

"She talks to me the way she is supposed to," said Mohan. "It is why we hired her."

"She does not know her place."

"You surprise me, Charanjeet. She knows her place very well: It is to take care of me. In fact, she does her work far better than I could have imagined."

"Well, I do not like her ways."

Mohan studied his son. "Are you jealous. Charanjeet?"

"Don't be ridiculous, Daddy. I am just looking out for your welfare. And why does she dress that way, like an American teenager? And wearing that ridiculous scarf."

"Don't you find her the least bit fetching?"

"Don't be ridiculous, Daddy. What are you thinking?" Mohan smiled, which caused Charanjeet to say again, "Don't be ridiculous. You're being *completely* ridiculous."

Of course Charanjeet found her fetching. He just could not admit it, to his father or to himself. Although, even in his confused state of mind, he had to admit, albeit reluctantly, that she was a very effective caregiver for his father. In the few weeks she had been attending to Mohan, she had not only gotten him out of bed and on his feet, but had also gotten him taking daily walks. They were not yet long walks, only to the park and back. But they were walks he would never have taken otherwise, and at her urging, they were getting longer all the time. Mohan still leaned on her arm, even though, Charanjeet suspected, he no longer needed her support. And on the walks he pretended to tire so that they could sit together on a bench in the shade.

Abinaash had also forced Mohan to modify what he ate in strict accordance with Dr. Burgati's recommendations, which was something of a miracle. Golapi and even the cook had been persuaded to change their habits too. Sometimes, to everyone's shock and chagrin, Mohan invited Abinaash to sit with him for a meal. She of course declined because it was a scandalous suggestion, but that did not stop Mohan from asking.

Charanjeet tried his best to avoid Abinaash. Seeing her confused him. He must not find her attractive, and yet he did. Her smooth, dark skin, flashing eyes, and white teeth made her arresting to look at. The way she moved because of her injured leg accentuated her lithe and curvaceous body, the sight of which caused Charanjeet unease and pleasure at the same time. Pleasure because she was beautiful to see and unease because this pleasure was one he did not dare allow himself. He was the son of wealthy and cultured Brahmins; she was a lower-caste peasant girl. She had no education, no sophistication, and no claim on happiness.

Charanjeet had never been in love before. He had only had sex a few times, and that had been with prostitutes in London and New York. The experience had been mostly furtive and perfunctory. But he now found himself having the most arousing amorous fantasies. *My mind is infected*, he thought. He attributed this "infection" to his time living in the west, away from the norms and strictures of his own society. Women were loose in the West, and castes did not exist. Despite the egalitarian principles of Islam, castes still had a strong foothold in Pakistani society.

Charanjeet had expected that his parents would select a suitable wife from among the children of their friends, but they had made no move in that direction. In fact quite the opposite: They seemed to have decided that he should be at liberty to do as he pleased. "You have come home to a different Pakistan," said Mohan, and he did not seem unhappy at the change. Charanjeet looked to his mother to contradict his father, but she only smiled at him and nodded.

The more Charanjeet rejected any thought of loving Abinaash, the more he found himself drawn to her. And because he tried to avoid her when he was at home, he encountered her at every turn. He would round a corner in the garden, and she would be coming toward him with an armload of laundry. He would stop in to see his father, and she would be taking his blood pressure. This happened more than once in fact. It seemed to Charanjeet as if Mohan was always having his blood pressure taken.

"Roll up your sleeve, Charanjeet," said Mohan one morning. "Abinaash will take your blood pressure."

"Don't be ridiculous," said Charanjeet and wondered in the same moment why he kept saying ridiculous over and over. He was an educated man; could he really not think of anything else to say? "I don't need my blood pressure taken," he said.

"Your blood pressure is high," said Mohan. "I can see it in your face. You are wound too tight. Take his blood pressure, Abinaash." Charanjeet had to roll up his sleeve and submit his bare arm to Abinaash's ministrations. His heart was pounding. Her fingers brushed his skin as she wrapped the cuff around his arm, and it was like a small electric shock. He closed his eyes. She positioned his forearm on the arm of the chair and held the end of the stethoscope—the same one Sister Hildegard had given her—against his pulsing vein. He imagined kissing her. She began to pump up the cuff, and he thought he would explode. He opened his eyes and looked at her, but her gaze was fixed on the gauge as she released the air. "One hundred sixty over one hundred ten," she said.

"That is very high," said Mohan. "I told you so. You are working too hard."

"Don't be . . . It's not that."

"Then what is it?" said Mohan.

"How should I know?" said Charanjeet.

"It could be any number of things, sir," said Abinaash. She was looking straight at Charanjeet as she said it.

LIII

DIMITRI ADROPOV SAT IN THE car and watched as Charanjeet left his parents' compound and walked toward the Fine Fabric Works. "Follow him," he told the driver. Charanjeet was a few centimeters taller than Jürgen. He was a little thinner too, but then he was not a pastry chef. Otherwise, the resemblance was astonishing. "He's Jürgen," said Dimitri without realizing he had spoken aloud. *"And he's Jeremy Gutentag."*

Once James Wyatt Cheswich, the Trinity headmaster, had given Dimitri Mohan's name and the city of Lahore, an Internet search had led to the Chamber of Commerce and from there to the Fine Fabric Works. The Chamber of Commerce site, with its list of member companies, gave not only company addresses and phone numbers, but also company officers, including Mohan Kapoor, retired president and chairman, and Charanjeet Kapoor, president and treasurer. A search of the name Charanjeet Kapoor turned up the fact that he had become president and treasurer of the company not too long after Jeremy Gutentag had disappeared. Dimitri thought it likely that Charanjeet was Jeremy Gutentag.

Charanjeet walked the few blocks to FFW and went in through the gate. He went over the pending orders with Hashinur. They broke

at eleven to have their morning tea. Then Charanjeet shut the door
to his office. It was the last time anyone saw him.

Charanjeet was reported missing the next day by his father. "It is
not like him. He came home every night for dinner. And he never
missed breakfast with me." Mohan choked on a sob. The police
searched Charanjeet's rooms for clues, but did not find anything out
of the ordinary. They spoke to the staff—the cook, two servants, and
Abinaash. The father and the nurse had seen the son leave for work.
But no one had noticed anything or anyone out of the ordinary.

The police then went to the factory. The police sergeant in charge
of the case, a potbellied man with a great handlebar mustache, conducted interviews while two detectives examined the area.

"When did you last see Charanjeet Kapoor?" The police sergeant
sat at Charanjeet's desk.

"After morning tea," said Hashinur. Even when he was standing
at attention, his beard barely cleared the top of the desk.

"And what time was that?" said the sergeant.

"Eleven-fifteen," said Hashinur, except he said it in Swedish.

"What?" said the sergeant.

"Eleven-fifteen," said Hashinur. He pronounced it in Punjabi this
time, and anticipating the sergeant's next question, he added, "It is
when we always end morning tea."

"Did you notice anything unusual yesterday morning?"

"An order of bobbins did not arrive as it was supposed to."

"What?"

Hashinur repeated himself in slow, deliberate Punjabi, as though
he were talking to a schoolboy. "An order of bobbins was supposed
to arrive. It did not arrive."

The sergeant stopped writing and looked at Hashinur. "Anything
that might concern the disappearance of Charanjeet Kapoor?"

Hashinur scowled. "I do not know what might concern the disappearance of Mr. Kapoor."

"I see," said the sergeant. "And how closely did you work with
Mr. Kapoor?"

"I was his foreman. He was my superior."

"And did you work closely?"

"Of course."

"So how did he seem to you yesterday?" said the police sergeant.

"He was a conscientious and bright young man who threw himself into his work."

"Normal?"

"He was a bright young man, full of ideas and energy—"

"Was?"

"Is. *Is* a bright young man."

"Is this where you met in the morning?"

"It is where we met every morning."

"And where did you have morning tea?"

"It is also where we had morning tea. *Have*—where we *have* morning tea."

"Did he do his work with paper and pen or—"

"He worked with a computer."

"And was his computer here this morning when you met?"

"It was here, and now it is not. It was a foldable computer."

"You mean a laptop?"

"He used it on his desk."

"So, was it a laptop computer?"

"Yes."

"So it is missing?"

"It is not here, is it? So it must be missing."

"Did you use his computer?"

"I did not. I do not believe in computers. Although he tried to teach me."

"I see," said the sergeant and brushed his mustache with the back of his hand. "Did he have a girlfriend?"

"You mean *does* he have a girlfriend? I do not know, but he is in love."

"Really?" The sergeant stopped writing and looked up. "And how do you know that?"

"I can tell by looking at him."

"You can tell just by looking?"

"Yes. For example, I can tell you are *not* in love."

"And whom do you think he was in love with?"

"I think it is his father's nurse."

"But she is a peasant."

"*I* am a peasant."

"And why do you think he is in love with her?"

"Because she is smart and beautiful and very competent."

"No, I mean what makes you think he is in love with her."

"Because he does not like even the mention of her name."

"You take that as proof that he is in love with her?"

"A sign. I take it as a sign that he is in love with her."

The sergeant put down his pen and studied Hashinur. "Are you a detective?"

"Of course not," said Hashinur and saluted the sergeant. "But I was at one time."

At that moment one of the detectives who had been examining the premises entered the office. "Sergeant, I have found something you should see."

The sergeant followed the detective, and Hashinur started to follow as well. "Wait here," the sergeant said to Hashinur. Hashinur saluted again.

"This way," said the detective. "There," he said, and pointed to a small dark puddle by the entry gate. "It looks like blood."

LIV

ONE MORNING THERE WAS A loud knock on Louis's door. When Louis opened it, there stood Peter Sanchez accompanied by Renard and two other men. Louis stepped back without saying anything, as though he had been expecting them, and the four men came in. Peter Sanchez spoke first. "These two gentlemen—Monsieur Hubot and Monsieur LeBroc—are from the Police Nationale, the French National Police, fraud division, Louis. I'm sure you know why we are here."

Louis thought for a moment. He looked at Renard. Renard met his eyes but gave nothing away. "I don't. Why don't you tell me?"

Peter deferred to Hubot. "We're here, Mr. Morgon," he said in French, "investigating the theft of money from the Charter Island National Bank in George Town on Grand Cayman Island. The money was recently removed from accounts registered—through various aliases—to St. John Larrimer."

"I know the money is gone," said Louis. "I've been watching it."

"You've been watching it? I see."

"No, I don't think you *do* see. I've been watching it on the Internet," said Louis and gestured toward his computer.

"Which gave you ample opportunity to take it," said Hubot.

"It might have. Except I didn't. I want nothing to do with it. I only wanted to monitor it and to arrange, as best I could, for it to be returned to its rightful owners."

"Its rightful owners?" The policemen looked at each other.

"To arrange, as best I could," said Louis, "that it be returned to them, whoever they might be. That would be determined by the authorities appointed to see that that is done. The American president recently appointed—"

"We know you have been following St. John Larrimer and his money for months, and you have said repeatedly that you meant to get him and it. You—"

"You surprise me." Louis switched to English to be certain that Peter would understand every word. "I am amazed that Peter Sanchez was able to persuade you to pursue a case—if you can call it that—founded on such circumstantial evidence. No, I take that back. It's not even circumstantial; it's Peter's ridiculous imaginings and nothing more."

Peter Sanchez exploded. "Goddamn it, Louis! Don't play your fucking games."

Louis stared at Peter. So did the other three men. "Let me explain something to you, Peter," said Louis, "something your people may have missed while they were watching Charter Island National Bank. There was no way these men could have known this, but *you* should have. Don't your agents even talk to each other?

"Richard Smythe. Does that name mean anything to you?" Louis paused a moment. "No? I see. Well, Richard Smythe is Larrimer's friend and co-conspirator. A fellow thief, as far as I can tell. They went to Yale together. Didn't you go to Yale, Peter?" Louis continued before Peter could respond. "Anyway, Richard Smythe *is* Charter Island National Bank. He founded it, he owns it and runs it—the bank where St. John Larrimer stashed his ill-gotten gains. Charter Island is, you probably know—or maybe you don't, a money laundering service and Smythe's personal money machine. And, by the way, Smythe was stealing from Larrimer, siphoning money out of his accounts, before Larrimer or someone else emptied the account.

"St. John Larrimer is beyond your jurisdiction, and so is Smythe. And, I might add, so am I. But Dimitri Adropov may not be—do you think you can find him? He's been chasing Larrimer's money. And there's someone else you probably don't even know about— Carolyne Bushwick, Larrimer's ex. She's got a phony real estate operation in Bridgeport—that's in Connecticut, Peter—through which she has been funneling Larrimer's loot. It's amazing that I have to do your work for you, and in return all I get is harassment."

Louis turned back to the two policemen. "I suggest you come back when you have some actual evidence against me."

Louis had not expected Peter Sanchez or the policemen that morning, but in considering the situation later, he was not sorry they had come. It had been the perfect moment to feed Peter some information. That would allow the CIA and FBI to follow up on some of his hunches, and it had the additional benefit of embarrassing Peter in front of the French National Police.

"He left angry," said Renard later. They were at the Hôtel de France. He wrapped his hands around his coffee cup.

"I'm glad he did," said Louis.

"Why?"

"Because it might help him focus. I like it better when he's on the case."

"Even when he comes after you?"

"Even then. He can actually do something about Larrimer, find his money, find him. Peter's pretty competent when he's not distracted."

"What do you think happened to the money?"

"Exactly what it looks like. I think Larrimer moved it."

"Why?"

"I can only guess," said Louis. "He must have suspected it would be found. Also I think his good friend Richard Smythe may have been stealing from him and he may have discovered that. In any case, now it's gone."

"And we're no closer to Larrimer or his loot than we were at the beginning."

Louis looked at Renard. "We?"

Renard shrugged.

"We may be farther away," said Louis. "Zaharia tells me there is nothing more he can do to find it. It's essentially gone. That's what laundering is for, I guess. Mixed with all the other money. It's disappeared into the vast and endless sea of capital, of world commerce. And Larrimer seems pretty untouchable too. He slithered back to his island without the slightest difficulty and took his thug, Nigel, with him. He must have lots of powerful people in his pocket. Maybe the story has simply run its course."

Renard looked at his friend with a doubtful expression. "In a way, I hope it has. At least your part in it."

"I'm with Renard," said Pauline when Louis told her about the whole episode. "I definitely hope it has run its course."

"I knew you'd be relieved," said Louis.

"I never liked your taking the law into your hands. And I certainly didn't like your using Zaharia the way you did."

Louis didn't say anything. What could he say?

It was a warm, sunny day. By noon the blustery north wind had dropped and a southerly breeze had come up. Louis and Pauline had pulled on their walking shoes, snugged them up and tied double knots. They put sandwiches in a small pack and walked out into the rising warmth. The freshly turned soil in the fields smelled rich.

They walked out to the quarry above the Beaumont château, then back down to the Dême and then farther than they normally went along its banks. They sat with their eyes closed and let the sun warm them, in a spot out of the wind. They ate their sandwiches—Comté cheese and green onions on baguette. Each seemed relieved for his own reasons that the story was over.

Of course the story wasn't over. Its direction and momentum had just changed. Louis could not see that yet, but it had become a different story. Nothing had run its course, and nothing would. Nothing ever does. One story feeds into the next, which feeds into the next. Like the river of Larrimer's money dispersing itself into the ocean of world commerce, where it would be stolen by someone else, or earned, or donated, or invested over and over again.

St. John now had an incipient conscience of sorts, and one could be forgiven for thinking that that fact alone could turn things around for Louis and for everyone involved. A thief who grows a conscience, even a minuscule, malfunctioning one, could possibly send the story in a happier direction. A Scrooge-ian resolution might even be possible. The grasping villain could see the error of his ways and do his best to make things right.

It had even entered St. John's mind during another fitful night spent under the stars on his vast porch, that one way to gain peace in his soul and maybe even mitigate the heat building around him would be to return all the money he had stolen. Well, not all of it. He had to live on something. But if he could devise some means to make a significant gesture of restitution, he might feel better. And the law might leave him alone. It could even set off a chain reaction of some sort that could redound to his benefit.

Of course St. John knew that that would not happen, *could* not happen. Fairy tales may work that way; life never does. In life nothing works out that logically or predictably. Certainly not justice. Americans claim they're a nation of laws, which is supposed to mean that they are an orderly people. But their laws, and the justice they imply, are incomplete and extremely disorderly.

St. John was a crook, but he was a prudent and cautious crook. He had made substantial contributions to a number of members of Congress. They would take his phone calls and even spring into action on his behalf if need be. He had made certain in each case that some of the contributions were in direct contravention of the campaign finance laws. In other words, the politicians' grateful receipt of his illegal contributions assured him twenty-four-hour leverage and their undivided loyalty. They had taken the money; they were crooks too.

LV

Since coming home from Newark, Lorraine Usher had made certain that her pistol was nearby, safety on, but loaded and ready to fire. She had been to a shooting range and had taken instruction. She was able, after several lessons, to put all her shots in the black. "You have a gift," said her instructor, a note of admiration in his voice. She had learned to dismantle and clean and reassemble her pistol. Its oiled, black parts slid together with a series of comforting clicks and clunks under her deft fingers. And Lorraine kept the pistol in a drawer in the small table beside the sofa. Her baseball bat still leaned beside the door.

Lorraine heard someone come up on the porch. She laid the book she had been reading aside. Arthur jumped down and scurried off to the kitchen. There was a loud knock on the door.

Lorraine looked out and saw a large man in the uniform of a mail carrier. His mail cart was on the walkway. He held a thick envelope.

Lorraine slid open the small drawer and then opened the door. The mailman smiled and offered her the envelope. "Special delivery," he said. "Registered. Sign here." He pointed and handed Lorraine his pen. She wrote her name, he tore the slip off the envelope. "Have a good day," he said. She took the envelope, shut the door, and watched him go. Sometimes the mailman was just the mailman.

The envelope contained a thick packet of negotiable bonds with a face value—once she added it all up—of one hundred and fifty thousand dollars.

"Isn't a hundred and fifty thousand how much you had with Larrimer?" Louis said. Lorraine had called him wondering whether he had somehow gotten hold of Larrimer's money and sent her the bonds. She didn't think that was likely, but it was the only explanation she could fathom. Louis assured her that that was not the case. Larrimer had moved his money some weeks ago, Louis explained, and as far as he knew, nobody knew where. "But it must come from him. You say there was no name on the envelope and nothing in the envelope but the bonds? No sales receipts, tracking slips, nothing?"

"Nothing."

"And the postmark is New York?"

"Does that mean Larrimer is here?" Lorraine wondered.

"It doesn't mean anything," Louis said. "And if the money's in bonds, it's as good as cash."

"But why did he send it to me?"

"Maybe he's afraid of all the information you have. He hopes to buy you off."

"Now? All this time later?"

"You're right," said Louis. "It doesn't make sense."

"What should I do?"

"Do you have a safe deposit box?"

Lorraine was the first, but over a period of the next several weeks, St. John sent packets of negotiable securities to dozens of his victims, the value of each packet a percentage of the money St. John had stolen from them. He had selected those to be "compensated" based on his assessment of who was deserving and who was not. Lorraine was the only one to receive the full amount she had invested, not because she was more deserving than the others, but because St. John had felt "bad" from the beginning for having cheated her. The fact that she would be the most damning witness against him had also entered his mind.

St. John studied the public records of the charitable organizations he had cheated, and deducted his estimate of the percentages they had spent on fund-raising before he had bankrupted them from the amount they had lost. Then he made further deductions based on his assessment of the value of their charitable work.

Those individuals he reimbursed were evaluated as to his calculation of their deservedness as well, and, to some degree, the wretchedness of their current condition. St. John had spent a considerable amount of time working out his hierarchy of reimbursements. He would have been the first to admit how subjective these judgments were. But he could not pay everyone back; the pot of money he was using was considerably smaller than the amount he had stolen. He had spent many millions while the Ponzi game was going on, many more since it had closed down. Yes, he had tens of millions in his various homes and his yacht, but he thought it reasonable that no man should have to give up his homes. Plus he had to allow for the millions he needed each year just to meet expenses.

Still, St. John was paying reparations, which he regarded as evidence of a profound transformation tipping the good-evil scale in his favor. He was not an Ebenezer Scrooge or a Jesus Christ, or any other fictional characters. He was, rather, in his estimation, a more realistic, more practical version, a *real life* version of a "good man." He was someone who had seen, or at least glanced at, the error of his ways.

St. John derived pleasure from doing these "good deeds." He felt a definite sense of joy and relief. He thought the joy and relief came from repaying what he had stolen. What actually gave him his newfound joy was what always had given him joy—playing God, by deciding who would receive bounty from his all-powerful and benevolent hands, and who would not.

Louis dug out the list Lorraine had given him of Larrimer's victims. He had decided to call a few of them to discover whether they too had received reimbursement from Larrimer. He began with the charities.

"This is the Heartfelt Foundation. May I help you?"

"Yes. My name is Louis Morgon. I am from SIPC, the Securities Investor Protection Corporation."

"The what?"

"We are charged with the task of insuring the losses investors have suffered because of securities fraud. May I speak with Father Ian Wilson, please?"

"This is Father Wilson speaking."

"You are the director of the Heartfelt Foundation, Father Wilson?"

"The founder and the director, yes."

"Our records show, Father, that your foundation lost twenty million dollars to Larrimer, Ltd., and that you have applied to be reimbursed for your losses as well as the money Larrimer, Ltd. claimed you had earned at the moment they went bankrupt. Is that correct?"

"Twenty million is correct in round figures. It's actually a bit more."

"And have you received any reimbursement recently in the form of bonds or other negotiable securities?"

Father Wilson was silent for a moment. His foundation—which now consisted of Father Ian Wilson alone—had, in fact, received a packet of municipal bonds worth a total of five million dollars the day before. At first Father Wilson did not know what to do, but his conscience had found a way to think of the money as manna from heaven, a moment of divine intervention, definitive proof of God's goodness and mercy. And it was just between him and God.

Considering how much had been stolen from Heartfelt, and considering that the gain on Heartfelt's more than twenty million dollars should have been almost eight million according to Larrimer's false statements, Father Wilson had not the slightest compunction about accepting the paltry five million dollars in bonds as his, that is Heartfelt's, money.

"I don't believe we've received any reimbursement," he said. "I will however check with the appropriate department here, Mr. Morgon.

Although I'm quite sure there has been none. No, I'm quite sure. Of course, if any reimbursements do come in, I will notify SIPC."

"Thank you, Father Wilson. I'm sure you will."

"Go with God," said Father Wilson and hung up the phone.

LVI

Despite the denials by Father Wilson and the others Louis called, he believed that Larrimer—or someone—was sending money to his victims, and that Father Wilson, among others, had gotten some. Louis also believed that it was extremely unlikely that any one of them would ever admit receiving that money. It could not easily be proved that they had. He could imagine what they were thinking: They were *owed* that money, it was *their* money. They had learned their lesson; they did not intend to ever part with it again. Larrimer's bonds disappeared into safe deposit boxes all over the world, waiting for an opportune moment to become cash again.

"Do you know what SIPC is?" Louis asked Lorraine. Of course she knew. She had, like all shareholders, received a packet of papers from SIPC not long after the Larrimer fraud had been discovered.

"Did they send a form to be filled out in the event you recovered your money?" he asked.

"They did," said Lorraine. "I haven't sent it in. What will happen if I send it in?"

"The government will probably confiscate the money and, along with all recovered money, it will become part of a general fund, part of which will be used to repay the victims of fraud."

"Part of which?"

"I'm just guessing here," said Louis, "but I think much of it will likely go to the agency overseeing the distribution to cover their administrative costs."

Lorraine hesitated. "Still," she said finally, "I think I'll send in the form."

"May I ask you to do one other thing, Lorraine?" he said. "A phone call. To *The New York Times*. A tip. Alex Purfoy has been covering the story. It would be better if it came from you."

Two days later, the article appeared.

St. John Larrimer Makes Secret Payments
By Alex Purfoy

NEW YORK, March 31, 2010. The New York Times *has learned that St. John Larrimer, the fugitive financier who defrauded several thousand investors of billions of dollars, has been making secret payments to some of his victims. The Securities Investor Protection Corporation (SIPC), the federal entity that oversees the reimbursement of defrauded investors, has received "several" declarations of reimbursement, according to an SIPC source. The source also said that they believed a "significant number" of reimbursements have been made without having been declared. "Some people may believe the money is theirs and may have chosen not to report it," an SIPC spokesman said.*

SIPC has notified all of Larrimer's former clients that they have thirty days from the time they receive any reimbursement to file the appropriate declaration. If they do not do so, they could be charged with a crime. "How could you be charged with stealing your own money?" said one investor, who declined to be named. "Of course, I didn't receive any money. But if I had, I would consider it mine."

SIPC today released a statement reiterating the obligation of those who have been defrauded to abide by the laws and not to engage in fraudulent behavior themselves. There is no conclusive

*evidence, SIPC says, that the bonds Larrimer's former clients are
receiving actually come from Larrimer.*

"Well, Christ on a crutch!" St. John had just read the piece in *The
Times.* "Who the hell else is the money going to come from?" He
had just spent another restless night on the terrace—it was becoming routine. St. John could not believe it; his luck was going from
bad to worse. Not only had he recently been blamed for every possible crime and misdeed imaginable, most of which he had not committed, but now, adding insult to injury, he was not getting credit
for the good he was doing.

These good deeds—returning some of the money—which were
entirely voluntary, he reminded himself, came at a heavy price. When
she heard the news, Carolyne had become furious enough with him
to have broken off all communications. St. John was certain she had
left the country. And he was now hearing from her lawyers, that same
smarmy band who had tried to take him to the cleaners during their
divorce. She was probably trying to cut a deal with the legal authorities and would, he was absolutely certain, soon be giving evidence
against him. He could hear it now: Yes, she had helped him launder
money, but she had done it out of love. He had made her do it, for
the boys, and so on.

And Richard Smythe, his oldest friend and most intimate confi-
dante, had also gone strangely silent. St. John was pretty sure Richard had been siphoning money from his accounts before St. John had
emptied them. Even Nigel was looking at him funny.

St. John called Wallace Jimrey, at Jimrey, Newbawer, LLC. He
had not had contact with his lawyers since he had gone from being
a money wizard to being a crook. But they took no notice of his
changed status. They welcomed his call as though he were a long-
lost brother, as he knew they would. The secretary did not bat an eye.
"One moment please, Mr. Larrimer." He was put right through to
Wallace Jimrey, who seemed his old self—competent, reassuring, and
properly obsequious.

"A new team is in place, St. John," he purred. "We've been in a ready mode, waiting to hear from you. We should meet soon, somewhere . . . mmm . . . convenient. We need to go over the various contingencies, outline possible strategies."

"That sounds like a good idea," said St. John. "I want your best people—"

"That goes without saying."

"No . . . conflicts—"

Wallace Jimrey anticipated his concern. "Everyone at Jimrey, Newbawer, has diverse and well-dispersed portfolios of assets, St. John. As do our families. We are extremely careful to anticipate and avoid all . . . inconvenient situations, shall we say? Everyone on your team has been vetted. We're all at your disposal, St. John."

"All?"

"Three criminal, two contract, and two financial. All partners or senior partners."

St. John allowed himself to be reassured. "Excellent." Who needed friends when you had lawyers? Especially if they were a pack of jackals like Jimrey, Newbawer.

"Just let us know when and where you can meet. A week's notice should suffice," said Wallace.

"I'll send the plane," said St. John. "You'll be my guests of course."

Not long after Lorraine had returned the forms to SIPC, two men arrived at her door. One claimed to be a representative of SIPC; the other flashed FBI identification. Lorraine got out the bonds, despite her suspicions. What choice did she have? The men collected the bonds in exchange for a signed receipt. As it turned out, they were *not* Dimitri's colleagues or one of the many other thieves who would have loved to get their hands on her little stack of negotiable bonds. They were exactly who they said they were. Their identification cards were genuine and they did exactly what they promised they would do: They took the packet of bonds back to SIPC's

Manhattan office and put them in the safe from where they were transferred into a Federal Reserve safe deposit box.

Lorraine received a letter from SIPC thanking her for her cooperation and explaining yet again that she had done the right thing. Lorraine called Louis and read him the letter. "And what do we do now?" she said.

"Wait and see," said Louis.

"Wait for what? What are we looking for?"

Evidence of Larrimer's redemption maybe? Louis thought about it. But he still didn't believe it, and he didn't say it. Anyway, what difference could it make?

"Do you think other people who got money back from Larrimer turned it in?"

"Not many," said Louis.

LVII

IN EARLY JUNE Louis and Pauline drove to the Dordogne River Valley for a four-day walk—Trémolat, Les Eyzies, Beynac, Sarlat. At the end they joined a tour through the cave at Lascaux. Louis's eyes took a while to adjust to the darkness, but when they did he was dumbfounded all over again by the ancient bulls and antelopes cavorting across the ceiling in all sizes and colors.

"You're right, you know," said Pauline.

"About what?"

"About Picasso," she said. "It's all here already."

"Yes. Picasso knew that. He was here, you know. He had a private tour. I can see him, taking off his hat and bowing deeply."

"Did he really do that?"

"It's what I imagine. Of course it would have been in the other cave. The original."

"It's easy to forget this is a reproduction, isn't it?"

"A magnificent fake," said Louis. He laughed, and others on the tour turned and scowled at him. The many visitors after the cave was first discovered had led to the degradation of the original paintings. So the French government had caused this replica to be built. It was correct in scale and configuration down to the centimeter, a remarkable achievement of engineering and art.

"This red bull." Pauline pointed above her. "It looks like your Picasso."

"It does a little. Yes."

"You still think of Larrimer sometimes, don't you?" she said.

"Sometimes. Yes."

"Do you think anything will ever happen to him? Will he pay for what he did?"

"Too many people have been stirred up for it to just die. The Russian's still out there. Peter Sanchez. And Jeremy Gutentag's yet to be heard from. I think something will happen. Somebody will do something."

"But Zaharia is out of it?"

"Yes. He did what he could; he's out of it altogether."

"I'm glad."

"I know. I am too."

"I hope it's over."

"I know."

They squinted against the light as they left the cave. It was raining lightly and they hurried to the car. They drove to a small café on the far side of Montignac.

"And do *you* sometimes think of Larrimer?" Louis wondered.

"No. I think of Jean-Baptiste."

"And you hope for justice."

"Justice is too much to hope for. And too frightening."

"Too frightening?"

"Well, what exactly would justice be for Larrimer?" Pauline said. "And if one hopes for justice for him, doesn't one have to hope for justice for oneself? We tend to be well aware of all the suffering we have endured, don't we? But we don't know much about the suffering we've caused. I'd be very careful about wishing for justice."

"I wasn't thinking in such . . . biblical terms."

"But you of all people should, Louis. You became an avenging angel of sorts. You set forces loose in the world. You don't know what you may have caused."

"What do you *think* I may have caused?"

"I don't know."

"What do you *hope* then?"

Pauline thought. "Remorse," she said. "I hope you've caused remorse."

"My own?"

"That too," she said. "But Larrimer's would be more interesting."

"That won't happen," said Louis.

"How do you know?" said Pauline.

"I'd bet on it," said Louis. "People like Larrimer don't work that way. The world doesn't work that way."

"Never?"

"Rarely. And never with guys like Larrimer. How could he feel remorse now if he has gotten this far without feeling remorse?"

Pauline studied Louis. She reached across the table and took his hand in hers. "There it is," she said. "At last." She smiled.

"What?"

"The limits of your wisdom. Your hubris, your idée fixe. Where your thinking ends and your faith takes over."

"My faith?"

"Your faith in Larrimer's villainy. You're not open to the possibility of redemption."

"The world doesn't work that way."

"Ever?"

"Rarely."

"I agree. Rarely. But rarely means it sometimes does. And when it does, you'll be blindsided by it. If Larrimer seeks redemption, you'll be defeated. You won't know what to do."

Louis studied Pauline's face carefully. "Have you been talking to Zaharia?" he said.

"No. Why?"

"Well. When I last talked to him, he asked, out of the blue, really, what if he—Larrimer—said he was sorry? I couldn't imagine it then. I still can't."

"Maybe you ought to try harder."
"I'm too furious."
"At Larrimer?"
"At all the Larrimers."
"Furious. Where does that get you?"

LVIII

Dimitri Adropov was furious. He had finally found St. John's bank accounts and had then watched helplessly as the money in them disappeared, like water swirling down a drain. And now—just back from godforsaken Lahore—he had to read in the newspaper that Larrimer was giving money away.

Dimitri cursed Larrimer, and cursed himself for not having just gone right for Larrimer to start with and squeezed the son of a bitch until he coughed up the money. He should have taken Larrimer's wife—Dimitri was sure she was in on it—and made her tell him what he needed to know. Or the Usher woman—he was more and more convinced that she was part of the whole scam. Instead he had pissed away precious time on Jeremy Gutentag or Charanjeet Kapoor or whatever his name was.

Dimitri had slipped into the Fine Fabric Works factory and waited until morning tea time was over. When Hashinur had left the office, Dimitri had gone in.

"Hello, Jeremy," he said.

Charanjeet's face went pale. "Who are you?" he said. His mouth hung slack, his eyes were wide with fear.

"Let's go, Jeremy. You and I, we take little ride." Dimitri took Charanjeet's arm in one huge hand and the laptop in the other.

"What do you want?"

"I want my money back."

"I . . . I don't know what you mean."

"Larrimer, Ltd. is what I mean."

Charanjeet tried to get free as they left the office. "Stop fighting," said Dimitri, and when he didn't stop, Dimitri punched his nose. A small river of blood ran onto the floor. Dimitri felt sorry. It was as if he had punched Jürgen. "You stop or next time I shoot you."

Charanjeet stopped struggling. "Please don't hurt me," he said. "Just tell me what you want."

"I want my money back."

"But I don't have your money. I don't know where it is. That's all Larrimer's doing. I just worked for him."

"You ran his trading. You got to know something."

"I did what I was told. Please. I'm in love." Charanjeet didn't know why he had said that last thing. He didn't even know if it was true.

Charanjeet had been gone for months now; he had vanished without a trace. Tests had shown it was his blood on the factory floor. Mohan and Golapi Kapoor were inconsolable. "You'll see: He will come back," said Mohan, always hopeful even when there was no reason for hope.

"He is dead," said Golapi.

"No, no, no," said Mohan, "he will come back. He always has."

Mohan had recovered his health, but his recovered health meant nothing to him. His recovery gave him no joy. And because Charanjeet had been in love with Abinaash, and Mohan had therefore come to imagine Charanjeet and Abinaash as a couple, had come to anticipate their marriage and children, *his* grandchildren playing in the garden, now his daily walks with Abinaash became bitter reminders of his son's absence.

With time Mohan almost came to blame her for Charanjeet's absence and for whatever misfortune might have befallen him. He could no longer bear the sight of her, and so one morning he called Caritas and told them he no longer wanted Abinaash as a nursing aide. Caritas sent a representative to inform Abinaash that she was no longer wanted in the Kapoor household.

She was of course astonished. "Have I not performed my duties satisfactorily?" she asked.

"That is not for me to say," said the representative. "But you must gather your things and leave by this afternoon."

Abinaash tried to approach Mohan. "Have I not performed my duties to your satisfaction?" she said. He turned and ran when he saw her coming. "I must have done," she called after him, "since you are running, and you could not even walk before I came."

Abinaash went to Caritas and asked for a recommendation for another nursing aide position. "We are sorry," the person in charge said, "but Mohan Kapoor is a very powerful and influential man. And without an endorsement from him, we are unable to recommend you to others as a nursing aide. You must understand that."

"And what about my studies?" Abinaash said.

"Because you have been summarily dismissed from a good position with a very powerful and influential family, the Caritas Foundation can no longer subsidize your studies or recommend that you be allowed to continue. We suggest you seek a job in another line of work, perhaps one where people skills are less important. I see from your paperwork that you were once a seamstress. Why not look for work as a seamstress?"

LIX

St. John decided to go see his attorneys instead of bringing them to Terre-de-Haut. He was certain he could get into New York unimpeded, though it did not seem a prudent thing to do. But he had to. He had been bamboozled in France by Louis Morgon, and had been feeling trapped on his little island ever since. He needed to feel his old invincible self again. "Into the lion's den," he said. He thumped his chest with his fist. Nigel looked at him with raised eyebrows, which St. John took to be a look of concern. "It'll be fine, Nigel. Don't worry."

St. John's plane landed at Long Island Islip Macarthur Airport late one night, dropped its two passengers, and took off again. St. John and Nigel sped into the city in a hired car. They drove to an exclusive boutique hotel. St. John had rented the penthouse suite under an assumed name.

Wallace Jimrey and his team of lawyers were ushered upstairs the following morning. St. John had arranged for a bar and sumptuous buffet in the conference room. The men talked preliminary strategy, but mainly St. John wanted to take the measure of the team Wallace had assembled. He told them about the payments he had made to his victims. He exaggerated the number of payments and the amount of money involved only slightly.

"Congratulations," said Wallace. "That is a wise and generous and possibly useful thing to do."

"Useful?" St. John had not considered how it could be useful.

"Yes, of course. Generosity is always useful," said Wallace. "And you have been extremely generous." He saw it as his purpose to prevent St. John from ever being indicted and, barring that, of ever being tried and, barring that, of ever spending a single day of his life behind bars. A tangible and irrefutable demonstration of St. John's remorse, such as his retribution payments, would serve admirably in case any of those eventualities came to pass.

Wallace changed the subject. "You shouldn't have come here. If you're found out, it will be seen as a provocation and will be seen as contradicting your avowed remorse."

It took St. John a moment to recognize what remorse Wallace might be talking about. "Oh, that. I have no intention of being found out," said St. John. "And I have business to attend to in New York."

"It can't be done from Terre-de-Haut?"

"It can't."

"Anything we can be helpful with?"

"No."

After two hours the team of lawyers left, and St. John and Nigel took a car uptown. They found Hamilton Jones at home. St. John was not convinced by Jones's repeated assurances that he had known nothing in advance about Louis Morgon or his fake paintings. He waited in the front room. He looked over Hamilton's pathetic art collection while Nigel took Hamilton into the bathroom and pistol whipped him until he was unconscious. Hamilton woke up between the toilet and the tub in a puddle of his own blood. He staggered to the phone. He was taken to the emergency room, where he required several dozen stitches to several cuts on his face. His eyes were swollen and bruised and he ached all over.

"Robbers," he told the police. "Two of them. I don't know how they got into the building."

As soon as he was home, Hamilton called Louis to tell him what had happened.

"And you're sure you're all right?"

"I've got a whopping headache," he said. "But I'll be fine. I thought you'd want to know he's here in New York."

Louis left a message on Peter Sanchez's machine that St. John Larrimer was in New York. Louis couldn't say how he had gotten there or where he was staying. "Good luck, Peter."

After hanging up he went back out to the terrace.

"I suppose," said Louis, "Larrimer's remorse hasn't come into play yet."

"I suppose not," said Pauline.

Lorraine went to the front door when she heard the knock. Before she could decide whether her eyes were deceiving her, Nigel smashed open the door and came barging in. St. John crowded in behind him. Arthur let out a cry and fled from the room.

"I'm sorry, Lorraine," said St. John. "I'm not here to hurt you, okay? But it has to be this way."

"Why? What do you want?"

"Lorraine, I need your help."

"Mr. Larrimer, really. You stole my money. You stole everybody's money."

"I gave it back, Lorraine. You got it all back, didn't you? Did you count it?"

"That wasn't mine."

"Of course it's yours. What do you mean?"

"It was money you stole. Did you give everyone their money back?"

"Don't be ridiculous, Lorraine. Just listen . . . think of it as—"

"No." She crossed her arms in front of her and turned her back.

"Damn it, Lorraine. I sent that money in good faith—"

Nigel stepped forward. "Come on, Mr. Larrimer, let's get out of here." St. John wasn't listening. Even a man as rich and corrupt and venal as St. John Larrimer can have moments when the winds of abandonment and loss seem to whistle past his ears, and this was one such moment. Beset by doubts, abandoned and betrayed by Carolyne and then Richard, St. John had somehow convinced himself that Lorraine Usher would be his last true friend. She had been faithful to him longer than anyone. After returning her investment to her, he did not think it unreasonable to expect to be greeted with gratitude and friendship.

"Please, Lorraine. Please. What do you want from me?"

Lorraine picked up the telephone receiver and held it toward St. John. "Turn yourself in, Mr. Larrimer."

Nigel leapt forward and tore the phone from her hand and crushed it back onto its cradle. Lorraine fell backward onto the couch, hitting the table as she fell. Nigel felt a sharp pain in his leg and looked down to see Arthur's green eyes looking up at him shimmering with unmitigated hatred. The cat sank his claws deeper into Nigel's calf.

"Jesus!" said Nigel and kicked out violently, sending Arthur against the wall with a sickening thud. The cat lay still on the floor.

Lorraine looked at Nigel in horror. And Nigel looked back at her just in time to see the brilliant muzzle flash, hear its terrible explosion, and feel his right kneecap shatter into a hundred pieces. His leg collapsed beneath him. "Oh, Jesus!" he said and rolled in agony on the floor. "Jesus!" He vomited.

That was how St. John came to be arrested. It was not Louis Morgon or the Russian, not the FBI or Interpol or the Police Nationale who arrested him, but patrolmen from the nearby station house who responded to Lorraine Usher's 911 call. St. John pleaded with Lorraine. He offered her a vast fortune. He proposed a partnership in some future enterprise. She sat silently with her pistol pointed at him. Her only words during the ten minutes while they waited for the police came when St. John seemed to get a little restless and appeared to be contemplating making a run for it.

Arthur staggered to his feet and stumbled toward the kitchen, meowing as he went. Lorraine seemed momentarily distracted by that, and St. John slid forward on his chair. "I promise you, Mr. Larrimer," Lorraine said, turning her full attention in his direction again and waving the gun slightly, "that was not a lucky shot." Nigel moaned.

The police knocked and came through the door. Six of them— four men and two women. "This is St. John Larrimer," she told them. They did not immediately recognize the name. Four policemen took St. John and Nigel into custody. Nigel was taken in an ambulance to the nearby Lady of Mercy Hospital, where surgery was performed to try to repair his knee. St. John was taken to the Queens courthouse to be arraigned, where he was met by Wallace Jimrey.

Two policemen remained behind and questioned Lorraine. She explained that she had felt threatened when Nigel knocked her over and then kicked Arthur so viciously, and so she had shot him. "I aimed for his knee."

"And the other guy?"

"St. John Larrimer is wanted for fraud and many other things."

"Larrimer . . . ? *That* Larrimer?"

"And what about the pistol?"

Lorraine produced her permit. Still, the police had to take the pistol to perform a ballistics test. They promised it would be returned as soon as the ballistics had been determined and entered into evidence. Bruno rushed up just as the last police were leaving.

"Are you all right?" He saw a rising bruise on her forehead where she had hit the table.

"I'm fine. I'm worried about Arthur." Arthur was still wobbling around meowing.

"At least you're safe."

"They took my pistol."

"Lorraine, listen. At least you're safe."

"There's still the Russian," she said.

LX

THE DISTRICT ATTORNEY, Elaine Degarza, a large, rotund woman with frizzy hair, asked that St. John be remanded to prison. "Mr. Larrimer is a longtime fugitive from justice, Your Honor, wanted and charged with multiple counts of fraud, money laundering, and a host of other reprehensible crimes. He still has access to the billions he stole. He also has multiple residences outside the United States and several passports. No amount of bail is beyond his means, and no amount, no matter how high, would ensure his return. If he is released, Your Honor, this is the last time we will ever see him."

"Your Honor, Ms. Degarza's indignation is misplaced and inappropriate." St. John looked contrite and ordinary standing beside his attorney. His fingers were laced in front of him. He wore an ill-fitting gray suit purchased hours before—his first off-the-rack in thirty years. "Mr. Larrimer has, it is true, committed fraud on an enormous scale. He has admitted to that. But he recently discovered he has cancer, Your Honor, and has, since that discovery, recognized and confessed the error of his ways. He came to the United States—"

"Illegally and under cover of darkness, Your Honor—" said Degarza.

"He came," Wallace continued, "after paying reparations to many of his victims. He came with the intention of visiting his victims and begging their forgiveness. . . ." As if on cue St. John opened his arms and spread them in a Christ-like gesture of supplication. He looked with widened eyes, as innocently as he could manage, in the judge's direction.

The judge interrupted Wallace's plea. "Mr. Jimrey, that is all very moving, but save it for trial. This is a bail hearing. . . ." The judge and Jimrey had been at Harvard Law together and had, at one time, played in the same weekly poker game. The judge felt urgently therefore that he had to demonstrate his strict adherence to the law and his complete and utter impartiality.

"Forgive me, Your Honor, but Mr. Larrimer's intentions and actions before being arrested speak directly and irrefutably to his trustworthiness. He went to the home of Lorraine Usher, his longtime assistant and loyal friend, after having paid back everything he had taken from her, in order to ask her forgiveness. He was arrested as he was trying to do just that."

"Your Honor!" said Degarza. She could not mask her astonishment and outrage. "Mr. Jimrey talks as though he's holding a royal flush when he's showing a pair of twos. This is a serious legal proceeding, not a poker game. Bluffs don't work."

Both Wallace Jimrey and the judge looked hard at Elaine Degarza as though they were seeing her for the first time. Did she know about their poker connection? Or had she just gotten lucky? In either case, it was now clear the judge could not afford to show even the slightest leniency. Degarza was probably right that Larrimer would disappear if allowed to go free on bail, and if he did disappear and it then came out that the judge and Jimrey had once been poker partners—all the players in that game had had nicknames: Jimrey had been "Slick," and the judge had been "Fingers"—if that came out . . . well, Fingers did not want to even contemplate that possibility.

The judge ruled that because St. John Larrimer was a confessed felon and a ruthless and unscrupulous one, he was indeed a serious flight risk. He would therefore be subject to house arrest with a radio bracelet attached to his ankle. The seriousness of Larrimer's crimes certainly suggested that he should be remanded without bail, but the judge felt he had to consider not just Larrimer's crimes but also past contributions to the community. The ankle bracelet was sufficient. He would not be allowed outside for any reason except to attend legal proceedings. No walks, no museum or opera visits. House arrest, period. That is how it happened that the hotel penthouse St. John had rented—all sixteen rooms—became his jail while he awaited further hearings and, presumably, a trial.

Louis and Pauline were making lunch when the phone rang. It was Lorraine with the news. Louis told Pauline the whole story while they sat on the terrace.

"And will he come to trial?" Pauline wondered.

"He might," said Louis. "Eventually. But not for a long time; it could take months, more likely years. Larrimer's lawyers will file motion after motion, and each motion will delay the trial. Then when the trial eventually starts, there will be further motions and further long delays and diversions. His lawyers will want to find his former wife so they can demonstrate that the entire Ponzi plan was hers and poor Larrimer was in her thrall. And when that fails they will find his banker, Richard Smythe, and prove that he was the reason Larrimer stole. Smythe was the driving force behind his thievery. And when that fails they will find . . . who knows, me maybe? And Hamilton Jones? And the Russian? All those who tried to trick Larrimer and steal from him instead of the other way around.

"They will paint the world as a morass of larceny; they will indict Wall Street and capitalism itself as the ultimate Ponzi scheme. They will say St. John Larrimer was only operating by the mores of the age and culture in which he lived. They will plead diminished capacity or insanity even. His lawyers will find witnesses who can attest to his extreme remorse and his efforts to make good on his debts to his victims. Lorraine Usher got money back from Larrimer, and she will have to testify that she received that money and that Larrimer came to her house at considerable risk to himself seeking her forgiveness."

"Did he do that?"

"Of course not. But a clever lawyer can conduct Lorraine's examination so that Larrimer comes out the saint and Lorraine the sinner. She pulled a gun and shot Larrimer's goon, after all, and she would have shot Larrimer. He was terrified for his life; he never meant to hurt her; he had only her well-being at heart. He was filled with regret, remorse, and a yearning to repair the damage and ease the suffering he caused. And she was about to shoot him."

"But he stole all that money," said Pauline.

"And he will probably be convicted of some charges," said Louis. "His lawyers expect that, and will conduct their entire defense so that it lays the groundwork for his sentence to be light. Larrimer will have a jury trial. He saw what happened when Madoff was sentenced by a judge. He'll plead not guilty and try to push the blame onto others. And the cancer—he supposedly has cancer—the retribution payments he made for whatever reason, all that will be brought into play early in the trial and kept alive until the end."

"You think the cancer is a lie?"

"I think it might be similar to his remorse. He may have cancer, but not as serious as his lawyers make out. He'll go to prison in Tennessee or some relaxed place, if he goes at all. He'll be a model prisoner and will be paroled after a couple of years."

A breeze came up and rattled the umbrella and the table. Louis stood up and carried the lunch dishes inside. Pauline looked out across the garden. It needed some attention after all the rain they had been having.

LXI

DIMITRI HAD ALL BUT DISAPPEARED, as far as Louis could tell. In fact, Dimitri had been probing here and there, like a desperate animal, trying to find a way to Larrimer. He still had someone watching Lorraine. He knew where Louis was and what he was up to. He had even showed up on surveillance film more than once outside the building where Larrimer was confined in luxury.

"Is like fortress," he told his associates at Gazneft. And it was, with twenty-four-hour police guards, plainclothes surveillance, cameras, you name it. The members of the Gazneft board were not mollified.

The day the trial began, Dimitri visited the courthouse, but realized he couldn't get anywhere near Larrimer. And even if he could, what good would it do? If he killed him or had him killed, he'd never get the money. Never.

The trial unfolded more or less as Louis had predicted it would. After eighteen months of delays concocted by the defense for various reasons it got underway in the Federal District Court in Manhattan. The courtroom was packed with spectators and press. St. John was thinner now. His skin was pale; his hair was going gray.

As the trial began Wallace Jimrey, who had elected to conduct St. John's defense himself, let it be known that St. John was undergoing treatment for his cancer. "But," he insisted, placing a hand gently on St. John's sagging shoulder, "he assures me, Your Honor, that, though the treatment continues, he is now strong enough to proceed. He wants a speedy trial in the interest of justice for all."

Jimrey realized full well that a jury of rich money men was beyond the realm of possibility, but he did his best to assure that those selected for the jury were not against acquiring wealth.

In their opening statements the prosecution made St. John out to be the worst villain that had ever walked the earth, and the defense presented him as someone who had been carried away by the opportunities for wrongdoing presented in a self-regulating capitalist system. "Free enterprise is exactly what it says it is," said Jimrey. "And being free, it is full of pitfalls and temptations into which St. John Larrimer"—and here Jimrey rested his hand on St. John's shoulder—"allowed himself to be lured."

The prosecution then began its case by presenting a parade of financial experts and bankers who, after describing in detail Larrimer, Ltd.'s wrongdoing, expressed their sincere contempt for St. John Larrimer. "He has sullied not only his and his family's name, he has sullied the name of American investment banking. We at Goldman Sachs have always operated, not only by the letter of the law, but with a conscientious concern for our clients and the American people. We feel ourselves to be serving a sacred trust."

"What Larrimer has done," thundered a former World Bank president, "is nothing less than to undermine the world's faith in the American financial system."

After two days of such presentations, followed by testimony from the most egregiously cheated of St. John's victims—the widows and orphans, so to speak—the prosecution rested.

The defense rose to present their case. They did not contend that St. John was innocent of wrongdoing, only that what he had done, while technically criminal, was in its essence—the acquisition of money from unsuspecting clients—no different from what other bankers did. And to prove it, they called a number of reputable economists and scholars of various political persuasions who, when pushed, had no choice but to admit, one after the other, that free market capitalism was essentially a giant pyramid scheme. Of course, the defense did not mention that this was St. John's own theory, which he had laid out in one of their strategy sessions. At that moment, Jimrey had recognized the bones of their defense strategy: St. John was guilty of nothing more than free market capitalism.

In a daring gambit to drive the point home, Jimrey called a number of St. John's victims to the stand. The first was Father Ian Wilson.

"Father Wilson would you remind us, please, of the amount of money your foundation lost to Larrimer, Ltd."

"The Heartfelt Foundation lost approximately sixteen million dollars through our investments in Larrimer, Ltd."

Larrimer's attorney pretended to leaf through his notes. "Did you say sixteen million? The SIPC report you filed said you had lost twenty-one million dollars. How do you explain that disparity?"

"Well, the initial report was filed as soon as the fraud was made known to us. A more recent examination of our books has, thankfully, allowed us to revise the amount downward. We now believe it to have been sixteen million dollars."

"I see. And I presume you have filed an amended report with SIPC."

"We have only recently discovered the disparity. We will report is as soon as we have completed our audit."

"Father Wilson, did you receive anything from Mr. Larrimer in repayment for your losses?"

"We received five million dollars in bonds. I assume from Mr. Larrimer, although there was no indication on the package who had sent it."

"When did you receive these bonds, Father Wilson?" The witness shifted uneasily on his chair.

"Please answer the question," said the judge.

"It was . . . about eighteen months ago," said Father Wilson.

"I see. Then I assume you must have reported the receipt of that money to SIPC within the thirty days the law requires. Is that correct?"

"Um, well, we missed the deadline. All our time has been taken up just trying to save the foundation, so we overlooked the deadline—"

"So, then, can I assume you have filed the report by now?"

"We will as soon as—"

"Father Wilson, I can't help but notice that you are quick to file reports when you lose money, but not all that quick when you receive it." The prosecutor objected vigorously, the judge sustained the objection and instructed the jury to disregard the defense attorney's remark.

"Father Wilson, I have one more question. When speaking of the Heartfelt Foundation you have repeatedly used the word *we,* the first person plural pronoun. Who is the *we* you refer to?"

"Well, once our finances were so severely decimated by Mr. Larrimer's fraud, we had no choice but to curtail expenses severely, so—"

"Father Wilson, is there anyone else in the employ of the Heartfelt Foundation besides yourself?"

"As I was saying—"

"A yes or no will suffice, Father Wilson."

"No."

"Thank you, Father Wilson. I have no further questions at this time." The prosecution chose not to cross-examine.

Lorraine Usher was called, and the treatment she received was not any kinder. "Isn't it true, Ms. Usher, that Mr. Larrimer sent you negotiable bonds for the entire amount he had taken from you?"

"Yes, that is true, but—"

"And is it not also true that he did so out of a sense of deep remorse?"

"That is what he said, but—"

"But you do not believe that he was motivated by remorse and the desire to make amends?"

"No, he—"

"So, is that why you shot his driver and threatened to shoot him?"

And so it went with witness after witness, each of whom was shown to be no less venal, or greedy, or malevolent than St. John had ever been.

St. John had not taken the stand, but he was permitted to make a statement before the jury began their deliberations. He said, in essence, that he expected to be found guilty and to be punished for his moral laxity. "I have fallen," he said, "about as far as a man can fall." And while he did not have the faintest idea how far a man really can fall—he knew nothing about Abinaash, or the millions like her—his contrition appeared to be sincere. The jury was out for six days and found him guilty of most of the charges against him, but they also saw his efforts at restitution as a genuine effort to right the wrongs he had committed. They even offered a plea on his behalf to the judge who was to pronounce the sentence.

The judge—not "Fingers"—was not entirely persuaded by St. John's contrition. But he did find the jury's sentiment convincing that St. John's sentence should reflect both his guilt and his efforts at retribution as well as his previous contributions to society. The trial had been widely covered on television and in the press. St. John represented something novel in the annals of crime, particularly white-collar crime: a convincingly remorseful crook. He had been a villain, but now he was redeemed. The press rolled out the Saint Paul on the Road to Damascus analogy again and again, even playing on his name. "*SAINT* ST. JOHN?" wrote the *Post*.

St. John was sentenced to five years in prison, with time already served—meaning his time in the luxurious penthouse apartment—reducing his sentence to three and a half years. He declined to appeal the sentence; he pronounced that he found it fair punishment for his crimes and misdemeanors. He was to serve his sentence in California so that he could be near his sons. He would be eligible for parole in eighteen months.

St. John was a model prisoner. Religion had never been of interest to him, but now he seemed to find God, or God found him. St. John read the Bible from cover to cover, and on Sundays he conducted Bible study for the other inmates, who were mostly small-time drug dealers and other nonviolent criminals. Most of his fellow inmates, all people without the means to have ever invested in Larrimer, Ltd., knew him only as a genuine gentleman who was concerned with their spiritual well-being and their final salvation.

"What kind of a name is Sinjin?" they asked.

"Just call me John," he said.

St. John was released on parole after eighteen months and allowed to serve out his parole in his penthouse apartment on Park Avenue. He was also allowed to purchase a new suite of offices on Fifty-seventh Street. Not surprisingly, the parole board was suspicious about his purpose, but once he explained that he intended to launch a charitable foundation called New Beginnings, they were willing to allow it.

"We'll have a close eye on you, Mr. Larrimer," said the parole board chairman. "We'll have complete and total access to your accounts, the members of your foundation's board, and a thorough account of all your business dealings."

"I would expect nothing less, sir. I think you will be amazed." They looked skeptical when he said that, but in fact they were amazed. St. John designed New Beginnings as a partner to, and intermediary between, business and nongovernmental agencies whose purpose was to improve wages and working conditions in factories around the world, starting in Mexico and Pakistan, but then expanding to all of Latin America and Asia. He hoped, he said, in partnership with his allies—he had already made contact with the Clinton Foundation, the Gates Foundation, and many others—to accomplish no less than the elimination of child labor, and the end of the exploitation of women and of poverty among the working men and women of the world.

He was invited to appear on *60 Minutes*. The interview took place in his Fifty-seventh Street offices. He wore a modest Glen plaid jacket with an elegant tie. Gone was the pocket square. He sat at the Andrew Carnegie desk, the only remaining trace of Larrimer, Ltd. to be seen.

"St. John Larrimer," Charlie Rose intoned, sounding like the voice of doom, "a lot of the people watching this right now are going to be asking, 'Why? Why should we believe this rich man. What does he even *know* about poverty?'"

St. John looked straight into the camera. "I know," he said, "that it needn't exist. Poverty need not, *should not* exist."

LXII

WITH THE PASSING OF MONTHS and now years, the anger of the Gazneft board members who had lost money to St. John Larrimer had begun to diminish. For one thing, Gazneft had become an even larger entity, taking over pipeline, oil drilling, and natural gas companies, not to mention several banks of its own. Measured against the amounts of money they were now raking in, the 2008 losses seemed less dire. Moreover, some members had left the board for even more lucrative enterprises. They just wanted to put the whole sorry experience behind them. Everyone except Dimitri, that is.

Dimitri could not let it go. He would be working along just fine, overseeing an acquisition or an expansion, when suddenly he would disappear. He would turn out to be off somewhere following yet another lead, trying another tack. And eventually he would come back to the board to report what he had discovered. But it always ended up amounting to nothing.

"Forget the money, Dimitri Adropov. It's gone."

"It's not gone," said Dimitri.

"Okay, then where is it?"

"Larrimer has it. He still has it."

"You're neglecting business, Dimitri. We have bigger things going on than the fucking money. You chose the EisenerBank; they lost the money. It's over."

"It wasn't me that chose that bank," said Dimitri. This was true enough. The man who had was no longer on the Gazneft board. It was not even certain he was still alive. In fact, Dimitri had opposed using EisenerBank. It was run by a bunch of innocents. "You thought that was an advantage, having a bank run by children. Remember, Vasily? Well, how the fuck did that work out?

"Now!" he said and raised his finger with a dramatic pause, capitalizing on his newfound, if brief, advantage. "Now that Larrimer's giving money away in his so-called foundation, I can get to him and get our money back with interest."

"Yeah, how? You can't even get near him. You never could, and you never will."

"Don't worry," said Dimitri. But it was a good question.

It looked like the end of the line for Dimitri Adropov. He had tried everything, and nothing had worked. Carolyne had flown the coop for who-knew-where. Jeremy Gutentag had been worse than useless. And Dimitri didn't dare go near Lorraine Usher. He could send somebody else, but what good would that do?

"Don't worry," he said again. He turned his back on the board and gazed from the window overlooking the great Gazneft works that he, Dimitri Adropov, had built and was now about to lose. The relentless push of time and fate: *that* was all Dimitri had left. Without an earthquake, a war, a tsunami, a rampant toxic cloud, a pestilential epidemic, something, *anything* to shake things up, his story was over.

At that exact moment, as though a prayer were being answered, a small asteroid entered the earth's atmosphere at a speed of over eighteen kilometers a second, which is fifty times the speed of sound. Small in the case of an asteroid means the size of a railroad car. Its ferocious velocity caused it to explode in a tremendous fireball twenty-three kilometers above the city of Chelyabinsk with the concussion of an atomic bomb. It was captured on a thousand automobile dashboard cameras and shown all over the Internet. It was written about in newspapers and broadcast on television around the world. It was the first recorded asteroid strike on the earth that had caused human injury and death.

The explosion shattered windows and caused buildings to sway all over Chelyabinsk. People were knocked off their feet. Irina Adropov, Dimitri's aged mother, standing at the sink peeling turnips, was cut on her hands and face by flying glass. She crossed herself and fell to the floor. Surely it was the end of the world. The members of the Gazneft board seated around the table were showered with flying glass and debris, their cigarettes torn from their lips. Dimitri, standing facing the window, got the worst of it. He was thrown to the floor. When he looked up and could not see, he reached up and found puddles of blood where his eyes had been.

At the Fyodorov Microsurgery Clinic in Moscow, Dimitri emerged after six hours of difficult surgery. A short time later he awoke in a private room. His mother, Irina, was at his side. Three days later the bandages were removed from his eyes. Special dark glasses were placed over his eyes before he was allowed to open them.

"You will see light and shapes to begin with, and with time your vision should improve, although it remains to be seen how much of your vision you will get back. What do you see now?"

"I see light and shapes," said Dimitri. He turned toward Irina. "I see my mother." She took his hand in hers and pressed it to her cheek.

Over time Dimitri's vision stabilized and he was given prescription glasses to wear. The lenses were tinted because he remained sensitive to light, and they were very thick, making his eyes appear smaller than they really were. Instead of softening his looks, the glasses emphasized his reptilian aspect and made him appear even more menacing than before.

Dimitri had had his own Road to Damascus moment. But he did not find Christ or goodness or even remorse.

Senator Bob LaPlacca had received outsized contributions from St. John Larrimer during the previous election campaign five years past. Thankfully, Larrimer had never asked anything of him, but the senator, who was watching the *60 Minutes* interview with intense interest, saw now how he could both repay Larrimer's largesse and do himself a favor at the same time.

As the chairman of the Senate Finance and Banking Committee, he had been conducting hearings on the exploitation of Asian workers by American companies, and in the process had called numerous witnesses—professors of economics, business analysts, other politicians—trying to gain some traction with the public. But no one was watching. It was an important issue, but who wanted to hear American business criticized? Certainly not the businesses themselves, and they were the ones that owned the newspapers and television networks.

"Jess," LaPlacca said to his administrative assistant, "this guy Larrimer is huge right now. Did you see *60 Minutes*? A thief gone good. No wonder he's all over the news. And you know what? Our hearings line right up with this foundation he's starting. Let's get him as a witness. It'll shine a spotlight on the issue, on his foundation, and on us. People won't have any choice but to pay attention."

"And it won't hurt your reelection chances either, Senator." LaPlacca was being opposed by the same Afghanistan War veteran as last time. And he would have lost, too, if it hadn't been for Larrimer's last-minute infusion of cash into the campaign.

"You know damn well, Jess, I don't operate that way. That's not what these hearings are about. Goddamn it, Jess!" The senator saw profanity as proof of his integrity and forthrightness. His great bushy eyebrows settled into a disapproving scowl.

"I'm only saying," said Jess, sucking deeply on his diet drink.

St. John was more than happy to testify. "Anything to bring the plight of the impoverished to public attention." He swore "to tell the whole truth, etc., etc.," and then was seated before an overflow audience in one of the large Senate hearing rooms. Flashbulbs popped.

Bob LaPlacca hadn't seen so many cameras pointed at him in a very long time.

St. John began his testimony with a brief recapitulation of his own wrongdoing and salvation. "I am not here to cast aspersions," he said. "I am not here to accuse anyone, or even suggest what anyone ought to do. Who am I to do so? I am the lowliest sinner." There was astonished silence. No one could remember such words ever having been spoken in the halls of the United States Congress.

St. John began his opening statement, which was an impassioned plea for the improvement of working conditions and safety standards around the world. He believed, he said, that remarkable improvements could be achieved in South Asia in particular, where the need was so dire. But they could be achieved everywhere in the world. Why not? Anything was possible. And, he went on, he believed, no, was convinced it could be achieved without harm to the overseas affairs of American enterprise. He thought, in fact, that instead of slowing the engines of free trade, by improving conditions, you would improve trade.

The solution to most of the world's problems was international cooperation. Cooperation would lead to reduced and more focused regulation. He believed that a free world marketplace with minimal government interference would cause prosperity to flourish and spread. Prosperity, he believed, was contagious. A well-ordered and transparent marketplace was ultimately, he believed, the best regulator of all.

Republican members of the committee praised his embrace of the free market; Democrats praised his call for improved standards and protections around the world. St. John dismissed their praise as undeserved. He had been a villain and now he was not, but his villainy was still the largest part of his personal history, he said.

St. John's forthrightness and humility only made them love him more. Every senator was in his thrall, but less for his plan, such as it was, and more for his demonstration of the miraculous power of public contrition. This man, a convicted felon, had reversed his fortunes and was on the road to achieving enormous influence by means of . . . repentance. He had stolen billions of dollars, and yet everyone loved him because . . . he was sorry.

The senators ignored his disclaimers. Instead they now tried to outdo each other by lavishing praise on him, praising his perspicacity, praising his plans. And each senator recalled his own personal stumble and subsequent salvation. "I was defeated the first time I ran for office," said the senior Republican on the committee. "Trounced, in fact. But it turned out to be the best thing that had ever happened to me." He did not say why.

"I was unfaithful to my wife, but she has forgiven me and, in so doing, made me a better man and a better husband. I love you, Betty," said another.

"I remember my dear little son looking up at me with tears in his eyes when I ran over his puppy. 'Darryl Junior,' I said, 'I didn't mean to do it,'" said yet another.

More than one of the senators managed to squeeze out a tear. Some invoked God, or Jesus, or God *and* Jesus. Saint Paul came up a few times. The trouble was each senator was new to contrition, and none was willing to confess to genuinely serious misdeeds, the kind that might land him in trouble with the Senate Ethics Committee, or the IRS, or that might land him in jail. No one regretted taking illegal campaign contributions or cheating on his taxes or lying under oath.

Anyway, St. John Larrimer had stolen *three billion dollars* and had been to jail for it. How could anyone compete with *that*? Still, when the hearing adjourned, each senator managed to feel cleansed and purified. Each felt that his soul had been purged of whatever darkness had once resided therein. The only exception was the senator who had confessed his infidelity. Betty had definitely *not* forgiven him, and as he was leaving the hearing room, he was handed a subpoena for his tax and financial records going back through the entire twenty-plus years of his marriage.

The launch of the New Beginnings Foundation in the Grand

Ballroom at the Pierre was attended by celebrities from every sector. An army of reporters and photographers circulated with microphones and cameras at the ready. *The New York Times* featured the launch in a front-page story and wrote a moving lead editorial about St. John's transformation from scoundrel to champion of the forgotten poor.

St. John Larrimer has gone from disgrace to admiration in a very short period of time, too short some might say, given the magnitude of his crimes. At the launch of his New Beginnings Foundation Saturday evening, he spoke with a newfound humility and contrition about his own conversion to the cause of poverty and workers' rights, which he has decided to make his life's work.

Despite a great deal of reporting by this newspaper and others over the years, there is still widespread ignorance about the unspeakable conditions under which many tens of millions of people who manufacture the things we buy must live and work. They are woefully abused, poorly paid, and live and work in conditions of constant deprivation and danger. "South Asia—India, Pakistan, Bangladesh—is where we will begin," Mr. Larrimer said, "but that is only the beginning. Few people are blessed as I have been blessed. And I freely admit: Few have squandered their blessings as I have. Until now.

"By the grace of God I still have great energy and great resources at my disposal. With the New Beginnings Foundation, I intend to use these resources, for the good of the world's poor."

One cannot help but admire the enormous breadth of Mr. Larrimer's vision and the seriousness of his purpose. One hopes that he is able to harness the forces he thinks he can harness. For if he succeeds, then the entire world will be all the better for it.

LXIII

IT WAS A SUNNY SUMMER day. The sky was an improbable shade of blue. You could never have painted it, thought Louis. It was physical, chemical maybe. You didn't just see it; you took it in. If you licked your lips, you could almost taste it. And the clouds, white at their feathery edges and lavender inside, barely moved and yet seemed to be dancing. Louis and Pauline were both in the garden, their faces in shadow from their broad hats. The short-handled hoes in their hands were all but forgotten as they looked around. A day like this made you greedy for more time.

They were standing in the garden watching the neighbor's cows grazing nearby when Renard came up the drive. The cows—Holsteins—black and white on a normal day, were golden and purple today and cast violet shadows beneath them. Renard got out of the car with a copy of *Le Monde* under his arm. The three friends greeted one another with kisses. "I'll make coffee," said Pauline. Louis and Renard sat down at the table while Pauline went inside. "You look tired," said Louis.

"I got called in the middle of the night. Madame Chalon wrecked her car."

"Is she all right?"

"Amazingly, she is. At seventy-five, all she's got is a few bruises. She was drunk and hit a pole."

"Uh-oh," said Louis.

"Yeah. She's going to jail. It's her second offense."

"You can't get her into a program?"

"I've tried. Several times. She won't go. Pierre can't walk anymore, and she's got to look after him. And now she'll go to jail. So who will look after Pierre? Anyway . . ." Renard slid the paper across the table and Louis picked it up. "Look at page three," said Renard.

Louis opened the paper and read for a minute. Then he closed it, folded it back up, and pushed it away.

Pauline came out carrying a tray with a tart and coffee on it. She poured the coffee and gave everyone a slice of tart.

"Mmmm," said Renard. "A good year for plums."

"What's in the paper?" said Pauline.

"A tale of redemption," said Louis.

Pauline opened *Le Monde* and read the story describing Larrimer's crimes, conviction, and the launch of the New Beginnings Foundation to fight against poverty and for workers' rights. When she had finished, she closed the paper, got up, and walked out to the garden. She looked out over the garden and beyond it for a while. Then she knelt and began weeding.

"Jean-Baptiste?" said Renard.

"She misses him," said Louis.

The men finished their coffee. Pauline waved as Renard drove off. After a while Louis walked over to where she was. "I'll finish the leeks," she said. "You do the spinach." They weeded the adjoining rows, each chopping with the hoe and pulling the weeds out by the roots. When they had finished both rows, Pauline said, "Let's go make supper. They put the tools in the barn near the fake masterpieces stacked in the corner facing the wall.

Pauline put on water for pasta. They sautéed garlic and onion and peppers and spinach in a little white wine. They drained the cooked pasta, put it back in the pot with the vegetables, added some chopped tomatoes, some white beans, and basil, and let it all simmer for a while. They carried it to the table outside and ate in silence.

"Do you believe Larrimer?" Pauline said finally.

Louis had been mopping up sauce with a chunk of bread. He stopped in mid swipe. "Believe him?" he said.

"Believe he's a changed man?"

"I don't know. He may be. I don't know what to believe anymore. Do you?"

"No," she said. "And even if I did . . ."

"It wouldn't matter," he said.

"No, it wouldn't matter. The people he cheated are still cheated. The lives he ruined are still ruined."

"And what about his rehabilitation and redemption?" said Louis.

"That's not rehabilitation. He went to prison and changed his mind. I don't see changing your mind as rehabilitation. It's too easy."

"Well, and I don't see the redemption either," said Louis. "What Larrimer got isn't redemption. He got a gift from a gullible world. It's drama, that's what it is."

"Yes," said Pauline. "But that's what redemption is, isn't it? It doesn't depend on regret or remorse or atonement. It comes because . . . it just comes, whether you ask for it or deserve it or not. God just reaches in, and you're redeemed."

"God, or the SEC or the US Congress," said Louis. "That's who redeemed St. John Larrimer," said Louis. "The SEC, the attorney general, Congress, and the Almighty Marketplace. He was redeemed because we liked his drama. We bought his story: from shameful avarice and crime to abject humility to punishment to a glorious epiphany."

"And will he do what he says he's going to do? Work to help the poor, improve conditions for workers, eliminate child and slave labor?"

"You know, Pauline, I deluded myself. I somehow imagined I could impose rough justice, when all I accomplished was to compound the disorder and unhappiness I was trying to fix. I thought he was a character in my drama, when in fact I was a character in his. Maybe I still am; maybe we all still are."

"You're still angry, aren't you?" she said. They carried the dishes to the sink and set them down. She put her arm around his back and pressed her face against his.

"Maybe," said Louis. "Yes. At him, and at the world that makes people like him possible."

"Well," said Pauline, "it's the world we've got. It doesn't behave like a storybook. The good are seldom victorious; the meek *never* inherit the earth. It's not a place where people are rewarded for their honesty. Sometimes the evildoers are punished, but only when not doing so would bring the game to an end.

"So, big deal: Instead of a resolution, the Larrimer story ended in unresolved confusion. The way real stories always do. Stop feeling sorry for yourself. You did a good thing, and in doing it, you made a bit of a mess."

"The Larrimer story isn't over," said Louis.

"You think not?" said Pauline. She pulled his head to her and kissed him. "I hope it's over."

"Larrimer has started plan B. And there's still the Russian. He's still out there," said Louis.

"There's *always* still the Russian," said Pauline. "He's *always* still out there."

LXIV

EARLY ON A SUNDAY MORNING as he was being served breakfast by his pool, Richard Smythe's cell rang. He was surprised it was St. John calling. He waved Carlos away and hesitated for a few rings more before he answered.

"Well, hello, stranger," said Richard.

"Hello, Richard," said St. John.

"My goodness, it's been a long time," said Richard. "What a lovely surprise. I'm delighted you called. How are you?"

"I wasn't sure you would take my call." St. John could hear parrots in the background.

"How could you think such a thing, Sinj?" said Richard. "I'm *so* glad to hear from you."

"Well, I'm assuming you know my story. I've been convicted of crimes, sent to prison, and now I'm in the process of turning my life around. So I just didn't know whether you'd want to talk to me—"

"My goodness, St. John, our friendship is too big for that to matter. I'm just very glad to hear your voice. Really, I am."

"Well, that's a relief. I'm glad to hear your voice too. And how are you, Richard?"

"I'm doing really well, St. John, really well indeed. The banking business is picking up as you must know. We're managing more money than ever. I'm in Acapulco right now. Listen: This will interest you. I've been looking at some Aztec artifacts: the most spectacular little pottery figurines. Sacrificial stuff, as I understand it. I'm in a bidding war with the Louvre and the Met. Great fun, great fun. And you, Sinj? I've been following your adventures. I want to hear all about everything. Are you buying art these days?"

"I'm fine, Richard. No, no, I'm not buying art. In fact most of my collection was confiscated and sold as part of the retribution process. I'm in Manhattan now, but I've got some important travel coming up. Of course I have to clear it with my PO. That means parole officer, Richard."

"Yes. I see," said Richard. There was something different about St. John, a newfound diffidence, a guarded quality. His voice seemed thinner, his expression flatter, less expressive, more cautious. Maybe prison did that to you. Or maybe someone was with him, listening.

"Not on Terre-de-Haut then?"

"No, Richard, not Les Saintes. Manhattan. That's where I'm working now. Working hard to build up the new foundation. We call it New Beginnings. A new beginning for me, of course. It's my way of atoning for my sins. But new beginnings for others too, for the oppressed and abused. And for the cynical, Richard. For the cynical."

Oh, brother, thought Richard. "Yes, I've read about it. But tell me more, St. John. I want to hear all about it *from you*."

"Well, Richard, that's what my life is about these days, improving working conditions for the poor around the world, and fighting poverty. There is no need for poverty. It's my belief that poverty can be eradicated in our lifetime."

"You haven't become a socialist on me, have you, Sinj?" Richard laughed, but St. John didn't. He remained silent for a long moment, as though he was allowing Richard's frivolity to dissipate.

"No, Richard. You don't understand. That's not it."

"You're right, St. John, I *don't* understand."

"The sins were mine alone, Richard. I'm not blaming the capitalist system. I'm talking about the next iteration of capitalism. Think of it: a smarter, even broader marketplace than we had before. I'm talking about a truly worldwide marketplace, where everyone, and I mean *everyone*, is a player, where avarice is replaced by generosity.

"The money, Richard, the sheer dollars available for an enterprise that can transform and save the world, it's mind-boggling. The foundation has taken off because people see the promise of an expansive and expanding system." St. John abruptly went silent. Then, just when Richard thought their call had been dropped, St. John was back. His voice was soft, almost a whisper. *"We have to see each other,"* he said.

Richard wanted to see his old friend, to talk things over face-to-face, to see what St. John was *really* talking about. It sounded vague and pie-in-the-sky, and nothing like the old hard-nosed, feet-on-the-ground St. John. Had St. John Larrimer really turned into the benevolent sap on the phone? "I'd love to see you, Sinj, I really would. But the territorial US is a little tricky for me right now. Still, we can make it happen. Can you come down here somehow? To Acapulco?"

"I understand, Richard," St. John said. "We have to make it happen; I owe it to you. I have to tell you more than I can tell you right now. This project, this next iteration"—there was that word again—"will blow your mind." Richard could have sworn he heard St. John chuckle just before he hung up the phone.